Like Family

Michele M. Feeney

Black Rose Writing | Texas

The author grants the final approval for this literary material.

First printing

ISBN: 978-1-68513-463-1
LIBRARY OF CONGRESS CONTROL NUMBER: 2024936727
PUBLISHED BY BLACK ROSE WRITING
www.blackrosewriting.com

Printed in the United States of America
Suggested Retail Price (SRP) $19.95

Like Family is printed in Minion Pro

*As a planet-friendly publisher, Black Rose Writing does its best to eliminate unnecessary waste to reduce paper usage and energy costs, while never compromising the reading experience. As a result, the final word count vs. page count may not meet common expectations.

Praise for
Like Family

"Feeney combines a wise heart with a keen intellect. Set during the flu epidemic after World War I, she brings together an abandoned child and a lonely teacher. Readers will find the progess of their friendship irresistible. An unusual story that is powerfully moving."
–Lynne Sharon Schwartz, author of *Truthtelling*

"In *Like Family,* Michele Feeney not only brings us back to the terrifying time when the Spanish flu had its hold on us, but also beautifully explores the meaning of family—the people we lose, the people we love, the family that, sometimes, we choose."
–Ann Hood, author of *The Knitting Circle* and *The Book That Matters Most*

"As fear of the 1918 Spanish Influenza tears a small Michigan community apart, traditional bonds are tested and surprising new sources of strength and connection are found. Feeney tells a beautiful tale of how we can choose to create a family from empathy and love that surpasses all else."
–Tara Ison, author of *At the Hour Between Dog and Wolf*

"We've all heard that history repeats itself, and never has it been so poignantly clear as it is in *Like Family.* When you sink into the era of the Spanish flu, you will be immersed in history while simultaneously planting your feet in our own present times. The struggle then reverberates with the struggle now. The reader will find new connections and support from those who lived generations before. What a lesson. What a comfort."
–Kathie Giorgio, author of *Hope Always Rises* and *If You Tame Me*

Author's Note

In the mid-1800s, a decade after emigrating from Ireland, my ancestors homesteaded a farm in Southeastern Michigan. The farmhouse they built, red brick and two stories, is a squared-off, front-facing, simple-but-inviting structure that I believe both exceeded their dreams and reflected their characters. When my mother passed in 2012, I inherited the farmhouse, as well as a portion of the money she had saved during her career as an elementary school teacher. I used my inheritance to restore the farmhouse.

The farmhouse is located on a dirt road. A mile north is a cemetery. When I was a child, my grandmother, born in 1892, often took me there to tend to the graves of our deceased relatives—her husband, sister, infant brother, parents, and grandparents. I asked her questions about many gravestones, not just those belonging to our family members. She told stories about the individuals and families buried there and their place and impact in the small farming community where she lived her life. By then, in the late-1960s and early-1970s, she was nearly the only one left of her generation and the ones before.

My grandmother once pointed out a gravestone shaped like a small obelisk, about waist high on an adult. Several names were engraved on the gravestone, a couple on each of the four sides. My grandmother explained that the modest obelisk was the marker for a family who died of the Spanish Influenza. The deaths occurred over a period of weeks during the summer of 1918.

Of course, when we faced the COVID pandemic in 2020, my grandmother was long dead. She had died in my farmhouse bedroom in 1982. I could not ask my grandmother about that family who died more than a hundred years earlier. I could not ask if the children had been her students in the one-room schoolhouse where she taught for decades. I could not ask how the community responded, or whether anyone from the family on the obelisk had been left behind. I couldn't even ask her if she contracted the influenza herself.

My grandmother lived through the installation of electricity and telephones and the advent of automobiles. Along with the influenza pandemic, she witnessed World War One; the Women's Suffrage Movement (she was twenty-eight when women earned the right to vote); the Great Depression; World War Two; the Korean War; Vatican II; the Civil Rights Era; the assassinations of John F. Kennedy (her political hero), Dr. Martin Luther King, Jr., and Bobby Kennedy; the Vietnam War; and the feminist movement of the nineteen-sixties and -seventies.

In June 2020, my teenaged sons and I traveled by plane to the farmhouse from our home in Arizona, as we had done since they were babies, but this time, we were masked and anxious. No vaccine was available, or even on the horizon. People were dying. We all wanted to get to the farmhouse, our refuge.

For all of us, the COVID pandemic established a bright line of before-and-after, and the same was true of my imagination. I found myself unable to work on stories set in the pre-COVID era or to imagine a post-COVID era. The characters and events I tried to craft were doing things we could not do and worried we might never do again. My grandmother's gift to me was the time I spent with her during my childhood. I listened to her so closely that I knew how she felt about most things and could imagine the story of Mollie and Cecilia. This is a story of loss, persistence, resilience, and love.

Like Family

Chapter One

The morning after her last day of school in June 1918, after Father and Hugh left for the fields, Cecilia helped Mamusia clear the breakfast plates and wipe down the scarred wooden kitchen table with warm water and vinegar, then rub the table dry with bleached white rags. When they were finished, Mamusia took the framed photograph of Josef, Cecilia's oldest brother, off the mantel and put it on the table. Mamusia then climbed onto the kitchen stool and removed the flour sack from behind the heavy pots on the highest pantry shelf and placed the sack on the table next to the picture.

Cecilia knew the flour sack did not hold flour. Instead, the sack, weighted with a few rocks from the stream that ran behind the house, and bulked up with dried-out corn husks, was where Mamusia kept her private things—hair ribbons for Cecilia to wear to school, a savings passbook Mamusia took to the bank from time to time, and a packet of sunflower seeds like those they'd planted early last spring. The sunflower plants had grown tall among the stalks of sweet corn in their garden. "Foolishness," Father had said, when he noticed the bright blossoms nodding among the cornstalks. "A waste of good money."

Mamusia poured herself a steaming cup of coffee and sat down in the chair that had its back to the door, the one where Father usually sat. She tucked the sack into her lap, then patted the seat of Cecilia's chair. Cecilia sat down next to her.

"You remember Josef?" Mamusia asked, tapping the glass on the frame with her fingernail.

"A little," Cecilia said.

She'd been four when Josef left the farm to take a job at the Ford Model T Plant in Highland Park, Michigan. Then, he was sent off to war in 1917, a war on the other side of the wide ocean. They'd received this news by letter, which had made Mamusia sad, because she hadn't said "a real goodbye." Now, for Cecilia, Josef was only a shadow in the vague shape of her older brother, Hugh. The framed photograph of the stiff young man in uniform—an image Cecilia saw every day—felt more solid than her memories.

"Is he like Hugh?" Cecilia asked.

Mamusia held the photograph at arm's length, her head tipped to one side, her expression happy, but careful, as deliberate as if she were checking a cake in the oven, determined not to jostle it into a fall. "Josef is a little quieter than Hugh. He loves to draw, like you."

"Where are his drawings?"

Mamusia shook her head and sighed. "Your father caught him drawing too many times when he was meant to be working. The drawings were then gone."

Cecilia thought of how stern Father became when he found her drawing rather than finishing chores and could believe that he'd ruined Josef's drawings. "He looks like Hugh," Cecilia said, then giggled. "Big ears."

Mamusia shook her head—she didn't like when Papa teased Hugh about his ears.

"Josef coming home?" Cecilia asked.

"Yes," Mamusia said. "He will come home from Kansas, but not until he is well." She crossed herself—Father, Son, and Holy Ghost.

"What is wrong with him?" Cecilia asked.

"I don't know," Mamusia said, and bowed her head.

Cecilia knew Mamusia's whispers meant she was praying for Josef's health and safety, just as the family did each evening when they said the grace prayer before dinner.

When she was finished, Mamusia untied the string wound around the top of the flour sack and removed a thick rectangle of brightly colored paper from the sack. The rectangle was the shape of a red brick from their fireplace, but thin like a pancake. Cecilia had never seen it before. Mamusia unfolded the rectangle, and it grew bigger and bigger, until it was a map like the one hanging from a pole on the wall in Miss Crowley's classroom. Mamusia pressed the crisp creases of the map flat, using the same stroke she used to smooth Cecilia's hair, which Mamusia always said reminded her of the palest and finest corn silk. The unfolded map, a sea of bright colors, not faded like the one in the classroom, covered most of the top of the kitchen table.

"This picture is the United States," Mamusia said, running her finger around the big shape that filled most of the page. Then she pointed to a yellow section in the middle of the map, and at the center of their kitchen table. "And this state," she said, "is Kansas. Josef is in Kansas. He is healing there." She marked the spot called Kansas with a heavy black pencil and said the letters—"K-A-N-S-A-S."

Cecilia found the mitten shape in the upper part of the map. "Michigan," Cecilia said, tracing the mitten with her finger, then putting her small hand into the shape, fingers together, thumb sticking out. "We live here," she said, wiggling her thumb. "In the thumb."

Mamusia nodded. "Clever girl."

"The blue is lakes. Miss Crowley taught us the word 'homes' helps remember the names." She shook her head. "But I not remember." She felt a quiver in her stomach, thinking about all the things she'd surely forget by the end of the summer, and how stern Miss Crowley would be.

"Huron, Ontario, Michigan, Erie, and Superior," Mamusia said, pointing to each one. Then she folded the map away, put it in the flour sack for safekeeping, put the sack back in its hiding place, and put Josef's photograph back on the mantel.

•   •   •

The summer passed, both slow and fast. Weeding was slow; sunrise was fast. Storms were terrifying but fast; the raspberries on the bush outside the kitchen door stayed green and hard for weeks. Cecilia could barely remember being in school, back when the chicks had hatched. But then, overnight, the chicks began behaving like grown chickens.

•   •   •

When they received a telegram that Josef was free to come home, it was from the Army, not Josef. Cecilia could tell by the way Mamusia fretted over the thin paper, reading it again and again, that she wanted more than to know Josef was still alive—perhaps she craved just a word or two in his own hand. Mamusia took the map out again and, over a few mornings, she made a long snaking pencil mark, which Cecilia traced over—Kansas to Chicago, then Chicago to Emmett. Mamusia said this was the path of the train that would bring Josef home. The train track ran along the north end of their property, and the train's whistle woke Cecilia in the morning and, again, late at night. She loved the sound— it was her own little *Dzień dobry!*—Good morning!—and *Dobranoc!*— Good night! It was the same rushing train that would bring Josef home.

•   •   •

The day of Josef's homecoming didn't come until late August, on Cecilia's eighth birthday. The Pokorski family—Cecilia, Hugh, and her parents—hitched up the horses to the wagon and went to meet Josef's train at the station near the grain elevator, even though it was the middle of a perfect haying day. On the way, Father said they'd "catch up tomorrow" and that the work would go faster "with another pair of hands." Mamusia shook her head, then Father added, "Maybe yet this afternoon."

As they drove, Cecilia snuck sidelong glances at Hugh. Would Josef be another Hugh, jokey and swift, or someone entirely different? Would he seem like a man or a boy? Would he be like Father, who always entered the house like a dark cloud? Mamusia seemed light and happy this morning, as if expecting a special gift. Cecilia decided Josef would likely be an older and larger Hugh, no more and no less, and she smiled. It would be good to have another brother. She imagined herself on the return trip home, sandwiched between the two of them, legs dangling over the back of the cart.

Once they were at the small station, Mamusia climbed down from the wagon and stood as close as she could to the westbound tracks, which she glanced down every few seconds. Cecilia and Hugh walked along the tracks, looking for the flattened pennies children sometimes left behind. Father stayed in the wagon. They heard the whistle in the distance before they saw the train. The massive clattering wheels came to a stop, blocking the view of the tracks running the opposite direction. Cecilia watched the conductor open the door and waited for a glimpse of her brother.

When Cecilia saw a single man ease himself from the end of the steps to the platform, she knew it must be Josef. Her scant memories, and her vision of a brother like Hugh, evaporated. The limping man who lurched toward them, then barely spoke, even to her parents, was a stranger. He didn't look as though he could climb onto the kitchen stool, let alone toss bales into the haymow. They rode home in silence, Josef up front next to Father, and Mamusia in the back between Cecilia and Hugh. There was no more talk of work to be done that afternoon, and no further mention of Cecilia's birthday either.

∞

Mollie Crowley was surprised to see Josef Pokorski and the Pokorski family a few rows ahead of her in the front pew at Mass on the Sunday of Labor Day weekend. Like many farming families, the Pokorskis rarely came to Mass during haying season. And regardless of the season, they would never have taken a front pew. There was an unspoken rule that those pews, identified by gold plates attached to the outside end of each one, were reserved for donors, like Mollie's family. Mollie and her mother, Catherine, sat in the same pew they'd occupied since she was a little girl. Mollie assumed Father Foley had invited the Pokorskis to take a special seat to celebrate Josef's return. She was sure of it when she saw Father Foley beckon Josef to an empty chair on the altar beside the head usher—it was the place of honor.

Ten years ago, Josef had been one of the boys in the back of the one-room schoolhouse during Mollie's first year of teaching. He'd been a head taller than her and came to school each morning smelling of the barn and perspiration. His gaze, when it landed on her, had been challenging. She'd faced Josef down the way she'd learned as a child to face off with the bull that often paced back and forth along the fence line of the Garveys' east field.

She still remembered her terror when she was a little girl and that bull chased her. The beast had come after her with his nose flaring, wet breath spraying the back of her legs. He'd been only inches behind her when she vaulted over the fence, breathless and shaking. It had been her father who'd taken her back to the field and shown her how to stand her ground. He'd told her that if she couldn't run faster than a bull, or a bully, she'd need to look him in the eye.

"Calm, confident, and quiet," had been her father's mantra.

Mollie had found the same approach held true with rambunctious boys. She only had to arrange a conference with Josef's father once— now she couldn't even remember what transgression had upset her. She'd started the conference by asking Josef a question, trying to provoke his cooperation. Mr. Pokorski had thrust out his arm as if to block Josef from entering a doorway before Josef could get a word in. Josef seemed to shrink on the spot. She'd softened her message; the father offered only a few grunts in response. But his gritty glare and Josef's pallor and quick apology let her know what Josef was afraid of— his father. From then on, corralling Josef only took an assured glance. Then, at the end of seventh grade, Josef was gone, working on the family farm. His brother Hugh followed within a few months.

The congregation was silent as Josef made slow progress forward, leaning on Hugh. When he settled into his seat, they gave a collective burst of applause. Josef clapped his hands over his ears, dipped his chin, and looked at the floor. The applause came to an awkward halt. Mollie snuck glances at him and noticed that he stayed seated for the Creed and the Gospel, like one of the oldest ladies or the mothers with tiny infants. During the homily, Father Foley said Josef's was the first of many homecomings. He called it a "true blessing." At Holy Communion, before attending to the queue in the center aisle, Father Foley went to Josef, who tipped up his head and opened his mouth like a hungry baby robin to receive the host.

This Josef was nothing like the tall, quick boy Mollie remembered kicking a ball across the dirt playground, darting away from other boys. This Josef was a bunch of bones with a gray face, disguised in a neatly pressed uniform. The uniform looked to be wearing Josef, rather than the other way around.

After Mass, outside the church, Josef stood stiffly, tolerating the hugs and tears of many mothers, celebrating his homecoming as though their own sons had returned, even though the Pokorskis were one of the few Polish families in the area, with customs and language strange to nearly everyone. Mollie did not hug Josef, finding the others' sentiment somehow simultaneously cheap and extravagant, but she did press his hands between hers. He didn't seem to remember her, and she wasn't sure she was distinguishing her memories of Josef from memories of Hugh. The Pokorski boys ran together in her memory; they'd both left school so long ago.

Mollie was surprised to find tears in her eyes as she walked away from the young man and crowd toward her car. She couldn't help but wonder if Josef's condition was a preview of what they should expect as other soldiers returned.

"That young man looked like death warmed over," Catherine said after they'd settled themselves in Mollie's car. "What was he like as a student?"

"I don't remember him well," Mollie said. "His family pulled him out of school early. Sad, though. He didn't have much of a childhood, and now it's clearly finished."

∞

The day after the Mass, Josef began coughing as though he would turn himself inside out. Mamusia begged Papa to fetch the doctor, and Papa finally agreed. He took Hugh with him, to help with English. Papa had never learned and wouldn't try.

Dr. Murphy, who treated Josef, said it was the "Spain Flu"—he was quite certain. "I've read about it, like everyone," he told Mamusia, "but I hadn't yet seen a real case. We've been sheltered here. Can you tell me where he's come from?"

"Overseas," Mamusia said. "Boston. Then, Kansas. Then, in Chicago a day to rest with family. Then, here."

"Family?" the doctor said. "From Poland as well?"

"Yes," Mamusia said.

The doctor rolled his eyes, dusted the sleeves of his coat, and took a few steps back from Mamusia. "We've been safe until now," he muttered. Then, he stepped outside the door, and gave Mamusia instructions from the porch. "Keep the windows open, keep him quiet, and keep this place clean." He sniffed as if he'd smelled the scent of pig *kupa* and winced.

Mamusia blushed scarlet.

·   ·   ·

At first, Cecilia didn't know what Spain was—a place? a food? a person? A day later, on his next visit, she overheard Dr. Murphy mutter, "The war wasn't enough? They brought this home, too?" So, maybe Spain was a place. Cecilia didn't remember Spain on the map, but there were so many words and places. And the "Spain Flu" had something to do with Josef's war. It was something he'd brought home with him, something unwelcome.

. . .

Josef passed during a night when Cecilia shook off deep sleep again and again, when it seemed the house was full of noise and movement. When she crept into the kitchen at dawn, she wasn't sure he was gone, whether she'd dreamed it or somehow overheard the news. She knew when she saw his photograph back on the kitchen table that he was away again, but also sensed that he would never return. Mamusia was weeping into her apron, bunched up into her hands. Father was already in the field, like always.

"Hugh is asleep," Mamusia said.

That was strange. Hugh was always up with Father.

"He was up most of the night," Mamusia added. "He helped move the body."

"Body?" Cecilia asked, looking at the face in the picture, then peeking over Mamusia's shoulder into the boys' room, where only the frame of Josef's bed remained—no mattress and no sheets or blankets. She hadn't thought about what was left when a person passed, hadn't realized it was like when an animal died. That there would be nothing, no sign the animal had ever lived.

"Doctor said, do it quick," Mamusia said. "The influenza—no one knows how you get it."

Cecilia put her arms around Mamusia's neck, and Mamusia pulled her onto her lap like she was a little girl again. Cecilia remembered the ride to the train station only a few days ago. It didn't seem possible that Josef was gone. It was as if the real Josef had never been there. It felt like the opposite of magic.

. . .

Mamusia told Cecilia that she needed to lie down in the middle of the next day. Cecilia had never seen such a thing—her mother in bed during the sunlight—so she ran to the field for her father, who fetched the doctor again.

This time, the doctor had a mask over his face and gloves on his hands. He confirmed what Cecilia already knew—Mamusia was ill. The doctor told Cecilia to make a bed for herself in the pantry and stay there. It was a tiny room off the kitchen. Cecilia remembered when Mamusia had tried to bottle feed an abandoned newborn lamb there after birthing season, to no avail. The lamb had died, and her father had made fun of Mamusia's soft heart. All day, confined in the dim pantry, Cecilia listened for clues about Mamusia, but all she heard were soft sighs and loud screams, and the sound of a door slamming.

By nightfall, Cecilia understood Mamusia was very sick—she'd never even come to check on her in the pantry; there could be no other explanation for that neglect. As the nighttime hours passed, Cecilia heard more coughing, not like when she had a cold, but more like an angry storm. She heard vomiting that was so much harsher than when she'd had the stomach bug last winter. She heard her brother Hugh screaming with pain in his head. The sounds grew louder as morning approached, and continued through the next day.

First Mamusia, and finally Hugh and Father.

Everyone was sick—everyone but her—and no one was getting better. Cecilia wanted to leave the pantry, for comfort, but needed to stay inside, for safety. She spent the night, and then the days and nights after that, curled in on herself like a single kitten. Each time Dr. Murphy knocked, she quickly opened the pantry door. He always backed far away, and always wore his gloves and a mask, which left only his stern dark eyes visible. He asked a few brief questions; Cecilia heard in his tone the disbelief that she was still healthy. She always found a basket of food by the pantry door, in exchange for which she shamefully exchanged the chamber pot she'd filled in the previous twenty-four hours.

It was the doctor who gave her the news of the deaths—first Mamusia, and then Hugh. That day, the doctor cried with her, but didn't come any closer. Hugh had been her only proper brother, the only other young person in the house that she could remember. He'd been up early every day with their father, in the barn or the fields, but still took time to push her on the swing he'd hung in the barn. The baskets kept coming even after they took the last body, her father's, the Sunday following the Mass where everyone welcomed Josef home.

Cecilia's family was gone, and she was alone. She waited to learn where they'd taken the bodies. Surely there would be prayers of some kind, like she and Mamusia had said over the lamb that passed, now buried next to the back garden. The people delivering her food baskets always rang the farm bell in the yard—the same bell Mamusia had used to announce dinner—and Cecilia always ran to the front door, but all she ever saw of the people making the deliveries was raised dust as their farm wagons travelled back down the lane.

Sometimes, the basket held a *maly prezent*—that's what Mamusia called small gifts. Unexpected kindnesses, like an extra sweet, another time fresh mint to put into her water, and then paper and colored pencils, which Cecilia used up in a few days. She'd drawn the apple tree in the backyard, shading in the pink ripening apples. She tried to capture the gold of the evening light shining on the tall cornstalks in the field, and then, using the last of her pencils, she drew her cat, Daisy, her belly round with the kittens she and Mamusia had been anticipating for weeks.

At night, even then, with the house empty, she stayed in the pantry, where she felt safer. It felt like where she should wait for her family. She fell asleep each night praying the prayers Mamusia taught her, hoping she would wake to a different outcome, but it was always the same— she woke to a silent house. Sometimes, in the night, she woke herself with her weeping, then quickly dried her tears.

"Tears solve nothing," her father had often said.

The days settled into a strange order. She heard Mamusia's voice in her head throughout the day, telling her what to do next—"make neat your bed," "water for the cat," "collect eggs," and then "prayers now," in the evening. She followed the same routine she and Mamusia had, as much as she was able—wiping the counters and tables with vinegar and water each morning, sweeping and then sweeping again, making her bed in the pantry neat and smooth. Each evening, she put the scraps left from the basket out for Daisy next to a bowl of fresh water. She turned every corner expecting to see Hugh's joking face, having a giggle at her expense. Her father she couldn't see at all.

Every few days, Dr. Murphy returned to the house empty of everyone but her, knocked, then waited at the bottom of the porch steps.

Each time she answered, he looked surprised she was still healthy. One day, standing at the bottom of the porch steps, he said, "We're still waiting for word from your people in Chicago."

"I don't know people in Chicago," Cecilia said, remembering that Josef had stayed an extra day there when they were tracing his path, but not knowing who he'd seen or remembering where Chicago was on Mamusia's map. "Where is Chicago?"

The doctor continued as though he hadn't heard her. "The priest wrote to the Polish parishes. Your mother told me Josef had stopped in Chicago to see family. We'll see if anyone turns up."

"So I stay here?" she stammered. "Alone?"

"Speak up," the doctor said.

"I stay here alone?" she repeated, her voice quavering. "How long? How long do I wait? How many more sleeps?"

"I am sorry—" he said. He shuffled his feet and looked off into the distance. "My wife…. well, she has babies of her own, and is terrified of the flu."

"But I not sick," Cecilia said. "Please."

"It won't be forever," the doctor said.

Cecilia didn't know how much time had already passed. It felt like forever. And it didn't seem there was any end in sight.

"She—Mrs. Murphy—doesn't know I'm here," the doctor added. He held out his hand as if to touch her forehead, though he was several feet away. "No fever? You're not hot?"

She didn't want the doctor to come closer—it was Mamusia she longed for. She missed her all the time. She wanted her now, or, if that was not possible, perhaps whoever was taking time to pack the sweet baskets. She put her hand to her own forehead—cool—and shook her head. Then, the doctor left, without saying when he might return.

Cecilia washed each afternoon on the porch, using the hand pump to lift water up from the cistern. Like the doctor, she disbelieved her continuing good health, but it remained. She was eight years old. She could take care of herself, even when the thunderstorms she so feared made the tin roof rattle overhead. She counted the beats between each crack of lightening and the rumble of the answering thunder, as Mamusia had taught her to do. The storms always passed, usually quicker than she thought possible.

Chapter Two

By the last Saturday in September, the Mass when the congregation had celebrated Josef's return was four weeks past, and only the Pokorskis had fallen ill. Mollie had listened for word of any further local cases of the influenza and heard nothing. Still, it was as though the community was in a state of waiting. How serious was "the sickness," as townspeople had taken to calling it? Had the Pokorski deaths been the worst of it? Would the influenza stay in far-off cities, be something they only read about in newspapers? As weeks had passed, people seemed to believe the influenza had come home with Josef, like an unwelcome interloper, and then taken its leave. They reassured one another that they would stay healthy themselves so long as they kept to themselves.

The Michigan governor had left the decision whether to open schools to each community, the town of Emmett left the decision to the town council, and the town council called a meeting and invited Mollie. They were full of questions. Did she have a plan to keep the children safe? Could she keep the children apart? Would she alert them at the first sign of trouble? What precautions would she take to cleanse and sterilize the classroom? Was she worried about the Pokorskis' deaths? Was there still a chance that a person who'd spoken to the Pokorskis at that Mass could be a carrier? Should they wait to re-open the school until the influenza was over for sure, even though no one knew when that would be?

Mollie held her patience throughout the long meeting, answering every question to the best of her ability, carefully and respectfully, basing all her answers on her research and reading, and the science available. Only in her own mind did she wonder why, at age twenty-six, with almost ten years of teaching experience, they didn't yet trust her? Didn't they think she'd done her homework? Didn't they think she could maintain order in the schoolhouse? She'd read every single word she could put her hands on, and all the literature said the critical period after exposure was seven days. They were well beyond that. The contagion period for the Pokorskis was long past. She was confident she could keep the children safe.

"Have you consulted with the doctor?" Michael Ryan, the father of one of Mollie's childhood friends, asked.

"Yes," Mollie said. "We've talked at length. Unless someone else falls sick between now and October 10, I have his support to open."

As the five council members looked on, chins in hands, she finished—with just the slightest edge to her voice—"Haven't I *always* had a plan to keep the children safe?"

The heads began nodding, and the town council delegated the decision to her.

As she drove home, she felt irritated that the task of proving herself might never end. Then she began to worry, to second-guess herself. Could she keep the children safe? What if the town council was wrong to place confidence in her, and the children got sick? Were they perhaps leaving the decision about whether to open the school to her in case things went awry? Were they setting her up as the scapegoat? Why was no one else worried about the children's schooling? Was there anyone in the township who shared her love of education?

As she passed over the train tracks on the road to the farm, she decided she couldn't focus on conflicts or her insecurities. She knew the right next step. No one knew how long this would go on; the students were falling further behind by the day. She had worked and worked to compress what she'd planned for September and October into a single month—her goal was to catch her students up by November 1. They'd have to work double speed, even triple speed, given that students always lost skills over the summer, but she was determined that they'd all start the new year in January 1919 unencumbered by the tiresome influenza. She knew the right protocols to implement. She would do her job and do it flawlessly. The school must re-open; it was the only responsible choice.

"Calm, confident, and quiet," she whispered to herself, evoking her father.

•   •   •

By the next afternoon, Mollie had posted a handmade sign about the new school start date—October 10—on the door of every storefront in the town. The signs detailed the symptoms to watch for, directed parents to keep children home from school if they showed any symptoms between now and the first day, and to keep children home for seven days after any illness once school started. The signs also recommended that no one travel outside the town. The signs requested that each child bring a mask to school and stated new school rules: masks at all times, no food sharing, no touching, and frequent hand washing. Mollie was confident that the children would be safe so long as the families and children followed the instructions. The post office at the south end of town was her last stop. She was eager to finish and get back into the car, where she could finally remove her mask—it was trapping perspiration in a thin wet line across the bridge of her nose and her breath smelled rank.

As she positioned the last sign on the post office door, two ladies deeply engaged in private conversation came up behind her. Mollie glanced at them and saw neither was wearing a mask, which made her wonder what she would do when families resisted her requests. She'd need to have masks ready in the classroom for children to wear—no point in fighting with parents. One more extra thing to do before the start of school—perhaps her mother could sew masks. There were plenty of fabric scraps in the sewing room. Good, thick cotton would be best. Each child could have a distinctive fabric, and she could wash the masks each night, dry them on the line, and then take them back in the morning. Mollie stepped out of the way so the ladies could pass, leaving them a wide path into the building.

"Never mind, dear," one said. "We can wait while you finish that. No hurry."

Mollie nodded. She knew her mask would muffle her voice if she spoke.

The ladies continued their conversation a few feet behind Mollie. The taller one mentioned that Cecilia Pokorski had been left alone in the Pokorski family house for almost thirty days. She was only eight years old, the other said. Then, "Poor little soul, it's not right." "I'm to drop a basket of food this afternoon—I'll put in some treats," the small one said, "and some fresh milk." "Poor little soul," was the last thing Mollie heard the two women say, it seemed in unison, as Mollie brushed through the door to the mailroom. She used her key to open the little gold letterbox she shared with her mother and took out three envelopes—a letter from her sister-in-law to both of them, a letter from the Michigan state government that was probably her teaching certification for the 1918-1919 school year—she'd been watching for that—and a flyer about a new tractor model for her father, John, now two years gone from heart trouble.

Mollie got back into her car, peeled off the mask, and took a few deep breaths. The women were still in front of the post office, chatting. She started the car and pulled away from the curb, disturbed by what she'd heard.

The Pokorskis were far from Mollie's favorite family. She didn't understand Polish customs—the pickling and brining, the language with its 'shhh' sounds every other word, the needlessly bright reds and yellows and blues on the house fronts and even the clothing. The Pokorskis had moved to Emmett from the west—Chicago—only ten years ago, rather than from the eastern states, like the other families in the village, who could all trace their roots back to County Cork and had practically traveled to the States on the same boat two generations earlier. The Pokorskis' homestead had angered most folks, especially those with relatives who might have liked to move to the township had they realized the claim was available.

The two boys—Hugh and Josef—were kept home from school whenever farm work took priority, which seemed just about all the time unless the Michigan winter had frozen over, and even then, there was the stock to care for—always an excuse. Mollie had seen it many times: the more a child was absent, the further behind they fell, and the further behind they fell, the less they liked school. She'd been angry the Pokorski family had broken the law that mandated students attend through eighth grade, but Mollie knew she couldn't win that battle. Still, she wished she could vouch that either Josef or Hugh had learned to read properly. Even more reason to get her enrolled students back in school for the precious few winter months when many were allowed to attend.

Cecilia Pokorski, a painfully quiet girl, had finished the second-grade last year and passing her had been a gift. Mollie could barely test the girl, who stammered and hung her head whenever asked a question. But Mollie had been afraid to hold her back. Perhaps the father would decide schooling was futile, even with such a minor setback, or decide school wasn't for girls. Then Cecilia would get no education at all. Still, as she drove along the tree-lined road, Mollie was horrified that she hadn't given the plan for Cecilia a specific thought since the family passed. She hadn't known the child had been alone for almost a month, fed, but little else, like a stray dog a person couldn't refuse but hoped might run along. Mollie had been busy with the plans to open the school and putting all the new routines and safeguards in place, but still she should have inquired after the girl.

•   •   •

When Mollie got back to the farm after putting up her signs, she pulled her Model T up to the front path of the farmhouse rather than into the barn. On a normal Saturday, she would have put the car in its designated spot, wiped it down stem to stern, and then sat down for a late lunch with her mother. Mollie was the only woman in the township who owned her own car. She was proud—and unashamed of being proud—to own the spunky little machine. She cut the engine, and the silence surrounded her.

Catherine was settled into her favorite rocker on the front porch. "Shouldn't you put the car in?" Catherine called. "It looks like rain."

"I'm going to get that child," Mollie called out.

Catherine stood and leaned on her gnarled wooden cane, then took a few steps toward the car. "What child?" she said.

"Cecilia Pokorski."

"The girl who survived the influenza? Where is she?"

"She's still on their place. People have been taking her food all this time. She's been on her own."

"Oh, my goodness. Who's been looking after her?"

"Aside from her basic needs? No one. I assumed her mother's people took her," Mollie said. "I'm horrified I never checked."

Catherine shook her head. "The child's been in that house alone? All this time? Why?"

"I expect people are afraid of her—afraid she's contagious."

"How old is she?"

"Eight. She was in my school last year. Shy little thing. Not that bright."

"I suppose eight is old enough that she'd kept herself alive, with some help," Catherine said. "But where are her people?"

"I don't know. I guess they would have come for her by now if they intended to."

"Where will she live?" Catherine asked.

"Here," Mollie said.

"Here"—the farmhouse—was a two-story brick house on a plot that had been homesteaded almost seventy years earlier when Catherine's parents moved west from New York, where they'd lived for just a few years after emigrating from Ireland. Catherine and Mollie's father, John, had built additions to the house when Mollie was a baby and her older brothers were teenagers, making it spacious compared to what most families had. Once an up-and-down rectangle, after a number of additions, the house was now more a horizontal rectangle. With just Catherine and Mollie living in the farmhouse, it was extravagant. And so quiet. The only sounds they ever heard were the occasional far-off mooing of the Garveys' cattle when the wind was from the east, the train whistling through late at night and early in the morning, frogs in the pond croaking in the summer, and geese honking as they flew overhead on their path south each fall.

"That girl was a change-of-life baby for the Pokorskis," Catherine said. "Their boys were nearly grown. She looked like a perfect miniature of the mother."

Mollie nodded. She remembered that Cecilia's mother's beauty was faded, and that she'd had wrinkles around her eyes. Mollie calculated that she couldn't have been much more than a decade older than Mollie. She'd just had a hard life. Mollie had been a change-of-life baby for her parents, too, more than a decade younger than the brother closest to her in age. Catherine, who'd stopped to lean on her cane at the end of the front walk, was old enough to be her grandmother. Mollie could barely remember when her brothers had lived at home. She put her chin in her hand and her elbow on the steering wheel.

"I can prepare a room," Catherine said.

"You shouldn't be on the stairs unless I'm here," Mollie said. "And we should keep her as far from us as possible. For at least seven days."

"Seven days?"

"Seven days is the maximum period between exposure to the flu and developing symptoms, based on my research."

"The last of her family—her father—passed far longer ago than that—"

"Yes, I know," Mollie interrupted.

"She's already been alone for almost a month."

"Please, Mother, just to be safe…." Now she was questioning her own instinct to pick Cecilia up. Though it was late afternoon, it would be hours until dark. Her stomach was growling. Maybe she should wait until the morning, see how she felt then. It wasn't as if Cecilia was expecting her, and the child had been fine up until now, for so many days and nights. Maybe someone else—

"The downstairs room, then," Catherine said, interrupting Mollie's thoughts. "I can prepare that room on my own, and not bother with stairs."

Mollie looked straight ahead, her hands on the wheel, making no move to get out of the car and crank the engine.

"Please tell me you're not too scared to fetch that child?" Catherine asked.

"Scared? I'm not *scared*—at least not for myself," Mollie said. "I've been exposed to *everything*—I never get sick." This was true. In her ten years of teaching, she hadn't missed a day of school due to illness, and only three times had she been thwarted by bad weather. "I'm worried for *you*."

Mollie thought of telling her brothers and their wives—who lived in Detroit and always thought they knew better—about bringing Cecilia to the farmhouse. They thought Mollie's purpose in life should be to care for her elderly parents, first her father as his health failed, and now her mother. Her older brother, Sam, had even suggested that Mollie take a year off teaching, while the influenza ran its course, with no worry for what would become of her career if she handed over the township school to another teacher. "Why not?" he'd asked, and she'd recoiled at the thought of having to ask him for money—she'd always had money of her own. She could only imagine how they would react when they learned she'd brought a child exposed to the influenza into the farmhouse with their elderly mother.

Mollie and Catherine were both silent for a few moments.

"This can't go on," Catherine finally said. "If not us, then who?"

"Yes," Mollie said, and got out of the car to pull together some things for Cecilia. Now that they'd made up their minds, she didn't want the child to wait alone a minute longer than was necessary. But she also wanted to be prepared, and home again before dark. There were clouds forming along the horizon.

∞

In the days and weeks since the deaths, Cecilia had ventured into every corner of the house, straightening and cleaning as she'd seen Mamusia do. The house mostly looked just as it had before Josef came home—barn boots left outside on the back porch; a cleaned iron pot, long since dry, resting on the washboard; and a stack of folded sheets Mamusia had taken down off the clothesline, waiting in the basket to be put on the beds. In other ways, the house looked different—a kerosene light from the tiny parlor moved onto the kitchen table next to a pair of reading glasses the doctor left behind; the coffee pot left on the stovetop; a dark circle around the base of the icebox where the ice melted to water and the water slowly evaporated. Of course, the biggest difference was that the people were missing. It was as if they'd been lifted away. Cecilia remembered the final two days, when only she and her father were left. Dr. Murphy had told her to pray for her father's recovery so she would have a family. Cecilia had mostly lived in a nest of herself and Mamusia; she couldn't imagine being a family with just her father. He was silent and terrifying, smelling of the barns and sweat, always finding fault with one thing or another. He seemed to only have use for the work Josef and Hugh could do, and little use at all for her.

That wasn't the way it turned out anyway—she was alone.

In the days after her father's body was removed, Cecilia had taken to conversing with a ghost. Mamusia, she hoped. She tried to remember exactly what they had talked about all through the long days together. Now, she took both sides of the conversation. In her imagination, they spoke of the chickens and their eggs—and when and how to replace their dwindling supply of chicken feed—and then about the weather, and sometimes about the memories Mamusia had of her childhood. Sometimes the ghost whispered back with the wind, but never with words Cecilia could understand. Just sighs. At night, the wind chimes Mamusia had hung from the porch tinkled in response to Cecilia's prayers, the ones she and Mamusia had recited before bedtime. Then, she'd been able to whisper along in Polish. Now, she couldn't remember the words. The cattle in the pasture were ghosts, too. Cecilia had watched the neighbor herd them up and drive them down the lane. He'd called out to her, "I'll tend to them for now." The next day, he'd come and caught up the chickens in wire cages with a flurry of wings and squawks. Only Daisy, the barn cat heavy with kittens, remained. She wound herself around Cecilia's ankles as she sat on the porch, then snuggled with her in the pantry, where Cecilia still slept with the door closed tight.

Cecilia owned a book, *The Wonderful Wizard of Oz*. Miss Crowley had read it aloud each day after recess, the only time Cecilia had been allowed to put her head down on her desk. Miss Crowley had given the book to her on the last day of school. She'd forgotten how to read the words and had trouble recalling some of the names of the letters. But she turned the pages and looked at the pictures of Dorothy, the Tin Man, the Scarecrow, and the awful twisting tornado, and tried to remember what happened next.

∞

Listening for the sounds of thunder and watching for lightning, Mollie took a clean set of clothing from a box of things she'd worn as a child, including underthings. The sizes wouldn't be right, but the hand-me-downs would work for Cecilia for the time being. She filled two buckets with scalding hot water—the water would be warm when she got to the Pokorskis. The water in one bucket was laced with bleach. The other bucket, for rinsing, was clear.

"I just hope Cecilia is healthy when I get there," Mollie said. "It's been weeks, but I can't bring her here if she's sick. If she's good now, she should be fine. Then, if we keep her quarantined here for another seven days...."

"We already spoke about that," Catherine said.

"I know," Mollie said. "I'm just thinking out loud. I am trying—"

"You are trying to do your best. There is no perfect decision. But seven days alone in that room, so far from us on the first floor, while we sleep upstairs—heartbreaking to think about it when she's been all alone for almost a month. But I understand—there should be no question she's contagious. Though she's probably...."

"Perhaps the child was immune all along," Mollie said. "She'd just about have to be, correct? From everything I've read, children are especially vulnerable."

"That's an excellent theory," Catherine said. "Who should we tell she's here?"

"Father Foley and Dr. Murphy," Mollie said. "But not until tomorrow. Not until she's settled. What about Dan and Sam?" Dan and Sam, Mollie's older brothers, were the people she dreaded to tell. They'd always thought she was spoiled and impulsive, and it seemed that nothing she did altered their opinions.

"Not yet," Catherine said.

Mollie raised her eyebrows but didn't answer. It was unlike her mother to openly defy her older brothers. Catherine's deference to them usually maddened her.

"I never thought I'd appreciate that your brothers moved away," Catherine continued, "but today, I do. By the time they're here again, she'll be ours."

Ours? That was a leap, Mollie thought. She just intended to care for the girl until something—a permanent arrangement for the child— could be worked out.

Before she could respond, Catherine added, "Be sure to leave a note for the people who've volunteered to bring the baskets. They'll think she's been levitated."

"Thank you," Mollie said. "I'm not sure I would have thought of that. Can you imagine the reaction if she just disappeared?" She shook her head—this was what it was like to be impulsive. She would have forgotten the note.

•   •   •

Mollie and Catherine liked to visit cemeteries. Once each summer, they went by train to Saginaw to visit the graves of a branch of the family Mollie only knew through Catherine's stories. It was their big excursion. This summer, they'd missed the trip because of the advisories to stay close to home. The cemetery where her family was buried—the family Mollie knew—was at the end of their road, just a mile from the house. They visited each Sunday, from the time the snow melted in the spring until the time the snow blanketed the graves again in the winter. They made sure their family plot was free of weeds, nicely mowed, and heavily planted with bulbs in the fall. When the bulbs' blooms died out, they were replaced with well-tended summer annuals. All the families did this; keeping the graves nice was a sign of love and remembrance, just as neglecting the graves was a sign of disregard, one that made Catherine tut-tut-tut in disgust. Their trips to the cemetery were mostly silent, though sometimes Catherine complained about Dr. Murphy. She believed he should have saved John, that a better doctor would have. She called him a "lazy thinker"—a true indictment. It wasn't that she didn't understand that John was terribly ill. It was just that the doctor seemed to have given up on him with no fight whatsoever. He'd allowed John to fade away without protest.

That afternoon, on her way to get Cecilia, Mollie stopped the car and got out at the cemetery. Her father's grave looked beautiful, as did the graves of his neighbors, with heavy blossoms and brighter colors than was typical in fall, as if in defiance of the news of illness. All the graves were laid out with individual headstones, in neat rows of rectangles.

Mollie located the Pokorski family graves, four grassless rectangles pointing out from a center point, like the spokes of a cross wheel. A limestone-white gravestone shaped like a spike—perhaps three feet tall, listing to the north, and clearly new—was the center point of the circle. The gravestone was far from the other families' markers, which all seemed to be clustered together. It was a modest thing, perhaps eighteen inches square at the base, tapering to a point of nothing, the tip level with Mollie's waist. There was a name on each side of the spike—Aloysius, Frances, Josef, and Hugh. The display was paltry compared to what was customary in the community. There was no space on the marker for Cecilia; all four sides bore a name. Cecilia would spend the rest of her life trying to create new connections, in pursuit of family. Catherine's phrase—"She'll be ours"—now echoed in Mollie's head. Mother is less torn about what to do than I am, Mollie thought. She already doesn't think anyone will come for Cecilia. She is already prepared to claim Cecilia as our own if need be.

Of all the dozens of students Mollie had taught, none of the children were hers. She knew that while she might understand children in the classroom, outside the classroom was entirely different. Before too much longer, students she'd taught in the beginning, now in their twenties, would have children of their own sitting at the kindergarten table. She didn't mind the thought of caring for Cecilia for a few days or even weeks, but what if it was forever? And why Cecilia—such a pale shadow of a girl, nothing special—when there were so many others with whom she'd had more affinity? She'd missed marrying and starting a family with her peers, and now accepted that ship had sailed. She'd settled into her independence. She was comfortable.

"Who were you?" Mollie whispered, looking at the four spokes. She touched the side of the marker that bore Cecilia's mother's name, Frances Pokorski, and whispered, "Where are your people?" The breeze rustled the leaves above her head. Then, she hugged herself at the thought of Cecilia left behind, alone in that house. There must be someone—surely this was just temporary. She had to be the least likely person to assume the care of an orphaned child.

Catherine had never asked how Mollie felt about being left behind as all her girlfriends married and had children. Mollie had never felt she belonged with those girls, so predictable and compliant. Catherine never wondered, out loud anyway, why Mollie was so different, why she stayed apart and worked so hard, and so valued her independence and so prized having her own income. Catherine never asked why Mollie so loved her little car, her status in the village, or when everyone deferred to her about big decisions, like opening the school. Catherine didn't seem to understand. Mollie remembered the prickle of anger she'd felt when Catherine suggested she was too scared to go for Cecilia—it had been her idea in the first place.

Mollie was *never* scared.

It was her father, buried just a hundred feet to the east, who had understood how she made the choices that led to her unusual life. He was proud of her completion of the year-long program at the teachers' college. He'd framed her certificate and hung it on the wall of the farmhouse dining room. He was interested in her students, and always read the books Mollie chose along with her, then discussed them far into the night. It had been her father who took her to buy the car, so proud, but he died before she learned to drive. She had to go to the hardware store in town and offer to pay the owner, Tom Reid, to teach her. She looked back at her father's grave, so well-tended. Tears welled up. She wished she knew what he would have advised. She still missed him.

What exactly am I doing, she thought, looking again at the Pokorski graves, in their strange, circular configuration. With its shared headstone and grassless rectangles, it was surely the cheapest and least thoughtful burial she'd ever seen. Whoever put it in hadn't even bothered to get the marker to stand straight. It was as if they'd plunked it down and run off, without even bothering to secure the sorry thing. Mollie walked between two of the graves and tried to push it upright, but the stone was immovable. She imagined the eyes of all the Pokorskis' heads in the center of the circle, looking up at her, imploring her to help, trying to tell her what she needed to know to take care of Cecilia.

Mollie considered why her mother was so insistent she should fetch Cecilia. She's growing older, Mollie realized. She knows that one day, I will lose her too—unthinkable. I will then be completely alone; no more choices. Decades still ahead of me. Does she think this is my last real chance to build a family? Even a makeshift one? And what if I don't want a child, any child, not now and not ever. What will I do with Cecilia if no one ever surfaces to take care of her?

Mollie tried to imagine delivering Cecilia to the Children's Home in Port Huron, where orphans went when there was nowhere else to go. She couldn't picture herself doing that. This was a moment of decision. This was no small thing. She could end up with this child permanently if no one showed up to claim her. Could she manage that? Mollie brushed away the dirt and mud from the base of the Pokorski marker, and vowed to plant flowers here in the spring, regardless of what happened with Cecilia. Someone needed to mind their graves.

So, how does one start, with a child? *Really* start, not like a teacher at the beginning of a new school year, but like a parent, if it comes to that? Once I do this, can I ever turn back? Mollie felt a shiver chill her skin. The autumn air, almost begging for a storm, was heavy and gray. Is she to be only my student and a boarder, perhaps one day a help with my mother? A comfort, so I don't have to be alone? Or is she to be something more?

Am I scared?

In some way, I guess both Cecilia and I are leftovers, Mollie thought. Cecilia is an orphan, and I am an anomaly. I know not one other woman who shares my current path. She touched the cool limestone of the Pokorski marker, caught in a shaft of sunlight that pierced through the clouds. It hadn't started raining yet, but it would soon. It seemed so odd, to even think about that slip of a girl, sitting in the first row of her classroom, soon to be living in her home, maybe even joining her family.

She shook her head, walked across the damp grass to the car, turned the crank to start the engine, got in, and put her hands on the wheel. Though Catherine might say the girl was a godsend, Mollie didn't think that way. She was more practical. As Catherine had said, if not them, then who? No need to think beyond the present problem. She pulled onto the road and sped south, toward the Pokorski farm.

Chapter Three

Cecilia heard the rumble of an engine coming up the curved drive but couldn't see what or who was approaching. It wasn't the basket delivery—that had been delivered hours ago. She went cold all over. She had gone from expecting people around her—like sunshine or weather—to fearing people. A car pulled into sight. Behind the wheel was—she squinted to recognize the figure—her teacher. She remembered that Miss Crowley would dart into the schoolyard in that car in a cloud of dust, sometimes a few minutes after the students had arrived. It was the only time Cecilia ever saw a woman operate a piece of machinery. Her memories of that time felt like those of a different girl.

What was Miss Crowley doing here?

It was as strange as if a cow flew, as Mamusia used to say, to see Miss Crowley anywhere other than the schoolyard.

She wished she had time to go into the house and make herself presentable, but Miss Crowley's car had already skidded to a stop, and she was climbing the front steps. She was already closer than the doctor had been willing to venture.

∞

At the Pokorskis' house, which Mollie had only previously seen from the road, she drove right up to the porch, jumped out of her car, and climbed the steps. She was surprised to find Cecilia outside, dressed only in a white cotton slip, seated on a bench, her feet flat on the wooden slats of the porch next to a pan of soapy water. Clearly, the child was in the process of washing up, and hadn't anticipated any passers-by or company.

Why would she? The lady at the post office said the baskets were dropped off, so if the basket for today had already come, Cecilia would think she was on her own to spend the hours of the afternoon and evening. She'd been alone for weeks—the house had a pox on it. Mollie thought of the interminable days of quarantine with just Catherine for company. Imagine how lonely the isolation must have been for a child—and how frightening.

Cecilia crossed her thin arms over her chest, and Mollie could see the heat of embarrassment in her cheeks from several feet away. To be found partly naked on a porch by one's teacher was an embarrassment even an eight-year-old could feel. Cecilia reached up with one hand to smooth her hair, a white-blond rats' nest.

"It's all right, sweetheart," Mollie said, getting out of the car. "It's just me, Miss Crowley."

"I wash up," Cecilia said. "The basket already came. That's why I outside."

This was more words than Mollie had ever heard Cecilia say at one time. "I know," she answered, thinking that Cecilia must have established her own routine, arranged around the delivery of the basket, and taking advantage of the warmest part of the afternoon. Quite resourceful for such a young child. Still, she looked "like no one loved her," as Catherine always said when Mollie, as a girl, was disheveled and dirty after a long day playing outdoors with the Garvey girls.

"I've come to take you home with me."

Cecilia stood and took a step toward Mollie, leaving the outline of two wet footprints on the dry boards of the porch. She held out her arms. Mollie could remember only a very few of the girls hugging her—

she wasn't that kind of teacher—and never Cecilia. She'd barely been able to get the girl to look her in the eyes.

"Stop," Mollie said, putting her palms up like a warning. "We need to be careful."

She walked back to the car and pulled the first of the heavy five-gallon buckets from the back of the trunk. The water was now just pleasantly warm but reeked of bleach. She set the bucket with bleach on the bottom step of the porch and returned for the second bucket of clear water, as well as the bag containing the fresh clothing from the passenger seat. She hoped she could trust her research, which established that Cecilia was both non-contagious and probably immune.

Perhaps she should still make Cecilia wear a mask? But for the whole seven days? And who was to say she wasn't a bigger risk to Cecilia than Cecilia was to her? Perhaps it was more sensible for her to put her own mask on. But the only one she had was the one she'd left in the car, and she'd been wearing that one in town. It felt soiled and smelled bad. Plus, she had no intention of wearing a mask in her own home and, within the hour, Cecilia would be in residence there.

This was all so new.

Forget the mask, Mollie decided. If she is coming home with me, we both must take some risk. She picked up her buckets and took the last few steps up the porch stairs.

"This is going to burn," Mollie said, dipping a dry rag into the bucket, then extending the wet cloth to Cecilia. "Wash every inch. Then, we'll rinse you right away with water from the second bucket and then the pump, and—" She remembered the ointment she kept in the glove compartment for the long winters when her hands were always raw and chafed— "I've got some lanolin you can rub in right away. I'll get it."

Once she was back on the porch, she turned her back while Cecilia sponged herself off, her only reaction to the bleach a quick intake of breath. Mollie winced—the water laced with bleach must be so harsh.

But what was the alternative? She opened the jar of lanolin, happy to see that the warm afternoon temperature had softened the balm.

Mollie turned when she heard another gasp of pain. "Let me pour this clear water over you to take out the sting," she said. "I won't look." Mollie sluiced the second bucket she'd brought, full of clear water, down Cecilia's bare back, then filled the bucket two more times from the cistern. The cistern water was ice-cold, and the breeze made goosebumps rise along Cecilia's skin. Mollie draped a clean towel around Cecilia's shoulders and rubbed until the girl stopped shivering. Then, she extended the small pot of lanolin ointment. "Use it all," Mollie said. "Rub it between your hands to soften it before you put it on your skin."

Cecilia rubbed the ointment onto her arms and legs, and then turned for Mollie to rub it onto her back, and Mollie guessed that must have been her habit with her mother. As she rubbed in the lotion, she recalled doing the same for her father in his last days and realized that she hadn't touched another person so intimately since. As Cecilia put on the white linen dress Mollie brought, much too large for her, Mollie fetched one of the left-over signs about the school's opening from her car, turned it over, and wrote:

Saturday, September 28

Cecilia Pokorski is now residing with Catherine and Mollie Crowley at the Crowley farm. Thank you for the baskets—no longer necessary.

Mollie Crowley

She tacked the sign to the Pokorskis' door. By dinnertime tomorrow, the entire village would know Cecilia's whereabouts, the news traveling along whatever gossip tree that accompanied the basket deliveries. So much for restricting the news to Father Foley and Dr. Murphy. She imagined their angry voices on the telephone in the farmhouse; she now regretted having it installed when her father got

MICHELE M. FEENEY   33

sick. Perhaps she should call her brothers herself, before anyone else got to them.

"How could you put our mother in danger?" they would ask. They would be livid, and likely would not listen to any explanation that Catherine had taken equal part in and approved the decision. Still, the brothers might be right; only time would tell.

She'd call this evening. Or, perhaps it would be better to wait until their weekly Sunday phone call tomorrow afternoon. She would act matter-of-fact, Mollie decided, like this was a temporary solution until they could find a better option. Perhaps it was. Of course, they would say the damage was already done once Cecilia was in the house. Mollie dreaded conflicts with her brothers, but it seemed there was no avoiding this one.

"My things?" Cecilia asked. "I be quick."

"No," Mollie said, and shook her head. "No one knows for certain how the contamination spreads—that's why I brought the clean clothing. No need to take unnecessary risk. Don't go back inside. We can perhaps come back another time."

Cecilia closed her eyes briefly, then nodded.

Cecilia's white cotton slip, abandoned after her wash, lay like drifted snow on the porch. It looked spooky, as though the girl had evaporated. Mollie shivered and put the image out of her head. She'd replace the girl's toys and books, perhaps from the farmhouse attic. She had a few things left over from her classroom last spring, too. Catherine would need to alter some clothing, so Cecilia would have something to wear. She'd also need to sew the masks Mollie intended to keep just inside the classroom door for all the students.

"Come along now," Mollie said. "Don't dawdle."

They settled into the car just as the storm broke, quickly, with pounding raindrops making rivulets in the dust on the windshield. Mollie navigated around the potholes on Fox Road and was relieved to find the stream north of their house hadn't yet risen over the bridge. As she turned the corner onto Webb Road, she glanced over at Cecilia.

The girl's face was turned away from her, looking out the passenger side window. The white linen dress was draped across the seat and clung wetly to her narrow chest and thin arms. The skirt was muddy along the hem; they'd dashed from the porch to the car just as the rain began to fall. Cecilia still smelled faintly of bleach, and her hands were raw and red from scrubbing, much like Mollie's were most of last winter, when her eczema got so bad that her dry skin bled and her nails cracked down the middle. Cecilia's white-blond hair clung to her scalp, and her ears were pink around the rims, as if sunburned.

"What on earth have you been doing in that house all by yourself, child?" Mollie asked. "How have you managed?"

Cecilia turned to Mollie. Her eyes filled with tears, and she began to sob. She sobbed all the rest of the way home, past the school, over three miles, as they drove through the rain. It was as though she'd needed a witness before she could let her tears go. Mollie reached over and put her hand on Cecilia's arm but couldn't imagine what else to do or say. As much as she missed her father, she knew she had never experienced a grief like Cecilia's. She was an adult when her father passed and his health had progressively failed over several months. The child had to have been not only lonely, but terrified, and grief-stricken—she'd lost everyone over the course of just one week, then been abandoned for several weeks more.

There was no going back, Mollie now knew. She would never have the heart to cast off this child. Unless a family member claimed Cecilia, she was theirs. Mollie felt a rush of gratitude that her mother was at the farmhouse. Catherine would know how to settle Cecilia and how to respond to further outbursts of grief. Then Mollie remembered that fetching Cecilia had been her impulse. She was the young and healthy one in the farmhouse, the one at the proper age to take over care of Cecilia. She was going to have to figure out how to make Cecilia see Catherine as a grandmother, not a mother, even if this was temporary. It was only fair. This was hers to manage.

∞

The car stopped in front of a farmhouse that Cecilia had never seen before. The broad face of the house was covered with trails of green ivy. The long narrow windows looked like eyes wide open with happy surprise. There were daisies in pots on either side of the front door. Cecilia remembered there were flowers in the pots next to the schoolhouse door last spring—she'd taken several turns watering them, as had the other younger students. The house was huge—much bigger than their house and even bigger than the schoolhouse. A tall, thin, gray-haired woman sat on the porch, waiting.

"That's my mother," Miss Crowley said. "I live here with her."

Cecilia's eyes narrowed. Who else lived here?

"Just us," Miss Crowley said, as if she had heard the question. "Just my mother and me, and now you."

They got out of the car, and when they reached the porch, the gray-haired woman said, "You can call me Grandma Catherine. Everybody does." She reached her arms out to Cecilia.

Miss Crowley reached out and cupped Cecilia's shoulder. She understood—she was not meant to go any closer. But, she wondered, why didn't Miss Crowley wear a mask like the doctor had, and why was she touching her? Did she think she was safe? The grandmother didn't have a mask on either.

They were acting as though it was before the sickness.

•   •   •

A few moments later, Cecilia stood in the entry to a bedroom with a bed tucked into the corner, covered with a bright patchwork quilt. The three windows were wide open. There was a blue nightgown draped across the bed. The bed looked big enough for several of her, but soft and warm. The breeze, fresh from the storm, lifted the light drapes away from the windows. Someone had put a bunch of white roses in a vase on the bureau.

"This was my daddy's room," Miss Crowley said. Then she blushed and smoothed her skirt with both hands, the way she did before starting a new lesson in the schoolhouse. She moved a few steps further into the room and Cecilia followed. She pulled the door partway shut behind them. "See," she said, gesturing to the wall behind the door. "Hooks. For your things."

"My things left behind," Cecilia said.

"I mean," Miss Crowley said, her blush deepening. "When you get things. Of your own. Or when we go back to your house."

"Where is father?" Cecilia asked. She imagined a crotchety old man, with a temper like her father's and a severity like Miss Crowley's in the classroom. Even though Mamusia had always said her bark was worse than her bite, Cecilia had feared Miss Crowley.

Miss Crowley had tears in her eyes, and her cheeks were now mottled and pink. "I'm so sorry," she said. "I didn't mean to mention that first thing. He passed. Two years ago. At the end, he couldn't get up and down the stairs. So, he slept in here."

"Father died here?" Cecilia asked, looking around the room.

"Yes," Miss Crowley said. "This was his room." Her cheeks grew even redder and the mottling spread down to her neck. "You can stay upstairs if it makes you, well…." She seemed to be fumbling for a word she couldn't remember. "Or we can figure out something else."

Cecilia felt surprised. She had never seen Miss Crowley embarrassed or flustered. "He nice?" she asked.

"Very," Miss Crowley said. "I miss him."

"Then good," Cecilia said. "As long as a nice ghost, like Mamusia. Like brothers. Maybe he whisper to me in night, like them."

Miss Crowley's stern teacher-look passed across her face, but she didn't tell Cecilia to "behave" or say anything at all. She didn't say there was no such thing as a ghost. Cecilia watched Miss Crowley cross herself—Father, Son, and Holy Ghost—like they did at church. A few seconds later, a wistful look settled onto Miss Crowley's features, like she perhaps wished her father might whisper to her. Maybe he would have, if Miss Crowley ever slept in this room, Cecilia thought. She knew one thing—she wasn't scared at all anymore to stay in a house where people had died. This pretty room would be just fine—so much nicer than she'd imagined.

"I wish whispers of my family would follow me here," she said, too softly for Miss Crowley to hear.

∞

"I held dinner over," Catherine called from the kitchen. "Whenever you're ready."

Mollie smelled the roast chicken and the scent of pie. Cherry? Apple? No, peach—her favorite. Her mouth watered and she could only imagine how Cecilia craved a hot meal.

Oh, no, Mollie thought, rushing to the kitchen. Did her mother really think they should all eat together around the small kitchen table? Had she already forgotten the seven days? Mollie wanted to be able to tell her brothers, truthfully, that she was taking every precaution to keep her mother safe and that they planned to observe the seven-day quarantine period. They could not possibly eat at the same table.

"Wait here," Mollie said, and when a look of terror passed over Cecilia's features, she added, "Just for a minute. I'm not going to shut you in. I promise."

As she entered the dining room, Mollie saw Catherine had set the long table—not the small table in the kitchen at the northernmost end of the house—with one setting at the end for Cecilia and two place settings at the opposite end. They only used the dining room, with its polished walnut sideboard and eight carved chairs, on holidays. Catherine's arrangement left space for at least four people—two on each side—between the two seats at one end and the single seat at the other. Mollie made a mental note to handle Cecilia's dishes after the meal, or better yet, have her handle her own dishes. She could slip them into boiling water with plenty of soap. Or maybe they should set dishes aside only for Cecilia's use?

Catherine appeared in the doorway. "I thought you and Cecilia would sit down there," she tilted her head toward the two seats at the end of the table, "and I would stay here. It's greater than six feet. You're going back to school anyway soon, correct?" Catherine sat down in the chair she'd designated for herself. "I'm going to have to create my own safe zone. Quarantine myself. Because you will not know who might be infected. I will have to assume you're contagious, all the time. You've been with Cecilia all afternoon—you could already be contagious."

Mollie realized that she hadn't only left off her own mask, she hadn't asked Cecilia to wear a mask when she entered the farmhouse either. And Catherine was now distancing herself from both Mollie and Cecilia. Catherine was the one outside the loop.

Mollie felt herself falter. What would Mollie do if her brothers insisted on taking Catherine home with them because of what they would call her foolishness? And, if they did that, how long before they made noises again about selling the property? Mollie had avoided discussing the ownership of the farm since her father passed, because talk of wills and such upset Catherine. Now she'd have to start all over again. If they had their way, she'd end up a boarder in an upstairs bedroom of some stingy farm family, perhaps one of her student's families. God only knew what would happen to Cecilia.

Cecilia entered the room, and Catherine nodded toward the place she'd set for Cecilia. Mollie reluctantly took the seat next to Cecilia, so far away from Catherine.

What had she done?

∞

That night, Cecilia learned Miss Crowley and Grandma Catherine's nighttime ritual—they took turns cleaning their teeth and washing their faces in water pumped into a big bowl in the kitchen sink. Then

Cecilia waited with Miss Crowley as Grandma Catherine crossed the grassy yard to the outhouse. When she was finished, Mollie and Cecilia took their turns. Then, the three of them, wearing their nightgowns, traveled into the house and quietly said evening prayers together, back at the dining room table, with Grandma Catherine at a distance.

Miss Crowley accompanied Cecilia to her room and pulled back the bedcovers and smoothed the sheets. She waited for Cecilia to slip in, tucked the quilts around her, and then hugged her. The hug was stiff, not warm like Mamusia's, but Cecilia clung on anyway, because it was the first hug she'd had in weeks. In a moment, Miss Crowley softened into her—Cecilia could barely believe that she was the same person she was so terrified of at school last year. Miss Crowley smelled of clean soap and roses and stayed put until Cecilia let go first.

When she was alone, Cecilia found the house soundless. Wherever Miss Crowley and Grandma Catherine were, she could not even hear the rhythm of their voices. The room smelled of nothing more than clean sheets. The bed felt large around her, so much bigger than the little bed she'd had at home before she had to sleep in the pantry. It was deep and warm, like a nest. Miss Crowley had said her father had stayed in this room when he was sick, and that he'd died here. This must've been his bed, Cecilia thought, but the thought didn't bother her.

Instead, Cecilia wished she didn't feel so comfortable. She couldn't help it. The soft air coming through the open window felt fresh and cool, not like the closed-in feeling of the pantry that always had the disgusting and embarrassing scent of her chamber pot. The sheets were smooth and crisp, and smelled like she and Mamusia had just pulled them off the line and out of the sunshine. The blue nightgown she'd seen earlier lying across the bed had been meant for her. It felt like it had been washed a hundred times and dried on a line in the sun. The quilts were pleasantly heavy on her skin. She knew that Miss Crowley and Grandma Catherine were in the house. She wasn't alone. Cecilia's head on the pillow felt heavy. She felt strange, but also comforted. She closed her eyes.

Five minutes later, she opened them. If only she had thought of Daisy before she left the farm. She hadn't even stopped to feed Daisy scraps from the baskets, as she'd been doing every day, or to give her fresh water before she'd left. She heard her father's voice saying how Daisy was a barn cat, meant to survive in the barn, but she wasn't sure. She wished Daisy was here in the bed with her, curled into her belly like a warm ball, just as she'd been for so many long nights in the pantry.

Cecilia heard a long, low whistle, faint at first, then loud. There was a rhythm now, clacking, and she couldn't figure out what it was—it scared her. Before she could work up the courage to slide out of bed and look out the window, the whistle had faded away and the clacking sound was gone. She struggled to recall where she'd heard the sound before and realized she'd last heard it when Josef came home. The farmhouse must be near the train track and the church and the village. Then, she fell into a deep sleep.

Chapter Four

Early Sunday, before dawn, Mollie woke with a start. Her head was filled with a vision of parading into the church with Cecilia in tow. Everyone would know who Cecilia was and what had happened to her family. Mollie pictured people moving away from them the way ground pepper moved across the surface of soapy water when she did the science experiment at school, the one about the tension of water molecules. Seeing Cecilia with her could make people think she was rash and irresponsible, just like her brothers did. Maybe they'd think twice about sending their children to school the following week. By the time she had dressed for breakfast, her stomach was sick with nerves.

"How would you feel about staying home this morning and saying the Rosary instead of attending Mass?" Mollie whispered to Catherine, as they both sipped their first cups of tea at the long dining room table.

"Everyone will think I've taken sick," Catherine said. "That's what they always think if an old person misses Mass."

This was a new perspective. Mollie hadn't realized that Catherine was sensitive about growing older. Of course, it would be the first time they'd missed Mass that Mollie could remember since the last days of her father's illness. Even then, they'd taken turns with Mollie attending one week and Catherine the next, so he was never left alone. Catherine being sick was the logical assumption others might jump to if their pew was empty this morning.

"I understand," Mollie said. "But I think we should talk with my brothers before taking Cecilia anywhere public. I want them to hear about it from us first. Plus, given the note I left, I think people may assume our absence has to do with Cecilia. I hope they don't think she's sick...."

"I expect it can't be helped," Catherine interrupted. "Let them think what they will." She stirred her teaspoon absently in the tea. Her voice was resolute, but her expression was anxious.

Was Catherine second-guessing Cecilia's rescue? Mollie always had her dark moments of self-doubt in the night; Catherine tended to worry in the morning before the day started properly.

"By next week, this should have all sorted itself out," Mollie said. She stood and went to the drawer of the sideboard where they kept the rosaries. Hers was a mother-of-pearl design she'd received for her confirmation. Catherine's was a simple thing made of jade beads that had been passed down from a great-grandmother in Ireland. Her father's Rosary was made of black wooded beads separated by metal links. He'd hated saying the Rosary and was prone to "lose" his; she'd purchased this one for him from the gift closet at the church, just months before he died. She set the black one aside for Cecilia.

"Yes, I agree," Catherine said. "For today, the Rosary is best."

Mollie sighed, anticipating the repetitive and numbing recitation of the Rosary. There would be five cycles of the Apostles' Creed, Our Fathers, Hail Marys, Glory Bes, Fatimas, and Holy Ghosts, each cycle intercepted by one of the Glorious Mysteries—the Resurrection, the Ascension, the Descent, the Assumption, and the Coronation—with nothing to look at and not even the freedom to let her own thoughts wander, as she normally did during Mass.

Mollie's aversion to the practice of the Rosary started with the nuns, who disciplined children by making them say the Rosary. Mollie most often got this punishment for talking too much. She much preferred the public school practice of a simple prayer to start the day and a grace before lunch. She otherwise kept religion to a minimum in her classroom. Still, there was no helping it. They'd be best to stay home.

"I wonder if the child has ever said the Rosary," Catherine said.

"We'll get started," Mollie said. "And let her join in when she wakes. No need to make a day of it."

"Mollie, you're exaggerating," Catherine said, shaking her head. "The Rosary doesn't take a whole day."

"No, only the soul of one," Mollie answered, and rolled her eyes.

"No more than twenty minutes," Catherine said.

"An eternal twenty minutes for a child," Mollie said.

"I suppose so," Catherine said, and laughed. "We'll recite quickly. I suppose we are also on inspection. Let's make a good first impression on the child."

∞

After the Rosary, which Catherine sped through, and of which Cecilia only caught the tail end, they had a breakfast of oatmeal and ripe peaches at the long dining room table, with the same seating arrangement—Mollie and Cecilia at one end, and Catherine at the other—as at dinner the night before. Then, after breakfast, Mollie read with Cecilia from a picture book she kept at home, dismayed at all the words Cecilia seemed to have forgotten. As the minutes passed, she wondered if Catherine was dreading the sound of the phone bell as much as she was. The phone was so often the bearer of bad news.

At exactly eleven o'clock, the phone in the kitchen rang, as it always did just before Sunday lunch.

Mollie took the receiver from the big black box on the kitchen wall and sat in the chair they kept next to the phone, twisting the long wire between her fingers. "Hello, Sam," she said, willing starch into her voice.

Sam talked for a few minutes about life in the city—because of the pandemic, the Detroit Public Schools had not opened yet, "might not open until the new year." He and his wife had no intention of sending their two boys anyway, he said, and Mollie bit her tongue about her plan to re-open the school the following week. There were masks everywhere in Detroit, and funerals too. Sam's wife was frightened to leave the house for any reason, sure the "vermin" that caused the illness was everywhere, "floating in the air." He finished, "I am so glad you and Mother are there, where it's safe. So far from neighbors. You can keep to yourselves as long as necessary. And now that the Detroit schools have remained closed, your decision about your school is obvious. You can't open."

Silence.

"Please tell me you don't intend to open," Sam said.

"We actually haven't had any incidents at all here," Mollie said, "except the Pokorskis, and that was weeks ago. So, I read the guidelines Governor Sleeper sent, and it seems we can open. The decision is up to me. That's my plan, along with a lot of precautions."

"What date?"

"October 10. Weeks later than usual. The students will be so far behind. But I think by November 1…."

"Dan and I discussed this," Sam interrupted. "If you insist on opening, we will come out today to get Mother. We will not allow your poor judgment to jeopardize her health. We can be there long before supper."

"Don't you think…." Mollie started, but before she could finish her thought, she heard the click. Now they'd be on their way, here in a few hours. At least, with Cecilia there, they wouldn't insist on staying the night, as they usually did. They paid no mind to whether she had time to get rooms ready for them, but just dropped in as if it were their right. Her stomach soured again; the breakfast she'd just eaten was threatening to come right back up. She felt her fury at Sam's disregard for her informed judgment change into apprehension. Her heart sped up in fear. She'd rather be anywhere other than facing down her brothers. They always treated her as if she was a silly, willful child. And they didn't yet even know about Cecilia.

∞

Three hours later, seated on the front porch with Grandma Catherine and Miss Crowley, Cecilia heard a car approaching. Grandma Catherine got to her feet before the car had fully stopped. Two men were seated in the front of the car, and the driver got out quickly. She and Miss Crowley stayed in their places on the porch bench to Grandma Catherine's right. Cecilia wondered if the arrival of the two men had something to do with the whispering in the house earlier that afternoon.

"I won't go," Grandma Catherine said, standing and stepping forward, her cane planted in the soil of the yard like a sturdy fencepost.

The other man slammed out of the passenger's side and put his hands on his hips. Cecilia thought they both looked stiff and sour.

"Who is she?" the first man asked, squinting at Cecilia.

"Cecilia Pokorski," Grandma Catherine said. "Cecilia, these are my sons." She nodded toward the taller one. "That's Sam," she said, then tilted her head toward the other one. "And he's Dan."

"What is she doing here?" Dan asked.

"Mollie and I agreed that she should stay with us."

Cecilia wondered who Mollie was, then realized Grandma Catherine was referring to her teacher, Miss Crowley. Mollie must be her name. She hadn't known.

"Is that the girl whose family passed?" Sam said, taking a step back, just as the doctor used to step back from the pantry door, then later, step away from the front porch steps.

Dan was still standing next to the driver's side of the car.

"Yes," Miss Crowley said, and stood up.

Cecilia stepped under Miss Crowley's arm. She did not like men, or at least bossy men like her father, but she kept that a secret and tried to give each man a chance—not to jump to judgment. That's what Mamusia had said, anyway—lots of men were nice. Hugh was always nice to her.

These men, the "brothers," as Miss Crowley called them, looked like twins, like Hugh and Josef looked in the pictures from before Josef left home, except that one brother was taller than the other, who was rounder than the tall one. If they wanted to, they could pick Grandma Catherine up between the two of them and put her in the back of the car, and Miss Crowley couldn't stop them. That is what Cecilia's father would have done. Cecilia shivered and narrowed her eyes and felt Miss Crowley's fingers tighten on her shoulders—she was scared, too.

"You brought that child into the home with our mother?" Sam said. "Carrying vermin? What were you thinking? And why didn't you consult with us?"

"We talked about it first," Grandma Catherine said. "We reached the decision together. Cecilia was left alone for several weeks after she lost her family. What would you have us do? Leave her alone in a deserted house? I am disappointed in you both. Your father and I raised you better than that."

"You could have asked us if we could get a girl from the city to care for her," Dan said. "Many people, especially in the city, are out of work. Lots of people are looking for a way to live in the country, where there's more space and air. Perhaps we could have found someone who'd appreciate a decent place to stay and food, even with the risk."

Cecilia looked at Miss Crowley. She had that new nervous look again.

"If anyone was going to put something like that in place," Grandma Catherine said, "it would have happened by now. And it would only have been a temporary solution anyway. What's done is done."

"We took precautions," Miss Crowley said. "Bleach to sterilize her skin, clean clothing, her own room, and lots of time outside, like now. We don't eat together…."

"They don't eat with me," Grandma Catherine said. "I have kept my distance. It's been weeks since her family passed. I am perfectly safe."

"We've agreed you should come home with us," Dan said. "Even though you now present a risk to us and our families. We will leave Mollie to her own bad judgment."

Grandma Catherine stepped close to Cecilia and put her arm around Cecilia's shoulder.

Cecilia saw Dan, still standing near the car, wince.

"Step away from her," Sam barked to Cecilia, and Cecilia inched away, only to have Grandma Catherine hold her shoulder tighter and pull her back to her side.

They all stood frozen.

"You completely disregarded our wishes," Sam said, glaring at Miss Crowley. "You knew we didn't even want you teaching this fall. You knew we would *never* agree to have an infected child in the house."

"She's not infected—" Miss Crowley said.

"That girl is not like us," Dan interrupted.

"What do you mean, exactly?" Grandma Catherine said.

"She has people of her own. There are other Polish families in the township. Why not one of them?" Dan said.

"Why not, I wonder," Miss Crowley said. "Perhaps they feel as you do."

"If you were so hellbent on interfering, why didn't you go and stay there with her?" Sam said to Mollie. "Why did you need to put our mother at risk?"

"Cecilia *is* like us," Miss Crowley said. "And she is *not* infected."

"So now you're a doctor too?" Dan said.

"What does Doctor Murphy think about this?" Sam asked.

"I haven't—"

"Of course, you haven't," Dan interrupted. "You are *so* headstrong. I cannot *believe* you've done this. Why, Sarah—" A look of concern pinched his features. "Sarah—"

"Don't be silly," Grandma Catherine said. "You and Sarah have a new baby. No reason to introduce me into the mix."

"I will take Mother," Sam said. "She can quarantine at our house, then stay safe with us through the winter."

"No," Grandma Catherine said. "You're not listening. I am *not* going with you. I am not afraid of this child." She drew Miss Crowley and Cecilia even closer to her.

Now, Cecilia could feel both women close on either side of her, and she drew a deep breath. She'd been afraid the brothers would shake their resolve, the way her father made Mamusia seem smaller.

Cecilia exhaled.

Sam cringed. "You are willfully taking risk," he began.

"I will not live like, like—well, like Cecilia has been living the past several weeks," Catherine interrupted. "With people passing food through the door for me. Like an animal. With my own family afraid of me. I will keep myself safe, certainly safe enough."

Dan looked relieved.

Sam crossed his arms; he hadn't given up.

Grandma Catherine stood straighter. Miss Crowley said nothing.

Cecilia never saw a woman hold her ground like Grandma Catherine just had. Miss Crowley's scary presence in the classroom was beginning to make sense.

"There's nothing for you to do other than sit for a bit," Grandma Catherine said.

"I don't think so," Dan said, looking pale around the mouth. He put a hand on the handle of the passenger door of the car.

"Outside," Grandma Catherine said. "We'll sit outside. Get the chairs from out back, under the tree. Drag them up here." Then she headed to her chair on the porch and settled herself.

"There's no need for more talking," Sam said. "I hope you know we won't be bringing our children here for quite some time now that you've introduced this stranger. Not my boys, and not Dan's baby."

Cecilia understood what that meant. Grandma Catherine wouldn't be seeing her own grandchildren because she and Miss Crowley had taken Cecilia in. Grandma Catherine would miss seeing her new grandbaby. She looked at Miss Crowley, whose mouth was open in a round 'O' of surprise. Maybe she hadn't considered that outcome either.

The two brothers stood outside the car for a few seconds, then got back in. Dan rolled down the passenger window. "You're unbelievable, Mollie," he said. "Unbelievable. It's like you're on a different planet. Don't you know what's happening? How bad it is? You haven't heard the end of this," he yelled, as Sam pulled away.

∞

While she was relieved, Mollie also felt angry. She couldn't speak. Whatever she could have said would have been the wrong thing. Her brothers simply didn't understand that she and her mother were more like friends now than mother and daughter, and they would never believe that she and Catherine decided about Cecilia together. If anything, her mother was more for it than she was. They would never treat her as if she was an adult in her own home, free to make her own decisions. They would never respect her judgment. As Sam pulled away, Mollie took off walking down the dirt road in the opposite direction, fast and determined as the little tugboats on Lake Huron, capable of pulling freighters as long as trains, leaving Catherine and Cecilia behind. She could feel their eyes staring at her rigid back, and already felt guilty for leaving, but she needed a minute. More than a minute. An hour.

∞

From her spot at the dining room table, a safe distance away from Grandma Catherine, Cecilia saw Miss Crowley striding back up the sidewalk to the front door. The picture book Miss Crowley wanted her to study lay open on the table in front of her. She'd been trying to puzzle out words with Grandma Catherine's help. She would take a stab at the word, and was sometimes so far off, she had to spell out the letters— Grandma Catherine couldn't even guess, based on her pronunciation. At least she could remember the names of most of the letters. She finished a word—gust—which had a picture of wind with eyes and pursed lips—while Miss Crowley, who had just entered the room, watched.

"Gust is a verb, and also a noun," Grandma Catherine told her.

"A noun because the name of wind or because pretend man in picture?" Cecilia asked, then pursed her lips and blew out a strong puff of air. "A verb because of sound?"

"Smart girl," Grandma Catherine said. "But *the* pretend man," Cecilia," Grandma Catherine said. "*The* pretend man. And it's a noun because it's the way to refer to a particular type of wind. A sudden, brisk wind, specifically."

"*The* pretend man," Cecilia repeated. Mamusia had tried to remind her to use 'the' and lots of other little words too, but it was so hard to remember. "*A* type of wind," she added.

Then, Grandma Catherine turned and looked up at Miss Crowley. "We were worried about you," she said, lifting her chin. "Not sure how far and long you planned to go. You really can't do that when you have a child. Just run off like that."

"I just needed to clear my head."

"This time was all right. I was here, but you can't leave a child alone. Not any more than you can walk out of a classroom full of students."

"Isn't that what this trouble is about?" Miss Crowley said. "Me insisting that you can't leave a child alone, and going and fetching Cecilia?"

"Yes, in principle, that's what *this* is about." Catherine reached over and patted Cecilia's shoulder. "You are no trouble, sweetheart." Then, she turned back to Miss Crowley. "What I am saying is that you can't leave a child alone for even an hour. Especially not under circumstances like this, when this new place is still so strange to her and she's already frightened. You must stay close by."

"But you were here—"

"Please listen," Grandma Catherine interrupted. "If you're going to take care of this child, you are going to have to think of her first. Say out loud what your plans are and when you'll be back, so she'll know. Give her a chance to object, to tell you she's afraid."

Cecilia looked from one to the other. She didn't know what to think. She never imagined anyone scolding Miss Crowley. She was a stern teacher, with a bit of a temper. No one crossed her, or at least not twice.

But she was just a daughter in this house, and Grandma Catherine was the parent.

"Here," Miss Crowley said, pulling a red apple from the deep pocket of her skirt. "I brought this for you. I think it's ripe enough."

Cecilia reached out for the apple. "It is perfect," she said.

∞

Mollie waited until she thought the sounds of Catherine preparing dinner would drown out conversation from the dining room. She was still rattled by her brothers' visit and smarting from the scolding Catherine had delivered. "I was thinking of you on my walk," Mollie said. "That's why I got that apple for you."

It was the closest she intended to come to an apology. She'd done nothing wrong.

"Thank you," Cecilia whispered. "I not like when my father scolded me either. Even when he right." She dropped her eyes to her plate. "Mamusia never did."

Mollie held back from telling Cecilia she needed the word 'do' between 'I' and 'not,' and instead asked, "Never did what?"

"Never scolded *and* never left."

Mollie sat back in her chair and paused. Cecilia was saying that she wasn't comfortable with either Mollie or Catherine's behavior over the last hour. She put out a finger to tip up Cecilia's chin so she could look into her eyes. "My mother was right. I shouldn't have done that. I will let you know when I'm leaving, and I will let you know when to expect me back. I'm sorry."

"I am new for you. You were the baby of Grandma Catherine? Like I the baby of Mamusia?"

"Yes."

"So, you and me, we are the youngest. Not the ones who know to watch out for littler children."

Catherine, entering the room, laughed. "Again, smart girl," she said. She placed a platter of cold chicken, rolls left over from the previous night, and cheese on the sideboard, fetched a bowl of cucumber salad, and took her seat. Then she stood and returned to the kitchen. She set a small plate next to Cecilia—it was Mollie's apple, sliced into crescents and arranged in a perfect arc. "You two help yourselves first," she said. "I'm sorry to be harsh. We are all learning one another."

When they finished grace, Catherine asked, "Cecilia, would you like to tell us about your family?" Then, she put her chin in her hand and waited.

Mollie leaned back. How could her mother jump right in like that with such an intrusive question? Why would she ask about what had to be the worst thing that ever happened to the child? She gave a slight shake of her head.

Catherine raised her eyebrows at Mollie, as if to say, *You think she's forgotten about them?* Then, she smiled at Cecilia. "You probably can't think of anything but your family. If you want to tell us about them, or tell us how our house is different, I would be happy to listen."

"I would as well," Mollie said, realizing, once again, that her mother was right.

"I help Mamusia," Cecilia said. "We take care of house. Garden. We pick tomatoes and beans. I look like her, you think?"

"I remember," Mollie said, biting her lip to keep from crying over the child's use of present tense and her drift into the speech patterns of an immigrant. The project of correcting her speech would keep. "I remember she had blond hair like yours."

"Braids," Cecilia said. "We wear braids. I can't make them."

Mollie and Catherine waited.

"I not remember Josef. He left when I four. Hugh funny." She thought of all the times he'd pushed her on the swing. "He strong." Cecilia took a tiny bite of chicken.

Mollie wondered why Cecilia never mentioned her father, but she didn't want to pry. She remembered how afraid of his father Josef had seemed all those years ago.

The corners of Cecilia's mouth turned down.

"What is it?" Catherine asked.

"We go back for Daisy?" Cecilia asked. "I left her. Almost time for kittens."

"Kittens?" Catherine said.

"Yes," Mollie said. "Certainly. It's been a long time since we've had a mamma cat. That will be fun." She smiled at Catherine—she'd dragged home every manner of animal as a girl and protested mightily at the death of every cow, pig, and even chicken from their barnyard. They hadn't had a pet in years. Not since her father's old hunting dog wandered off, and she hadn't had much use for the smelly old dog anyway. A mother cat and kittens would be a breath of fresh air.

"She can live in the barn," Catherine said.

"The cat stays on the porch at our house, in a basket with blanket," Cecilia said. "We feed her on the porch." A worried look passed over her features. "Her name is Daisy. She can keep kittens this time?" She picked up her knife and fork and cut a morsel of chicken from the breast on her plate, carefully took another small bite, then wiped the corners of her mouth with her napkin.

Lovely manners, Mollie thought. It must have been her mother who taught her.

"When we go?" Cecilia asked.

"Soon," Mollie said, thinking of the prospect of a cat in a basket on the porch, birthing kittens. What would they do with the animals? They'd be cute for a few days, then forever underfoot. She waited for the next question. Although Cecilia looked unsatisfied with Mollie's answer, she didn't press.

"What like to live here when you a little girl?" Cecilia asked a few minutes later when they'd mostly finished their meals.

"What *was it* like to live here?" Mollie said before she could stop herself.

"What a good question," Catherine said.

Mollie leaned forward and put her elbows on the table, then removed them. Her manners weren't as good as Cecilia's. She couldn't recall a student ever asking her what her life had been like as a child or, for that matter, what she did after she left the classroom each day. It was as if she existed only in the front of the class, with a pointer in her hand, or at her desk, watching the students do their work. And, if Cecilia was trying to figure out what her life here at the farm might be like, Catherine was right. What an inventive, diplomatic way to ask. She was beginning to realize how deeply she had underestimated the child.

"Well," Mollie said, "when I was a girl, Dan and Sam—my older brothers—lived here. At meals, there would be five of us. My father sat where Grandma Catherine is sitting, and I sat where you are sitting." She pointed to the two seats on either side of Catherine. "The boys sat down there."

"So boys one side, girls other?"

"Why, I suppose so," Mollie said and laughed. "It didn't feel that way, but I guess it was."

"You—" Cecilia hesitated. "You...*were*...always with mother, like I *was* with Mamusia?"

Mollie didn't know how to answer. She didn't want to hurt Catherine, but she had always been with her father, their chemistry always better.

"Mollie was always with her father," Catherine said. "From the time she could walk. They'd go off together in the mornings, to the fields, to town—I often had no idea where they'd gone off to. Off gallivanting was all they ever said."

Mollie nodded, unable to speak. It was true. Her father had been her favorite. She had been his, and everyone knew it. And now her mother seemed so willing to give her away, push her to the other end of the table with this strange child. She and Cecilia were both orphans in a sort of way, the ones left behind. Her father was gone, her brothers wanted nothing other than to bully her, and her mother was trying to make this patched-together arrangement between her and Cecilia feel more permanent than the relationship Mollie and Catherine had crafted, bit by bit, over the past two years. She was the only woman with her sort of life in the township. It was all too much.

Chapter Five

It was into this mood the sound of a vehicle intruded. No, it was two vehicles, Mollie saw from her vantage point through the dining room window. Both stopped in front of the house. One brought Dan and Sam. The other brought Dr. Murphy and Father Foley. Four men, all with determined looks on their faces. Mollie felt a sense of unease wash over her—she had thought she had the school situation in hand. After diligent persuasion, Father Foley and Dr. Murphy had been on her side about re-opening. She could only imagine the interfering her city-smart brothers had done over the past couple of hours, with their hands and noses deep into the business of her home and her work. What must it have taken to pull Father Foley from his Sunday afternoon respite and his dinner of covered dishes from the Ladies' Guild? And Dr. Murphy was thought by both her and Grandma Catherine to be a lazy excuse for a man, let alone a doctor, even before he'd left Cecilia alone in that house without a plan to care for her. Yet, here he was, on their doorstep.

Who is here?" Catherine asked.

"My brothers. Father Foley. Dr. Murphy," Mollie said.

"This seems to be a day for spontaneous visits," Catherine said. "Let's go back outside." She stood, then looked at Cecilia, which caused Mollie to look at the child as well. Cecilia's chin had dropped, and she was looking at her plate, her meal only half eaten.

Should she and Catherine go outside, just the two of them?

If Cecilia went out with them, there was a risk the men, at worst, would talk about the child like she was vermin or, at best, a remnant left over after the church rummage sale, right to her face. If Cecilia stayed at the table, the wide-open window would allow her to eavesdrop, and they'd probably be even less diplomatic. She could send Cecilia to her room but knew how she'd have hated that when she was a girl. She always wanted to know what was going on.

Catherine, as though reading Mollie's mind, shook her head. "Nothing good comes of secrets," she said. "Let's all go outside." She laid a clean dish towel over the platter and slid the cucumber salad into the icebox.

A few minutes later, they were on the front lawn again, now with the four men. Mollie and Cecilia sat on one long bench they dragged from the porch, and the brothers sat on another. Catherine sat in her chair from the front porch and the priest and the doctor sat on dark wood chairs Mollie dragged out from the dining room. It was mid-afternoon and the light was golden, and the warmth of the Indian Summer afternoon was still enough, even without a wrap, but it wouldn't last.

∞

Cecilia followed Grandma Catherine out the door. She knew her lovely dinner was still on the table, and now it was spoiled, no matter what happened. Her stomach was already too stirred up by the return of the men to even think about finishing later. Were they going to make Miss Crowley take her back to the lonely house or, worse yet, to a place she didn't even know about, like she hadn't known about the farmhouse just two days ago?

Miss Crowley had been the last one out of the house. She brought a pitcher of water and a tray of glasses outside and offered everyone a drink. All the men declined. Now, Miss Crowley sat next to her on the bench, facing the setting sun. It would be dark soon—another night in the soft bed in her room in the farmhouse. Or so she hoped—the prospect of going back to the empty house and curling up again in the pantry terrified her. She couldn't imagine they would make her do that, but the doctor had known she was there all along and hadn't done anything to help her. If it were up to him, she'd be there still. Just thinking about it made her shiver.

She glanced at the doctor. He looked as squeamish as he had at their house, when he came back again and again to tell her no one had come to claim her and questioned her about where any family might be. He talked about people in Chicago, but she didn't know any people in Chicago. She studied the priest out of the corner of her eye without turning her head. The closest Cecilia had ever been to the priest was the Sunday he invited their family to sit in the front pew, and let Josef sit up on the altar. Then he looked tall and stern. Now, she could see the skin between the top of his stockings and the hem of his black pants and an undone button below his white collar at the top of his shirt. His belly pushed at his shirtfront and his cheeks were red. It was like the wizard in the book Miss Crowley gave her—the priest looked like a normal man now, just as the wizard had looked like a rumpled old man in the picture on the last page of the Dorothy story.

The two brothers sat next to each other, with their four feet parallel to each other like the arriving and departing train tracks in town. They reminded Cecilia of the matched salt and pepper shakers on the dining room table inside, shaped like a red rooster and a plump yellow hen. Cecilia had never seen anything like those shakers, never anything so precious, made that way just to be pretty and catch the eye. It was the kind of pretty thing Mamusia would have loved, though she probably would have tucked the pair into her flour sack. Cecilia tipped up her chin to look at the brothers' faces—their squinty eyes and straight lips looked fierce. They scared Cecilia and ruined the happy image of the salt and pepper shakers. She remembered when her father used to get angry; if she had enough time, Mamusia would send Cecilia to her room or outside. Now, Cecilia moved closer to Miss Crowley and felt her teacher's arm drape across her shoulders. She sat very still under the weight of the arm, as unfamiliar but welcome as Miss Crowley's hugs before bed.

Grandma Catherine was the first to speak. "Sam and Dan," she said, looking at the two brothers as though the priest and doctor weren't there, "I know you are both trying to do the right thing. I know you want us—me especially—to be safe. I know you are worried. Thank you. But why, pray tell," Grandma Catherine said, her eyes narrowed, "have you brought these gentlemen here? And why in the world would none of you have called first, so we could be prepared?"

Grandma Catherine's tone and expression, the same squinty look the boys had, and the way the brothers were seated next to each other on the bench like that, like the big boys at the back of the schoolroom, made Cecilia remember that Grandma Catherine was their mother, capable of scolding them just as she'd scolded Miss Crowley. They looked like they remembered too, like Hugh had looked on the rare occasions when Mamusia pretended to be very stern. Dan started nodding, and only stopped when Sam gave him a sidelong look.

Miss Crowley sat up a bit straighter. "I happen to know there are telephones in both the rectory and in your office, Dr. Murphy," she said.

The priest ran his hand underneath the stiff white collar and started to speak, sputtering like the car engine did the first few times Miss Crowley turned the crank.

Dan said, "Surely you're not suggesting *Father* needs an invitation or permission to come here? Or that Sam or I do? Or Dr. Murphy, especially after he was kind enough to interrupt his evening for this conversation?"

Cecilia saw Grandma Catherine raise her eyebrows—she didn't say, but Cecilia knew, the men had interrupted *their* evening as well. She felt a tiny smile at the corners of her mouth and looked down at her shoes. This was the kind of smile that would have made her father so angry, angry enough to throw a dish or yell, mostly at Mamusia, but sometimes at her. She willed her face back to blank and evened out her features before looking up.

Sam cleared his throat. "I am sure we would all prefer to be enjoying our Sunday in peace," he said. "But this is important. We've agreed. The best course is for Mother to come home with me. Also, Mollie, Dr. Murphy has reconsidered whether you should start school this fall."

"In the last twenty-four hours?" Mollie said, looking at the doctor. "We've been researching and discussing this for weeks. Nothing has changed."

The doctor looked away from Miss Crowley and off into the distance, as if the horizon held something more interesting than just the cornfield across the dirt road, with stalks as tall as a man, heavy with big ears of corn.

"Are you suspending Mass as well?" Grandma Catherine said. "If it's not safe for children to be at school, then it's not safe for any of us to be at Mass either."

"It's entirely different," the priest began, his nose now as red as his cheeks. "People *need* to be in Mass. It's a commandment. I would *never* cancel Mass. Why, even when—"

Grandma Catherine raised her palm. "I didn't suggest that you cancel Mass. Though it's good to know you aren't willing to do so, for purposes of this conversation. And it seems that Dr. Murphy isn't insisting that you do so." Grandma Catherine looked over at the doctor. "Am I right?"

The doctor's eyes dropped. He looked to be studying his shoes.

Grandma Catherine waited a second, then continued. "Mollie oversees the decision whether to cancel school. That's what the town council decided. Perhaps she feels about education as you do about Mass, Father Foley."

Sam shook his head, looking disgusted. "It is not the same—" he started.

"I think education is as important as religion," Miss Crowley interrupted. "Many people do. The same rule should apply to both."

Everyone fell silent. The priest's face grew even redder. A large black fly landed on the surface of the water in the pitcher. Cecilia held her breath. She wished she could reach in and fish out the fly but didn't want to leave her seat. Miss Crowley and Grandma Catherine weren't budging. Grandma Catherine was not siding with the brothers, Miss Crowley was still planning to open the school, and no one had even talked about her leaving the farmhouse. This differed from Mamusia, who would have smoothed things over, and—always soft-hearted—rescued the fly. Cecilia didn't care if she went to church or school at all if she could stay right here. She took a deep breath, and her stomach settled, like a key had turned in a lock. The fly crawled to the side of the pitcher, shook its wings, and flew away.

The priest finally shifted in his seat and turned to Sam. "This is such a beautiful farm," he said. "Exactly how long has it been in your family?"

"Almost seventy years," Sam said. "My grandfather homesteaded it and passed it to my father."

"He's been gone two years now, isn't that right?" the doctor said.

"You know well he was gone two years last June," Grandma Catherine said. "We asked for your help." She turned to the priest. "And you were here when he passed." Her voice was tight, and her hands twined together. Her knuckles were white. Cecilia could see her ring pressing into her flesh, making a white circle. It looked like it hurt.

"Didn't either of you boys want to farm?" the priest asked, as though he hadn't heard her.

"I work for the railroad," Dan said.

Sam sat up straighter. "I'm a banker," he said.

"This is a lot to keep up," the doctor said.

"I wouldn't say it's been kept up," Sam said. "It's gone down considerably since my father got sick."

Sam had been the one driving the shiny car. His bones were long and his frame looked sharp, without an ounce of softness. His hair was slicked back. Cecilia noticed his watch. It was gold like her mother's wedding band, burnished and bent, and was missing one of its three small red stones. Mamusia had loved her ring. It had been her grandmother's.

Where was Mamusia's ring?

"We didn't want to farm," Sam said, pulling Cecilia back to the conversation. "Neither of us. We—the family—may sell this place. It's hard to keep up without a man. Look at those tree branches, for example." He pointed to the tree branches that overhung the sidewalk. "A person can scarcely pass to the front door."

"Selling?" the doctor said.

"Do you know of anyone who might be interested?" Sam asked.

Grandma Catherine didn't say anything, and Miss Crowley didn't either.

Cecilia didn't know what that meant—could the brothers really sell the farm, even if Grandma Catherine and Miss Crowley didn't want them to?

The priest had a quizzical look on his face, as though he was searching his memory for a mystery letter during the spelling bee, or the name of a state during the geography match. Cecilia remembered she'd gone out on the word "Maine" last spring—that was the one shaped like a dog's head. She'd spelled it "m-a-n" and not understood when Miss Crowley had shaken her head with disappointment. It hadn't been until she looked closely at the map that she'd remembered about the silent letters.

"Mrs. Murphy and I—" the doctor started, just as the priest blurted out, "I'll keep my ears and eyes open."

Grandma Catherine stood. "I fear you've wasted your time. I'm not going anywhere. Neither is Cecilia." Then, she looked at the brothers, and narrowed her eyes. "Perhaps you've forgotten; we Irish don't sell land. It didn't come to us so easily. My parents left their homes and family to have this opportunity." She waved her arm across the horizon. "As for the school, that's Mollie's battle." Her fingers were clenched around the head of her cane, and her knuckles were still white. "Good evening."

Miss Crowley stood too. "I am following the governor's mandate about the school. I am within the law. I will take into consideration what you decide to do about the Masses at church; it will inform my decision. As to the farm, I can see some slippage. I can hire the help I need, just like I could purchase my own car. Just like I use my salary to pay our bills. My money is as good as yours. And I am happy to stay here with Mother for as long as she likes. This is her home."

And yours, Cecilia thought, and maybe mine as well. At least she hoped so. She stood up and followed Grandma Catherine and Miss Crowley into the house, where they sat back down at the table and pretended to finish their meal. They could see the four men still sitting on the front yard, talking, until finally the two brothers dragged the benches and Grandma Catherine's chair back to the porch and left. They left the two dining room chairs sitting on the grass. By Grandma Catherine's face, which looked sad and lined, and the two bright spots of color on Miss Crowley's cheeks, not to mention her hair, which was standing up in wiry clumps because she'd been running her fingers through it, Cecilia knew this was not over. When they finished eating, Grandma Catherine announced she would spend the twilight hour in her garden, and Miss Crowley cleared the table. Cecilia noticed she packed away more than what they'd eaten. It seemed they'd all lost their appetites. Cecilia went out to the yard and dragged the two dining room chairs back in herself.

Chapter Six

That night, Mollie couldn't sleep. She got up to shoo a mosquito out the window, sat down to read in the rocker in the corner of her room by the light of a kerosene lamp, then finally succumbed to walking back and forth in the narrow space between her bed and dresser, hoping to tire herself out. The most worrisome part of the day, with all its worrisome aspects, was her mother's fatigue and pallor after the showdown with her brothers. She knew Catherine's after-dinner trip to her garden was a signal she wanted to ruminate on her own in the place she felt most comfortable.

All evening, once the men left, Mollie had yearned to ask her mother about what Sam said about selling the farm, and whether he and Dan had the legal power to do that. Before her father died, it had never occurred to her to worry about who owned the farm—it simply belonged to the family. She'd tried to broach the subject many times since then, but her mother always put her off. This evening, her mother had been so quiet and looked so sad, she just couldn't bring herself to probe. Her mother would talk when she was ready, or maybe, the time would be right for her to ask. Leave it to the priest, a newcomer, to challenge things that were as old as the paint on the barn door and leave it to Sam to twist the knife.

Mollie shook her head at how annoyingly evasive her mother could be. What if something happened to Catherine while the issue of the farm's ownership was up in the air? Why couldn't Catherine be more transparent? Why couldn't she be more decisive?

Mollie knew the answer. Catherine prayed, sometimes out loud, for a better relationship among her three children. For as long as she could remember, her mother had tried to force affinity among Mollie and the two brothers, without success. It was almost as if Mollie came from a different family, a family of three—her father, her mother, and her. She knew that part of the problem was that her father was hard on the boys, always insisting they should behave perfectly and work harder on the farm, though neither of them had any inclination for farm work. He was soft on her, they said, so there was jealousy involved, as far back as Mollie could remember.

They'd also never understood her choices as a woman. They'd questioned—no, resented—her using the bulk of her savings to purchase her car, calling her irresponsible and spoiled. Their salaries had to cover the needs of their families, they'd said, and she was using hers for a personal indulgence. They complained her father had refused to take any money from her for room and board. She knew her own stubborn disposition contributed to the conflicts. She couldn't ever let anything go, even silly things like who got to pick the color of the front door or decide what to request for the holiday meal. Even small things seemed important enough to fight over where her brothers were involved.

When her father was alive, her mother had always tried to smooth things over between her father and the boys and between the boys and Mollie. This was the first time she could remember her mother firmly taking her side. While that felt good in the moment, she knew her mother's bravado sapped her strength. She remembered how wan and exhausted her father grew as he fought the heart disease that killed him. None of this, not even the farm, was important enough to let that happen again. She couldn't bear it if her mother fell ill because of her stubborn disposition and fussing with Dan and Sam. She sighed; her father would expect her to do her best to keep the peace, for Catherine's sake.

Mollie crept down the stairs, intending to get a drink of water, slip out to the yard, and sit in the moonlight under the willow tree she planted when she was a girl. The tree, started from a slip she took from the grove near the creek, was now as tall as the house. She pumped water from the spout next to the sink into a glass. As she moved toward the back door, careful to skip the creakiest boards of the plank floor, a white shape came out of the shadow, startling her and making her heart race. Cecilia was ghostlike in a too-large linen nightgown.

"Your steps loud above me," Cecilia said. "I hear you walk above."

Of course she had. The child's room was directly beneath hers. When her father used that room, she was always careful to be quiet so she didn't disturb his rest. She'd forgotten about that. "I'm sorry," she said. "Just restless."

Cecilia nodded. "I not asleep either. I not know what footsteps were."

"What did you think?"

"Ghosts?" She smiled. "Only at first."

Mollie rolled her eyes, then stopped because of the thoughtful look on Cecilia's face. She remembered Cecilia had said she talked to Mamusia back at her house—perhaps the child was comforted by the feeling she could still communicate with her family. Maybe she imagined specific ghosts in the crevices of this house. She seemed comforted by the ghosts, and there was no harm.

"It's an old house," she said, patting Cecilia's shoulder. "Lots of people have been born and have died here. But there are no ghosts that I know of. Even if there were, they'd be kindly ones. Anyway, those footsteps were mine. I'm the guilty party. No ghosts involved."

"I not know all sounds of house yet," Cecilia said. "But I know it is you. If Grandma Catherine, I hear cane."

"Would you like to go sit outside for a bit?" Mollie asked as she took her shawl from the hook next to the door. "I want to show you a very special tree."

"Yes," Cecilia said.

Mollie pulled another shawl from the next hook and draped it around Cecilia's shoulders. A whiff of lilac scent reminded her the shawl was her mother's. She quickly lifted the shawl away from Cecilia. She needed to keep trying to maintain the distance between Cecilia and Grandma Catherine. "Fetch a blanket from your bed," she said, and hung the shawl back up. When Cecilia returned with a wool throw around her shoulders, she held the door open as Cecilia stepped onto the first step. "Would you like some water?"

"No water. If I drink, I must go in there." Cecilia tilted her head toward the outhouse. "I not like—do not like—the spiders."

"I understand," Mollie said. "I don't like the spiders either. Especially not at night."

The two walked across the grass, wet with dew, in their bare feet. Mollie saw that Cecilia's nightgown was trailing along the ground. She reached down and tied the extra fabric into a knot that kept the hem gathered around the child's knees. Sitting next to her on the bench under the tree, she searched her mind for some words of reassurance that this was all going to be resolved, but she didn't like to mislead children, and she truly didn't know. There were so many things in play—their health, the school, and now, the new opposition of the priest, the doctor, and her brothers. She couldn't even think about the farm—it was the only place she'd ever lived, except for when she'd boarded in Port Huron during teachers' college. The thought of living anywhere else was, well, unthinkable. And then there were her haphazard attempts to keep her mother apart from Cecilia—what would she do if her mother got sick? She would never forgive herself. Also, there was still the question whether Cecilia had any family of her own.

"You wish you not fetch me?" Cecilia whispered.

"No," Mollie said quickly, surprising herself with the immediacy of the response and the vehemence of her tone. There was no part of her that wished she had made a different decision about Cecilia. Instead, she could barely believe that a few days earlier she hadn't a concern in her head about the girl. Even with all the problems, she was glad they were together. She reached out and put her arm around Cecilia's shoulders. Then, surprising herself, Mollie said, "This is going to be all right. I promise." She felt the child stiffen as she had on the yard, but this time she relaxed against her after a few seconds. Mollie only hoped she could make her promise come true.

∞

The next morning, when Miss Crowley knocked at her bedroom door, Cecilia was dreaming of Mamusia. In the dream, Mamusia was a girl riding a horse, which was silly because Mamusia feared horses. She had walked too closely behind one when she was eight and still had a notch out of her right ear from the unexpected kick. She feared other large animals as well, like cows and pigs. Mamusia didn't even like to go to the corncrib because of the raccoons that lived underneath and came out after dark, their starry eyes reflecting the light from candles or moonlight. The knocking interrupted the dream, where Cecilia wished she could stay. When her eyes opened, she couldn't place where she was or what had happened, or even who might knock at the door.

"May I come in?" Miss Crowley asked and pushed open the door before Cecilia had answered.

She heard Grandma Catherine coming down the stairs, two heavy steps followed by the plunk of the cane on each stair.

"I'm going to the schoolhouse today," Miss Crowley said, standing next to her bed. "I need to prepare for students. Do you want to come along, or do you want to stay here?"

Cecilia wanted to cuddle back into the nest of the covers and go back to sleep, maybe even rejoin Mamusia in her dream. But what if those men returned? The thought of being here without Miss Crowley was terrifying. If they decided to take her, Grandma Catherine wouldn't be able to stop them.

"I go with you," she said, sitting up. "Please—we visit my house?"

Miss Crowley stood beside the bed. She was dressed and had a bag over her shoulder. "Perhaps on the way back," she said. "If you want to go, get out of bed. Clean your teeth and brush your hair. I've already loaded the car."

"What's your rush?" Grandma Catherine said from the kitchen. "Let the child have a hot breakfast."

Miss Crowley was crackling with energy, as if she was already late. Cecilia slid her feet into her boots and pulled the dress she'd worn the previous day—which was several sizes too large—off the hook.

"Get my clothes?" she asked. "At house?"

She also wanted to see if she could find Mamusia's ring and Daisy. Maybe Miss Crowley would let her bring Daisy back to the farmhouse today. The kittens could be born here.

"No clothes," Miss Crowley said. "Not yet anyway. But maybe we'll stop and have a look. Wash up, straightaway please. I filled the basin in your bedroom for you. I'll pack a breakfast and a lunch. The car is out front."

Grandma Catherine, standing in the doorway, frowned. "I'm going to cut down some clothing for you today," she said, pulling the shoulders of the dress a few inches out on either side of Cecilia's shoulders. "You're swimming in that."

"Good idea," Miss Crowley said, moving toward the door. "By the way, do you think you could make masks for the students out of scraps? Some good, thick cotton? Maybe…"

Cecilia could almost see her tallying in her head. It must be multiplication—the number of seats per row multiplied by the number of rows. The fourth grade had been learning that when school left off in the spring.

"Maybe forty?" Miss Crowley said.

"Yes," Grandma Catherine said. "All distinct patterns."

"So each student can hold onto their own," Miss Crowley finished her sentence.

"You can bring them home each day and I'll wash them up." Grandma Catherine rubbed her hands together as though she was itching to start the task.

"Thank you," Miss Crowley said, picking up the overstuffed big bag near the door, from which a stack of papers slipped off. "That's what I was thinking. And *please* don't go back out into the garden until we come home. I will help you. It's not safe—"

Grandma Catherine's lips were pursed and she was not agreeing. It was like the way she had held her ground with the men.

Cecilia rushed to collect the papers, and Miss Crowley crammed them into her bag. "Thank you," she said, and opened the door. "I'll start the car."

This Miss Crowley was nothing like the Miss Crowley she'd seen in the middle of the night, sitting out under the tree with the long branches that draped around them like a veil. This Miss Crowley was who she remembered from the classroom last year, the one she was a little afraid of, always saying "yes" or "no" without explaining. Cecilia was wide awake now, and a little chilled—it was fall this morning. A new season.

"I'll help you in the garden when we get back," Miss Crowley said.

Grandma Catherine nodded, but she didn't look as if she intended to obey.

∞

As Mollie sat in the car, waiting for Cecilia, she felt irritated and resentful. She suspected the priest and the doctor, at her brothers' insistence, were probably doing whatever they could to rally support for keeping the school closed, preying on the fears of parents. She was so frustrated. She'd had the school situation settled. In retrospect, she wished she'd said nothing to her brothers, then remembered she hadn't volunteered the information about Cecilia. Cecilia's presence had surprised them when they got to the farm.

Mollie tapped the horn; what on earth was the child doing? The best tonic for the way her brothers made her feel small and incompetent was to dust herself off and get ready to begin something she knew she did well—teach. It was always a struggle to get children back in their seats during harvest season, and she knew this year would be even worse. She'd see who turned up on October 10. It was only a little over a week away—there was plenty to do. Most years, opening the small schoolhouse and preparing it for the students was one of her favorite days. She resented the cloud over her this year. To be fair, though, it wasn't just the cloud due to her brothers. It was the flu, the Pokorski deaths, her new responsibilities with Cecilia, and the delayed and still uncertain start date that now felt like it might yet be delayed again. Everything felt off, as if it was written in pencil. Eager to be in an environment that felt sane and ordered, she tapped the horn again.

Cecilia came out the front door, finally, and slid into the passenger seat.

Mollie put the car into gear and accelerated, calming as the car sped up. It was a perfect, crisp, fall morning, with leaves just turning to gold and orange and even plum. The sky was bright blue with no clouds. The tall corn stalks on either side of the dirt road made it feel like they were darting through a green tunnel. She hummed the morning song she sang with the students, wishing again she could afford a piano for the schoolhouse. She smiled at the high cloud of dust that was following them as far back as she could see. The front window was coated with the remains of flies; she'd have to wipe it down first thing. If they dried there, she'd never get them off.

Cecilia, in the passenger seat, was gripping the passenger door, and her lips were pressed together. Mollie saw her lips move and made out what she was saying—"So fast"—over the noise of the engine and the rattle of the machinery, loud as she hurtled over bumps and potholes. Mollie knew she was indeed driving too fast—as usual. She applied the brakes and saw Cecilia's grip release a little. She took a few deep breaths and willed her voice to be calm and her tone even before speaking to Cecilia.

"We can take our time this morning at the schoolhouse," she said. "We don't need to hurry. I always love shaking the bugs off the old building. The first day of school is my favorite day of the year, and we're overdue to prepare."

Cecilia nodded but didn't answer.

"Don't you love the first day of school?" Mollie asked.

•   •   •

Cecilia remembered the first day of school last year. Her name was written on a piece of cardboard clipped to the top of a desk in the front row, next to Louise O'Connell, the youngest of the O'Connell girls. Though Louise was her age, she was a much bigger girl with even bigger sisters, every other grade, like the rungs of a ladder. Louise made fun of Cecilia's tight braid and the colorful ribbons Mamusia tied into bows. She made fun of the way Cecilia spoke, saying she was a "baby" and "stupid." She knew she didn't speak exactly like them, but she understood nearly everything. She knew she wasn't stupid. They made fun of the "Polack" food Cecilia had in her lunch pail—green beans in vinegar with dill, a chicken leg with paprika, a hard roll, and a pretty red apple—and because Cecilia cried, they kept making fun of every lunch all year long.

Cecilia's lunch was the same one Mamusia prepared for her brother Hugh and her father—there was nothing wrong with it, although she didn't love beans. The ribbons came from the flour sack in the pantry and Mamusia carried them in her pocket and tied them for Cecilia just before they reached the school—one bow at the nape of her neck where her braid started, and the other near the bottom of the braid, brushing the small of her back. Her hair was straight and smooth and blond, like Mamusia's. It was not fuzzy, like Louise O'Connell's, or Miss Crowley's red mop. Her hair held its braid all day, not like the curls the other girls had, hair that looked like rats' nests by first recess. A braid was the best style for her, Mamusia said, and she'd loved the way Mamusia's fingers felt darting through her hair, making their hair look the same, until Mamusia wound hers into a bun at the nape of her neck.

The next oldest O'Connell girl, the meanest one, Jane, joined right in with Louise on the playground. The two of them knew to whisper and to keep out of Miss Crowley's sight when they bothered Cecilia. The only one she told about the teasing was Mamusia, who said Louise was jealous. Cecilia hadn't known what possibly could make her jealous, but then Mamusia said those girls looked unkempt. They were jealous of her smooth hair and pretty bows, and her clean clothing. Cecilia thought that might be right; they all looked messy. Also, their lunches weren't nice at all. Just bread and an apple and sometimes a bit of hard cheese.

"They all back each other up," she'd told Mamusia.

"Of course they do," Mamusia had said. "They're all jealous, and they're sisters."

That made Cecilia wish she had an older sister at the school, or even that Hugh still attended. It was hard to be on her own.

Mamusia was also the only one she told about the ugly word— "Polack." Cecilia hadn't known what the word "Polack" meant until then. The word was a rude way to refer to being Polish, Mamusia explained. Cecilia hadn't even known they were Polish until that day, and that most of the other students, including the O'Connells, were Irish.

"Why so important?" Cecilia had asked.

"That difference makes a big difference to some people," Mamusia said. "Some people stick together with those from their home country."

"Do you think it's a big difference?" Cecilia asked. "The difference between Irish and Polish?"

"My best friend when I was a girl was from Italy, not Poland," Mamusia said. "It made not a bit of difference to us, but it mattered to her brothers."

"What about Miss Crowley? Does she think I'm different?"

"I don't know," Mamusia said. "Miss Crowley is Irish, too. Like the O'Connells. You should ignore them. You are there to learn, not play."

After that, Cecilia watched Miss Crowley carefully. She must know how mean those O'Connell girls were—it was obvious. So Cecilia figured Mamusia was right; Miss Crowley would never take her part against the O'Connells. They were all Irish. So, Cecilia tried to stay out of the way of the O'Connells, and never responded to them, willing her face to stay as stony as possible, not learning to stick up for herself, but instead learning to hate recess.

Louise would be back this year—now, perhaps, she could ask Miss Crowley if she could sit next to someone else. But who? She'd been so shy last year that she didn't make a single friend. And how would other students treat her when they found out she was living with Miss Crowley? It might be they'd treat her better, but it could be they'd treat her worse. There was a skinny boy they'd called "teacher's pet" last year, and he'd suffered almost as much as she had. Perhaps no one would know where she was living now—best to keep it to herself if she could.

As they pulled up to the porch of the white clapboard schoolhouse and got out of the car, Cecilia realized she hadn't answered Miss Crowley's question about whether she loved the first day of school.

"I go two years so far," she said. "I not like leave Mamusia."

But by then, Miss Crowley was taking a box of supplies from the back of the car, and within a couple of minutes, she'd opened the front door of the schoolhouse with a big key, and they were inside. Cecilia hung back and wondered whether Miss Crowley had even heard what she'd said, or how she could make herself known before this year started out as badly as last. Sometimes it didn't seem that Miss Crowley listened at all, which made her miss Mamusia so much because Mamusia had been the best listener in the world.

That little flicker of unease wiggled in Cecilia's stomach again—it was going to be so different living with Miss Crowley. She and Mamusia used to walk to the school in the mornings, and Mamusia would calm her butterflies. Then, in the afternoons, she told Mamusia everything that happened to her, even the things that made her cry. She told her how Miss Crowley didn't seem to notice how mean the O'Connells were or didn't seem to care. Mamusia would listen and slip her bows back into her pocket before they got home. A wave of grief flooded over Cecilia, and her eyes filled with tears. She turned her head so Miss Crowley didn't see her tears, and bit her lip.

"Perhaps you can call me Miss Crowley here," Miss Crowley said, several minutes later, as though she'd been thinking the whole time of something completely different from what Cecilia had been thinking about, "and Miss Mollie at home. Or maybe just plain Mollie?"

Cecilia wiped her face on the sleeve of her dress and gulped back the tears. She couldn't imagine even in her dreams that she would ever call her strict teacher anything other than "Miss Crowley." She wished nothing more than she could turn back time to weeks earlier when she and Mamusia laughed about how they had most of the summer ahead of them.

∞

So much to do, Mollie thought, placing the box of supplies she'd collected over the summer on her desk at the front of the room, and not addressing the fact Cecilia hadn't responded to her suggestion about calling her something other than "Miss Crowley" when they were at home. Everything was covered with dust. The names directing the children where to sit were still there from last year. The windows needed washing, and the outhouse was undoubtedly nasty. Dead bugs littered every windowsill. She sighed—usually she would have started this process weeks ago. But with all the back and forth about whether and when to open, and then devising the new precautions, then posting the notices, she'd neglected the regular work of getting ready for school.

And was this all for naught, anyway? What if her brothers got their way? What if there were new cases and everyone needed to quarantine again? Everything felt uncertain. She couldn't even know which students were likely to return, and whether the parents would feel comfortable sending the youngest students who should be in the front row, where Cecilia was last year. It might not matter whether she executed every preparation perfectly—so many, too many, things were outside her control.

"Begin," Cecilia whispered.

Mollie startled—she'd forgotten the girl was there. This was a job she was used to doing alone, uninterrupted, the same way each fall. How and when to prepare this building for school had been something she was confident she knew how to do, the exact solitary work to calm her start-of-school nerves. She planned as much as she could in advance because the year always went better when launched correctly.

"Mamusia says," Cecilia continued, "begin. Begin what you no like. Mamusia hate vegetable garden—weeding, harvesting, and canning— tomatoes and beans and pickles. She hate"—here, Cecilia's shoulders tightened—"bugs. So, we do little bits when we can."

A memory flashed into Mollie's mind—Cecilia and her mother walking to the school in the mornings and then her mother waiting for her again in the afternoon. Frances' hair was in a braid coiled into a bun, and Cecilia's braid swung down her back, smooth and looking nothing like the mess Cecilia had made of it today. It looked more like a barn rope than a golden cord. Two miles each way, she calculated— eight miles every day for Cecilia's mother. They must have had so much time to talk. She must have told her mother all about her days, and all the things Mollie did that Cecilia didn't like. For now, she knew, Cecilia was anything but silent—that had been Mollie's wrong impression. The girl had so many thoughts and opinions of her own and was quite bright after all. And sensible—like telling Mollie to pace herself.

She nodded and smiled at Cecilia. "I have seven days to work. I don't have to do it all today." She walked to the supply closet and got a bucket and said, "I'll take this outside and fill it with water at the pump. Let's start with the windowsills and desks. And the chalkboards."

Cecilia nodded. "I like here with you. I not here before when quiet."

"Really?" Was it possible she'd never had an individual conversation with Cecilia, outside the presence of other students, for two years? She couldn't remember any. "You were never alone with me?"

Cecilia shook her head.

"It's quiet, isn't it?" she said. "Peaceful. This year, you will probably get here early with me and then leave later, when I do. You'll have a lot of time alone in here."

They passed the next hour in companionable silence, Cecilia doing tasks as Mollie requested.

"Why pick student seats before school begin?" Cecilia asked.

Cecilia's question interrupted Mollie's concentration. She'd been focused on making perfect letters for the placard she planned to place at Anne Crimmins' seat. That would make it easier for Anne to learn to make her letters properly—last year, Anne's penmanship had been sloppy.

"I like to be organized," Mollie said. "Usually, I put all the placards out, but I'll keep them in my desk until the first day this year, so I can see who comes to school. No point in having a bunch of empty seats." And no point in advertising which families kept their children home, she added to herself. She shook her head—those students were going to have such a hard time catching up. She couldn't think of a single parent who had the time or capability, let alone the interest, to work at home with their child.

"Why you not wait until you see who people like?" Cecilia asked. "Let people sit by someone nice."

"I like to sit students next to students that help them behave."

"That the reason I sit next to Louise O'Connell? So I behave?" Cecilia asked.

"No, you sat next to her so *she* would behave," Mollie answered, then thought better of it. She was gossiping about one student with another. This was going to be tricky. Even if Louise O'Connell was loud and obnoxious, just like her older sisters had been, it wouldn't do to be sharing that with Cecilia. It was going to be hard enough to have a special relationship with a student.

"Didn't you like sitting by Louise?" Mollie asked.

"No," Cecilia said. "She mean."

"In what way?" Mollie asked.

"All ways," Cecilia said. "She make fun of my food and family and call me names. She make fun about way I speak."

"What names?"

"Polack," Cecilia said softly. "She say I smell."

Mollie remembered the torment of the Jankowski family when she was a girl; they'd been the only Polish family in the township then. So, all that was still going on. She noticed the firm set of the girl's jaw. Cecilia was right—Louise was mean, just like the rest of the O'Connells—and if it wasn't one thing, it would be another. But she hadn't known Louise was nasty to Cecilia, who was always such a mild little thing that she couldn't imagine Louise putting forth the effort. She hated when things like this surprised her. She regretted she'd never noticed that the older girl was persecuting—bullying—Cecilia. What else was she missing?

Chapter Seven

Mollie and Cecilia had been working all day, with just a brief break for lunch, and were nearly ready to leave, when Cecilia heard a car approach. She stopped washing the chalkboard and looked out the window, her heart racing, expecting to see the brothers or the priest or the doctor, or maybe all of them, again. Miss Crowley, who had been washing desktops, was right behind her, peering over her shoulder, and she could smell the sour scent of Miss Crowley's perspiration and hear her ragged breath. She was scared, too.

Cecilia saw a green truck, dusty and old, park in the schoolyard. A man Cecilia did not know got out of the truck. He was a very tall, thin man, wearing a canvas hat like her father used to wear in the field. He didn't slam the door of the old truck, but instead eased it into place like he was afraid it might not latch. Then he let a black and white spotted dog out of the passenger side of the truck. Cecilia felt her shoulders relax—she liked the way the man touched the dog, scratching between its ears until it seemed bored. As the man and dog walked toward the schoolhouse, Miss Crowley pulled her back from the window.

"Tom Reid?" Miss Crowley said, her forehead creased. She sounded irritated. "What's he doing here?" When he knocked on the schoolhouse door, Miss Crowley called, "Come in. Not the dog, please."

Cecilia heard the man say, "Stay." Then he walked through the door, stooping a bit so as not to hit his head.

"How can I help you, Tom?" Miss Crowley said. "Is there something you need?"

"I was hoping I could help you. I saw all the signs you put up in town, and thought you might need some repairs done, maybe an extra pair of hands."

Miss Crowley had abandoned a half dozen tasks over the course of the day—a map that had come loose from the wall, a broken latch on the outhouse door, a window that wouldn't open, and others. Cecilia thought she'd jump at the offer of help. Instead, Miss Crowley's eyebrows shot up and she took a step back.

"No thank you," she said. "I don't need any help."

He looked at Cecilia. "Who's your little friend?" he asked.

"This is Cecilia Pokorski," Miss Crowley said. "She's staying with us. Cecilia, this is Mr. Reid."

He nodded and smiled at her. If he knew about her family or recognized her name, he didn't show it.

Maybe not everyone knew what had happened to her family— maybe she'd be able to act as though Miss Crowley was just giving her a ride to school. Though that might make people call her teacher's pet, especially if they didn't even feel sorry for her because she'd lost her family.

"You sure about the help?" the man asked, interrupting Cecilia's thoughts.

"No help needed today," Miss Crowley said, and crossed her arms.

Miss Crowley surely needed help—not just with the tasks, but with all the people who seemed to be against her. The only ones on her side were Grandma Catherine and now Cecilia. Mr. Reid was the first person other than the two of them who'd been even a tiny bit nice to Miss Crowley. Still, Miss Crowley seemed skeptical, and that made Cecilia feel uncertain.

"Good enough," he said. "I'll check in again tomorrow."

"It's out of your way," Miss Crowley said.

"Not so far," he said, then nodded. "I'll bring my tools."

When he'd left, Cecilia asked, "Who that man?"

"Who *is* that man? That's Tom Reid. He owns the hardware store."

She had heard something about that before—she searched her memory. "He teach you drive?" she finally asked. "After father die?"

"How did you know that?"

"You tell me."

"He did. He taught me to drive after *my* father died," Miss Crowley said. "But I paid him. I wouldn't have it any other way."

The look on Miss Crowley's face as the sound of the truck's engine faded away was hard to read. She hadn't been happy about the visit or the offer of help. Now Cecilia couldn't tell if Miss Crowley was angry or sad. Maybe she didn't like Tom Reid or maybe she just liked to do things on her own? Maybe it had been a mistake to mention Miss Crowley's father—perhaps that made her sad? But how could Miss Crowley think of anything else? Cecilia thought of her family all the time. Maybe Miss Crowley had been looking forward to having her father teach her to drive and no one else would do; that Cecilia understood. Her heart felt sad each time she'd done anything with Miss Crowley or Grandma Catherine that she and Mamusia had done together. She'd had to hide tears just yesterday when she and Grandma Catherine picked tomatoes. It didn't matter how kind they were. Cecilia wanted Mamusia.

∞

When Mollie saw Tom Reid's truck pull into the schoolyard, her already aching shoulders tensed up. It had taken half the day to get into the rhythm of completing the routine solitary tasks she did each fall and she'd enjoyed Cecilia's company. Now the calm was disturbed. She girded herself for another battle, fully expecting to see one or more of the men who she'd faced off against on the front yard yesterday afternoon. She'd been relieved it was just Tom, but he presented a different sort of discomfort.

Two years ago, when he'd taught her how to drive, he'd not seen it as a chore. He'd tried to return the payment she made in advance for his time, then tried to give her all manner of things to offset the payment—a repair to the sagging barn door, snow plowing even, an invitation to dinner. She'd declined them all.

Tom was as old as her brothers. Sam and Dan had always made fun of him. "Odd and quiet—bookish," they called him. She hoped Tom hadn't come by the farmhouse before going to the school, because her mother had thought she should encourage him, and all that would start up again. Her mother wouldn't go so far as to say, "Beggars can't be choosers," but that would be how she would interpret her mother's encouragement, since she and Tom Reid seemed to be the only two single people over twenty-five left in the township.

All the men Mollie used to dance with at the town hall on Saturday evenings had either married in their early twenties—like Jim McElpin, who she had planned to marry before she broke off their engagement—and quickly started families, or gone to war, as Josef had done. It felt like the eligible men had disappeared overnight. The life Mollie had assumed she'd lead had evaporated because of circumstances beyond her control. The break of her engagement, her father's death, the war, and now the influenza. Tom Reid was not the worst option, she knew, but a chill ran across her shoulders, and she shivered. She was simply not interested. She already decided she was through with all that. She was far too set in her ways to think of taking up with a man. She liked her independence. She was content living with Catherine in the farmhouse.

"Let's go home," she said to Cecilia. "Enough for today."

"We stop at house?" Cecilia asked, as they turned onto Fox Road.

Mollie had forgotten all about her half-baked promise to stop at the Pokorski farm. She was a little squeamish about going to the property at all, though she knew it had been vacant, except for Cecilia, for weeks. Surely nothing could hurt them there. The child had asked at least three times to go. She understandably wanted to collect a few of her own belongings and her cat; there was no harm in that. "Yes," she said. "We can stop."

"Drive just ahead," Cecilia said.

"I know. I was there just days ago."

"From different direction it look different?"

Mollie looked over at Cecilia, once again taken aback by her intelligence. Surely an awareness of direction, and how things looked from different approaches, would be beyond most eight-year-olds? So, she was smart and forgot nothing? How had she been so wrong about this young girl's intellect? How had she missed her sensitivity?

Mollie stopped the car at the front porch, positioned the same as a few days earlier when she'd fetched Cecilia. She cut the engine, and the silence surrounded them. The air was still. It was as if the whole place had died and was now nothing more than an empty stage set. It was like entering the classroom in mid-July, weeks after classes ended, and weeks before they would begin again. She needed to steady herself. She thought they should talk about how to approach the house, or whether they would even go in. But Cecilia was already out of the car and on the porch, pulling the door open.

Why was she rushing so?

Mollie had no choice but to follow. When she passed through the front door, she could hear Cecilia's footsteps moving toward the back of the house. She took a quick look around. It seemed she was in an area that combined all the family's functions. The place was simple, but clean. There was a soft easy chair in a corner, a table with six seats, and a serviceable kitchen. She could see a large, discolored spot under the icebox where the water had leaked. She smelled the faint smell of mold and felt her nose wrinkle. There was a light layer of dust on the higher surfaces. That made sense—Cecilia had said she'd been doing her best to keep it up just as her mother had. She wouldn't have been able to reach the higher areas. Mollie followed the sound of the girl's footsteps to the back of the house.

At the door of a bedroom, she stopped. Cecilia was standing, looking at what Mollie assumed was the parents' bed. It was unmade and there were rust-colored stains she recognized as dried blood on the white pillowcases. She remembered the accounts she'd read of the influenza, the young soldiers bleeding from their ears and noses, even their gums and eyes. She could understand why no one had attempted to clean the room or the bed linens—what was the point? Especially with the worry and the uncertainty about how the disease was transmitted. To be honest, even if the blood had dried weeks ago, she wasn't willing to do it even today. The thought of it made her stomach turn. Why should anyone else have taken it on?

What must Cecilia have thought, the weeks she'd been here alone? What must she have told herself, sweeping around the unmade bed with its stains? Or maybe this was her first time in the room? Maybe she hadn't been able to bear to go in? She crossed the room and put her hands on the girl's shoulders.

"I not know what to do," Cecilia said. "Doctor say I not leave pantry, so I think I not touch anything."

"The pantry?"

"He say stay in pantry. They sick. So I not get sick. I show you."

They went back to the kitchen, and Cecilia opened a door in the corner. In the small closet, with shelves of preserved fruit and vegetables, there was a narrow compartment, which was probably just long enough for Cecilia to stretch out at night. There was a chamber pot in one corner, and a pile of blankets in the other. "You stayed in here?" she asked, aghast. "While they were dying?"

Cecilia nodded.

What sounds Cecilia must have heard! The headaches were reported to be so severe, hardened soldiers cried out in agony, screaming for relief. What conversations must the child have overheard? Probably just whispers—not enough so that she could know what was happening. That would have been worse than knowing the truth. How long this had gone on—days, or perhaps as long as a week? How could anyone subject a child to that, then leave her behind? She felt a rage rise through her—it was just like when her father died. That damned Dr. Murphy was no good at all at taking a stand. He probably hadn't been able to cross that wife of his, with all her silly affectations, and make proper provision for a healthy child, perhaps even take her home. Why would a woman even marry a country doctor if she wasn't stoic and capable? If she didn't have a big heart?

"Mother kept special things in flour sack," Cecilia said, looking up at a flowered sack on a high shelf. "Father kept papers in a drawer in their bedroom."

Mollie scooped the sack off the shelf. It was heavier than she expected. She couldn't ask the child to go back into the bedroom, with its blood-stained sheets, to fetch the papers. "Which drawer is it?"

"One on top, next to window," Cecilia said. "Will you look for mother's ring?

"Where?"

"Little jewelry box in drawer on the other side. Maybe there."

"Why don't you go outside and call for your kitty? Maybe she's in the barn."

Cecilia looked uncertain but went out the back door. Mollie could hear her calling for the cat; "Here, kitty, kitty, here Daisy." Her voice faded as she walked away from the house.

Being in this house chilled Mollie. She hadn't expected to feel so queasy and spooked. Still, she had no choice but to collect the papers and look for the ring, now that she was here. It was likely there would be information about the family in the drawer. She must go into the bedroom again, if only long enough to scoop the contents into the flour sack. She crossed the small common area quickly and found the bureau in the bedroom right away. The jewelry box was right where Cecilia had told her to look, but it was empty. Mollie even took out the little cardboard liner—nothing. The other drawer was crammed full of papers. On the top was the claim to the homestead of their farm signed with an 'X' next to the name Aloysius Pokorski. So, the Pokorski father couldn't write. Perhaps that was why he had such an ugly attitude about school. Next to the 'X' was the name 'Frances Pokorski,' written in beautiful script, even lovelier than Mollie's schoolteacher script. She pulled layer after layer of papers out of the crammed-full drawer and shoved the papers into the flour sack. She thought she would look for Cecilia's room. Maybe there was something she could take back to the farmhouse to make her room there seem more familiar. Surely, any threat of contamination had passed by now.

Just then, she heard a terrified scream from the barn. She dropped the flour sack on the bedroom floor and took off running. As she approached the barn, she could hear anguished sobs alternating with more high-pitched screams. What could it possibly be, after all that happened, that would so frighten and upset Cecilia? What could be worse than what the child had already seen?

Cecilia was sitting on her knees, leaning forward, hugging herself, rocking back and forth, bent over something on the floor.

As Mollie grew closer, she saw it was a cat with a grossly distended belly, with froth at its mouth. Something had already ripped at the belly of the animal. A cloud of flies swarmed around the carcass. The smell was fresh and nauseating; the cat had not been dead long. She looked away—she didn't want to know if the bodies of unborn kittens were visible in that bloody mess. "Get back from that," she said. "It's nasty."

"Daisy," Cecilia said, then screamed again, and sidled closer to the animal, still on her knees.

Mollie grabbed Cecilia's shoulder and pulled her to her feet and back from the animal. Mollie had never seen anyone so upset and had never heard keening like what was coming out of the child. She turned Cecilia so that her body blocked the sight of the dead and eviscerated animal from Cecilia's view. She held Cecilia, still rocking violently, as tightly as she could, keeping her from getting back down next to the animal. She was stunned by the child's strength.

They stood there like that for many minutes, while the storm of emotion waxed and waned. Each time the girl calmed, it started again. The sobs went on and on, far longer than she would have expected for any pet, much less a barn cat. Farm children were used to enjoying live animals, but also accepting their deaths. This meant that Daisy was more than a barn cat, Mollie realized. This was the last living piece of Cecilia's family. Now she was completely alone.

When the sobs subsided somewhat, she looked over the girl's shoulder at the animal. It looked rigid, like it had been struck by lightning. "I wonder what happened," Mollie said out loud. "I've never seen anything quite like that."

"I know," Cecilia sobbed. "I hate him."

"Who?" Mollie said.

"My father," Cecilia choked out.

"Oh, Cecilia," Mollie said, "You shouldn't—"

"Rat poison. He put in barn to kill rats and mice. Daisy ate dead mice, so she die too. Same for our dog. That why we feed Daisy up at the house. If she full, she safe—that's what Mamusia say. Then, when I go, no one feeds her. She come to barn for food. My fault. All my fault."

No, Mollie thought. It's not her fault at all. It's all *my* fault. Why didn't I listen yesterday, or the day before, when she asked to come and get the cat? Why did I let that silliness with my brothers distract me? I should have known that the pet was more important. A wave of grief and guilt washed over her. This was nothing she could control and nothing she could fix. This was something Cecilia would never forget. And, undoubtedly, no matter how carefully she watched and worried, the future held more of the same. Innocent sins that would cause grievous harm.

"Let's go home," Mollie said. "I am so sorry."

"Leave her here?" Cecilia said. "Like this? What if what tore her comes back?"

The child was right. They had to protect the body. Mollie pulled a horse blanket off a hook on the wall and grabbed one leg of the dead cat between her thumb and forefinger and dragged the surprisingly heavy body onto the blanket. Once it was on the blanket, she wrapped it tightly, almost like a swaddle, and picked the bundle up. She felt her stomach heave and bile come up into her throat, making her gag. She was surprised. She'd seen many dead animals on the farm. Why was this so upsetting? As her lunch roiled in her stomach, she dropped the bundle and heaved into a pile of straw.

"I can't," Mollie said. "I thought I could but I can't."

"Mr. Reid?" Cecilia said. "He come and take her? We bury her at farmhouse?"

Mollie wracked her brain for options—she didn't want his help, with all its strings attached. But who could she call to come and pick up the cat? Maybe she could do it herself with a night's rest when she had a chance to get used to the idea? When she wasn't so alarmed as she'd been by the hysterical screaming?

She considered the bundle, contemplated picking it up and hoisting it into her car, then disposing of it in a field or ditch when they got home. But she took an involuntary step back. She'd rather leave the dead animal right there. It could disintegrate over the course of the fall and winter. No one would be the wiser. No one except Cecilia, to whom she could tell any story she wanted about what had happened to the carcass. But the cat had been Cecilia's pet—a living creature Cecilia and her mother had tended—and Mollie understood that those little remembered sweetnesses were precious and finite. The girl was sobbing hysterically. She'd already failed the child. Catherine was right—no good came of secrets. Or lies. She couldn't tell her this was going to be all right—it wasn't. She couldn't pretend she'd given the animal a proper burial if she'd instead left it to rot. She had no words.

It was likely Tom Reid, with his affection for his dog, would know what to say to the child, and how to bury the pet without doing any more damage. Mollie didn't have a better idea.

"I'll call him when we get back to the farm," she said. "There's a phone in the hardware store. Let's pick up the papers from the house and go."

∞

Cecilia took a step back from Miss Crowley. Miss Crowley's hand reached for her, but she was already too far away. "No. I not go," she said. "I stay with Daisy." She sat down on a bale of hay within an arm's length of the bundled cat, remembering how Daisy had wound herself around her ankles on the sunny front porch and cuddled with her in the night, pressing one front paw after the other against her stomach. "Kneading bread," Mamusia had called it.

"Don't touch it," Miss Crowley said.

"Daisy," Cecilia corrected.

"Daisy." Miss Crowley's arm dropped to her side.

Cecilia anticipated the teacher-voice that would come next, but it didn't matter. She shouldn't have left Daisy in the first place. She'd been purely selfish—like her father always said, and not appreciative of valuable things or good food or a tight roof over her head. If she'd taken care of her pet, instead of rushing away with Miss Crowley, Daisy would still be alive.

"Animals get the sickness?" Cecilia asked, wondering whether the cat had gotten infected like her family did. If it had taken this long for the cat, maybe she would get sick too.

"What?"

"Animals get the—" She searched for the correct word. "Influenza?"

Miss Crowley hesitated—she must not know the right answer. Finally, she said, "I don't think so. I've read a lot about this influenza and there's nothing about taking precautions with any animals, not pets or farm stock. Plus, it's been too long."

"She not die of flu?"

"No, I don't think so."

"She eat poison, and then something got her. If I here, I keep Daisy fed and safe, like Mamusia and I keep her safe all summer."

"You stayed with your family, and it didn't help," Miss Crowley said, as if she'd read her mind. "Your being here wouldn't have changed what happened to the cat. Sometimes sad things just happen."

Cecilia shook her head. "We keep her safe all summer."

Miss Crowley sat down next to her on the bale. "How did you do that?" she asked.

"We feed her on porch after Father and Hugh go to field, and in afternoon before they come back. We made a little nest for her under the porch, with her basket, where only we knew."

"Did you do that after…?"

Although Miss Crowley's voice had trailed off, Cecilia knew what she meant. "When they sick, I sneak out early and put food out. At night, I let her sleep in pantry with me. Mamusia never let her in house. When Mamusia alive, we lock Daisy in the root cellar at night."

Miss Crowley sighed.

"We have kittens now, if we took her on Saturday?"

"I don't know," Miss Crowley said, then tears began dropping from her eyes. "I am so sorry," rushed out. "Can you ever forgive me?"

Cecilia stayed quiet. She'd obeyed Miss Crowley and gone with her, leaving Daisy behind, and look what happened. She'd thought of Daisy again and again, and asked for help to get the cat. She knew that if they'd gotten there in time, Miss Crowley would have allowed the kittens to be born on the farm. Now she'd never see them or see Daisy again either. Her eyes narrowed and she wrapped her arms around herself, pinching her skin to keep from crying. She would never forgive Miss Crowley or herself. "I not go with you," she finally repeated. "I stay here. I protect her."

"Well of course you're coming—" Miss Crowley said.

"No, I not," Cecilia interrupted, vowing to stay put forever if necessary.

Miss Crowley stood and stared, as if she had never been told "no" before.

There were rats in the barn—Cecilia had seen them often and heard their skittery scratches in the rafters. Even now, she could see their dark droppings littering the floor—tiny things in the shape of pitch-black eyebrows like that doctor's, always knitted together over his big nose. One time, when she came to get corn for the chickens, a rat ran right up the inside of her skirt, its coarse hair rubbing along her leg. Even now, she shivered to think of it. She'd screamed so loud that Mamusia came running and searched her flesh for bites. She'd continued to scream and couldn't speak to tell Mamusia she was scared, not hurt. Mamusia beat at the side of her skirt until the rat broke loose and ran away. From then on, they got the corn and fed the chickens together.

"It was rats," she said, trying to push the image of the tortured cat out of her mind.

Miss Crowley shivered, too, and hugged herself.

Cecilia was scared to stay in the barn alone. But, she said, "I not scared," which was a lie. Then, again, "I not leave. You find help."

Chapter Eight

This was how Mollie found herself tearing down the roads between the Pokorski farm and Tom Reid's hardware store in a disheveled frenzy, feeling like an incompetent hazard in every area of her life. She prayed the hardware store was still open. It was nearly five, but Tom sometimes stayed longer in the store, she suspected even until sundown, to accommodate the farmers who needed something at the end of the workday, especially now that everyone was desperate to get the hay off before the autumn rains.

If the store wasn't open, she'd have to go to his house, the big two-story one across from the church, and bang on the door or search through the barns for him. If she had to do that, surely someone would see her and wonder what in the world she was after. Going to his door when he was alone—suspenders eased off his shoulders, perhaps in his socks—would be more humiliating than she could bear on this already horrid afternoon.

Maybe Tom had locked the store and gone somewhere else. His mother had passed last spring. What did he have to go home for, rattling around in that big house, large enough to house ten children? She could remember the younger Reids, the ones her age, all tumbling down the front steps just minutes before the nuns rang the convent bell. They'd all moved away, leaving just him, the oldest son, with the farm and the store. Would she have heard if he'd taken up with someone new, and was spending time with her in the evenings?

What was she going to do if he wasn't at the store or his house?

Her lips tightened. Oh, how she hated asking for help. But Cecilia was distraught, understandably so, and she couldn't physically scoop her up and forcibly take her home. She understood why Cecilia didn't want to leave her pet's body until they'd made proper arrangements. Getting help for Cecilia was more important than her feelings, especially since she'd created this mess. There was no other way.

Yesterday, she'd reassured Cecilia that she had no second thoughts about fetching her, but in just over forty-eight hours—hard to believe it was only Saturday when she took her from the Pokorski farm and now it was just Monday—her life had become a whirlpool. There had been so much upheaval, on top of the pandemic and all the uncertainty about starting school, and now there was the resistance from her brothers and the priest and even the doctor, who had been in her corner as recently as the previous Friday. She could barely reconcile her present circumstance with how she'd felt a few short months ago, when it seemed she could move through tasks like a hot knife through butter.

Mollie had sometimes wondered if she was missing out by not having a family—but now, she couldn't help wondering if she'd tossed her peaceful existence out the window. Was this how parents lived? Had she invited all this pain? Worst of all, she was making a mess of absolutely everything—like the fiasco with the cat. And there was no predicting what tomorrow would bring—the world seemed as fickle as the Michigan autumn weather. This afternoon had been lovely and warm, and now it was clouding over. Tomorrow could bring freezing temperatures, pouring rain or, with her luck, even snow.

Should she expect this chaos to continue forever?

Mollie shook her head, even as she navigated around a deep pothole in the middle of the dirt road, then accelerated again. How had she missed the significance of the cat, especially when Cecilia mentioned the animal several times? She hadn't even remembered the name until Cecilia had said it a few minutes ago. Mollie turned left on Sparling Road and chanted a rare prayer to St. Jude—her favorite saint, the patron of lost causes—*Please, let Tom still be there, please let me get through this day doing no further damage, and please grant me grace.*

·   ·   ·

"Thank God for small favors," Mollie whispered, as she entered town from the south. Tom Reid's old green truck was still in front of the store, and she could see he was just locking the front door, that old hound next to him. She tapped the horn and startled them. Tom squinted, then once he'd realized it was her, raised his hand in a wave. She pulled across the oncoming lane, parked nose-to-nose with the truck, and bolted out of the car. I must look a fright, she thought—the perspiration dripping down under her arms had surely made wet circles under the sleeves of her thin cotton dress, the front of which was streaked with dirt from the day of cleaning. She reached up to smooth her hair but could feel it frizzed in a nimbus around her head—it was no use.

"Can you help me?" she cried.

"Of course," Tom answered. The keys to the store were still in his hand, and he sorted out the proper key and put it back in the lock. "What do you need?"

"Not here," Mollie said. "At the Pokorski farm."

His eyebrows raised.

Which made sense—he'd last seen her at the schoolhouse, where she'd acted like the last thing she could ever imagine needing from him was help of any kind. She shook her head and closed her eyes, then took a deep breath. "It's silly," she said, imagining how her older brothers would have responded to the problem with the cat. How small and helpless they would have made her feel. Her face grew hot—now she'd blush beet red on top of everything else.

"It's a cat. A dead cat," she said, her eyes still squeezed shut.

She opened her eyes. His face was still a question mark, like the big one on the strip of punctuation symbols she'd pasted above the blackboard just before she and Cecilia left the classroom. But it wasn't a mean expression, as her brothers' would have been—just confused.

"It's Cecilia's cat," she added.

Tom still looked confused.

She took a deep breath, willing herself to slow down and at least get a few sentences of explanation out in something resembling a calm manner. "She had a cat. It was…." What was the politest way to say pregnant? "With kittens. But something got to it, and now it's dead, and Cecilia wouldn't leave with me—" Despite her best efforts, her words had sped up and her voice quavered. "It's disgusting. And I left her there with it."

"You left her there?" he said. "The child? On that farm? Alone?"

"She wouldn't come," she said, feeling defensive, and remembering Catherine's scolding when she'd left Cecilia at the house to walk off her temper. "And I just left her for a few minutes. Long enough to come for help. She was there for *weeks* until Mother and I—"

"She's a brave little thing, isn't she?" Tom's tone was warm and neutral, not accusatory.

"Yes. I suppose she is." Mollie felt an unexpected surge of pride in Cecilia—she really was brave. To stay there like that after all she'd been through for the love of a pet. To square off against her, just like Mollie was prone to do when she made up her mind.

"I understand," he said, opening the store door. "Sounds like you need some help collecting and burying a dead cat."

"Yes, that's it." Mollie nodded.

"I'll get a shovel," he said. "Climb in the truck. We'll go together, and I'll bring you back up here to retrieve your car when we're finished."

As Mollie stood waiting, she saw the shape of his head and shoulders through the store window, moving through the stacks and dodging the large farm tools hanging from the ceiling, finding what he needed, without even turning on the light. She took her first deep breath of the last hour.

∞

Cecilia tried to block out the scurrying sounds coming from the corners of the barn. She didn't like that it was growing darker, she didn't like the scratchy sounds, and she didn't like the feeling of being the only living human for a long way in every direction. It reminded her of how she'd felt when she was alone for so many days and weeks after her brothers, then Mamusia, then Father died, and everyone went away and that doctor seemed like he'd be willing to leave her there forever. She could see Daisy's body, all wrapped up in the horse blanket, out of the corner of her eye, but she didn't like to look at that too closely. She was afraid she'd see something crawling or gnawing or even the signs of a kitten.

She didn't like to look too far into the corners of the barn either, for fear of seeing little beady eyes just waiting for a chance to dart out. And she knew the chirping sound she heard high in the rafters was bats. If she looked up, she might see them swooping in and out of the open window to the haymow. She remembered when Hugh used to tease her by putting his fingers in her hair and making the whirring noise he said sounded like bats.

Daisy isn't really Daisy anymore, she thought. Only a faint disgusting smell reminded her that Daisy had ever been alive at all. Then she imagined that no one in her family had their same shape anymore either, just like Daisy didn't have her shape. They probably didn't have any shape at all. She backed away from the thought of smell; Mamusia had smelled of lilacs, her father of what he called "the sweat of good honest work," and Hugh like fresh-cut hay. That's what she wanted to remember. Whatever was left of them had nothing to do with their bodies, just like Daisy had nothing to do with the lump wrapped in an old blanket lying at her feet in the dirt of the barn floor. Like puffs of smoke, they were really gone. Cecilia fixed a picture of Daisy in her memory, next to the pictures she kept there of Mamusia, Hugh, Josef, and Father. She hoped Miss Crowley would return before the barn was fully dark.

Cecilia stood when she heard a vehicle approaching. The sky outside the window was deep blue with a few stars. It was more night than day now. She'd been cold for a long time. This feeling reminded her of when she was here all by herself and how she'd hated when night came, even when she was in the house. She didn't like the mess of the cat—it wasn't Daisy anymore, she knew—and she didn't like the sounds in the barn. Back when her family was alive, there were cows and chickens here, so even in the dark, late at night, the barn had the feeling of being full of friendly, living things. If only she could put the rats out of her mind. And the bats. And imagine the homey feel of the barn when her family had been alive. Now, it just felt cold and damp, like it had been left to rodents and any other wild animal that needed a place to shelter.

It was a dead place.

∞

Tom pulled his truck up close to the barn door and positioned it so the lights would shine into the barn once they rolled the big door out of the way. Mollie was out of the truck before he cut the engine. She saw the girl's outline in the opened barn door, her hands shielding her eyes from the bright light. She must be blinded, Mollie thought.

"Cecilia?" she called out. "It's us. We're here. I'm sorry it took so long."

Cecilia ran to her and threw her arms around her waist. Tom and the dog followed them into the barn.

"Stay back," Mollie told the dog in a tense voice.

"The dog get sick, too," Cecilia added, looking at Tom. "The barn not safe. Father put out rat poison. Animals eat dead mice and rats, well...." She gestured toward the cat.

"He will not bother anything," Tom said. "Too smart for that. And fed too often and too well."

"Daisy's there," Cecilia said, still under Mollie's arm, and pointed to a spot a few feet further into the barn.

Mollie saw the shape of the swaddled carcass. At least she wouldn't have to look at the grotesque body again, or move the stiff, heavy body. She remembered the cat winding itself around Cecilia's ankles on Saturday, then scatting when she sluiced Cecilia's back with water. Why hadn't she scooped it up then? She felt so guilty, she couldn't speak, and suddenly, angry with her brothers and the priest and the doctor. She knew if she hadn't been so distracted by their bullying, she would have thought to come back yesterday. Maybe that would have been in time to save the animal. She looked at Tom, as if to say: 'Let's get going.' Prolonging this would not make it any easier.

"I'm so sorry, sweetie," Tom said calmly to Cecilia, as if he had all the time in the world. He reached down and scratched the dog's head again. The dog leaned in as if it experienced this small comfort many times each day. Probably it did, Mollie thought. "Was she your pet?" he asked.

"Yes," Cecilia swallowed.

Mollie could feel the lump in Cecilia's throat as though it was her own. "It's all my fault," Mollie said. "Cecilia asked to come back and get her, and I didn't listen. I am so sorry."

Cecilia stepped back from Mollie, and Mollie noticed the hard set of her jaw. She was willing to apportion fault to Mollie, and not yet ready to accept her apology.

They all stood in silence for a minute.

"You'll never get another cat exactly like Daisy," Tom said.

"Or kittens like those same kittens," Cecilia choked on the words.

"I know." Tom smiled, but his eyes stayed sad. "Lex here is my fifth dog. First, when I was a boy, there was Cindy. She died when I was six, just a little younger than you are, and I still remember her. Then, Mickey. Then, Pepper—she was prone to nip. Then, Tramp." He looked over at Mollie and shrugged. "And now, Lex."

"How they die?" Cecilia said.

"Old age, except for Mickey." His jaw hardened like Cecilia's had. "That was a farm accident," he added, and paused. "I cried over every one of them."

Cecilia nodded, and Tom's eyes filled at the memory of his lost pets.

Mollie looked away, thinking he must not want her to see his tears, though he wasn't making any effort to hide them. His description of the dogs and their long lives reminded her of his age, well over thirty. Almost ten years older than she was. Eyes downcast, she focused on his hand, still on the dog—Lex's—head. It showed his age, too. His knuckles were knobby from working in the cold winters, and his flesh was scarred from all manner of injuries. But he was touching the dog so kindly and he'd spoken of all his pets with such affection.

Finally, Tom swiped at his face with the back of his hand and pulled a pair of gloves out of his back pocket. "This isn't going to get any easier," he said, the same thing Mollie had been thinking a few minutes ago, but now placed at the correct moment, not too soon to show compassion. He moved toward the remains of the cat.

Cecilia stepped aside to allow him access. "We bury her?"

Mollie caught Tom's eye over the child's head. He nodded—he was going to help until the remnants of this animal were safely tucked into the ground.

"Yes," she said. "We're going to bury her."

"We bury her on farm?" Cecilia asked. Then, when Mollie didn't answer immediately, clarifying, "Your farm? Near farmhouse?"

So Cecilia wanted to bury the animal near the farmhouse, not here on her own family's farm. Could Cecilia's sense of home have migrated in just a few short days, however disappointed she may have been in Mollie? Mollie remembered how she'd been thinking, just an hour earlier, that perhaps she'd been too hasty with Cecilia. She choked up and nodded, even though a small part of her still wondered what she had gotten herself into.

"Yes," she answered. "We can bury her on the farm."

"What do you say I take her home with me tonight?" Tom said. "It's already near dark. I'll keep her safe. Then, we can find a perfect resting spot in the morning."

"Yes," Cecilia said. "You take her with you. Keep her inside?"

"Don't worry," he said. "Nothing will bother her anymore."

Cecilia sagged down onto the bale of hay and Mollie realized that she'd pulled the girl out of bed this morning with the chickens. The child had worked alongside her all day, and then confronted the sadness of the loss of her pet, not to mention what she must have felt about being left alone while she went to fetch Tom. She was, after all, just a little girl. Mollie pulled her to her feet and put her arm around her shoulders and led her from the barn, with Tom following, the bundled cat in his arms. Mollie ran back into the house to get the flour sack she'd dropped when Cecilia started screaming. Then, they sorted themselves into the tight cab of the truck, Lex curled at Mollie's feet and Cecilia in the middle. Mollie hoped her mother would have a hot meal ready for them. Then, she and Cecilia could turn in and face what awaited them in the morning.

Chapter Nine

After they'd collected Miss Crowley's car and were headed back to the farm, Cecilia felt her heartbeat slow and her racing breath return to normal. She sagged into the passenger seat. Daisy's body was safe until morning, thanks to Mr. Reid. She liked that he'd owned and cared for five dogs. She liked the tears in his eyes. She'd never seen that before—tears in the eyes of a man, although she thought she remembered tears in Hugh's eyes, but couldn't remember why or when.

As Miss Crowley braked to make a turn, the headlights illuminated a cluster of headstones. Cecilia realized she hadn't come to the farm this way before. Both the schoolhouse and the Pokorski farm were in the other direction. They were approaching from a different way.

"The burial place," Cecilia said. "I remember. Are they there?"

"Drat." Miss Crowley hit the steering wheel. "I should have turned a mile back and come in the other way. There seems to be no end to my stupidity today." She sped up, as though she meant to rush by. "That's where they are. We'll come back, one day, in the light."

"Please stop," Cecilia said. "I go there—now."

"*Really*? Are you sure? After the day we've had?"

Cecilia looked over at Miss Crowley. Her hair looked like red steel wool. Her dress was creased and covered with lines of dirt and chalk and even a dark stain Cecilia thought might be Daisy's blood. "Yes," Cecilia said. "I want stop. You know where they are?"

"Yes," Miss Crowley said. "I know." She peered out the car window, looking carefully at the gravestones, then finally stopped. The headlights pointed into the dark cemetery, making tunnels into the gloom. Each of the headstones cast a long shadow and the rustling leaves on the low branches looked as if they were whispering to one another.

"There?" Cecilia tilted her head toward a large, grey-white spike, tilted to the side. It was the marker closest to the car. "That it?"

Miss Crowley nodded but didn't move from behind the wheel.

"I get out," Cecilia said. "You stay. I go by myself."

"You want to get out?"

"Yes."

"Are you sure?"

"Yes. You no go." Cecilia took a deep breath. "I want to go alone."

Cecilia slipped out of her seat and walked around the front of the car. She heard Miss Crowley's door open and glanced back over her shoulder. She was sitting with her feet swung around to the grass but was staying put. At the marker, Cecilia saw something—names—scratched into the stone.

There they all were. Father—Aloysius. Mother—Frances—Mamusia. And Josef and Hugh.

She dropped to her knees, as if at Mass. Sodden leaves—all the colors of the fall rainbow—were bunched up around the base, and she felt the damp seep through her stockings. There were no flowers around her family's headstone. The flowers by the other headstones looked wind-chapped and tired. She could see the four rectangles extending from each side of the spike. Those must be the graves. The grass was just beginning to come up, like a man with picky whiskers, the way her father's face used to look. The spiky grass looked scratchy, not like a place anyone would want to relax. It looked so different from the day of the funerals, held outside here at the cemetery, when she'd stood alone, far from the priest and doctor, the only other attendees. She remembered how she'd ridden there and home in the back of the doctor's pickup, and that it already felt like her family had been gone forever.

She also remembered how hot she'd been that day, and how the doctor kept eyeing her warily, as if she might have a fever—like she was contaminated. She'd worn a mask that was so large it wrapped under her chin and almost to her eyes; she was the only one wearing one. Not a single person touched her that long day, not even come within an arm's length of her. She felt the priest and doctor looked at her with almost the same disgust Miss Crowley's face showed when she looked at the remains of what used to be Daisy. She tried to remember the prayer Mamusia used to say in Polish, and whispered a few phrases, but that really didn't help. She didn't feel the sense of anyone here at all—it was as if they'd been erased. The air was chilly—as if it had gone from late summer to fall in just a few hours. At least she knew where they were, she thought, and stood up to return to the car.

∞

As she came over the train tracks north of the farmhouse, Mollie wished she had called her mother at some point in the afternoon—she could have phoned when they left the schoolhouse or when she got to the hardware store. But how could she have known how the afternoon would unfold before they went to the Pokorski farm? And when she'd been at the hardware store, she'd been crazy to get back to Cecilia. Still, she knew she'd worried her mother—it was hours since they should have been home. She should have called. One more thing to regret.

She saw Catherine standing in the doorway as she passed the farmhouse. Had it been a fine evening, she would have left the car in front for a couple of hours and taken it to the barn after dinner, maybe even gone for a little spin by herself to calm her nerves, but tonight it seemed cold rain would start any minute and continue all night. At the barn, she threw her weight against the heavy sliding door to move it out of the way, then drove the car in. She collected her things and the heavy flour sack and noticed their masks lying on the back seat. She'd forgotten to wear hers around Tom and hadn't insisted Cecilia put hers on either. That was sloppy. In the flurry of activity, she had somehow eased into letting Tom feel like family.

"I am sorry," she called to Catherine, as she followed Cecilia up the walk, just as the first drops fell. "We would have been home hours ago, but…"

She saw her mother give a slight shake of her head over Cecilia's head, so she stopped speaking.

"Not to worry," Catherine said. "Tom called from the store. He told me what happened." She held out her arms to Cecilia. "Come here, sweetheart."

"Mother," Mollie said, grabbing Cecilia's shoulder. "You shouldn't be near her. Or me—I forgot all about the masks this afternoon, with Tom. He sees people all day long in the store. I haven't had mine on for hours."

"I don't care," Catherine said. "Who knows how long this is going to go on? It's not right to live like this. Keeping family so far from me—" She sniffed with disgust. "It's unnatural. I will be fine. Or I won't be fine. But I will not live like this. Now, come here."

Before Mollie could say another word, Cecilia had wrapped her arms around Catherine's waist. All Mollie could think was that she too wanted a long embrace, followed by a hot meal and a deep sleep. She couldn't do anything now about what she'd overlooked days or hours ago—she'd do better tomorrow. She dropped the flour sack with all the things she'd collected at the Pokorski farm inside the front door.

Catherine had prepared a simple dinner of roast pork and applesauce with sliced tomatoes, probably the last from her garden. It smelled like heaven. She'd set it up on the little kitchen table—another flagrant violation of what they'd planned only two days ago—but Mollie didn't have the heart to move it all, and suspected Catherine's choice of table hadn't been an accident. She had her mind made up; they were to behave as a family of three. Steam had collected on the inside of the window. It felt like they were the only people in the universe.

"We'll do better tomorrow," Catherine said, taking her seat, almost as if she'd read Mollie's mind.

Mollie ate for several minutes without stopping, then asked, "Where did the pork come from?"

"The Kellys dropped it off. And this is the last of the tomatoes. I made applesauce today."

"Who are the Kellys?" Cecilia asked.

"They own the pig farm we pass on the way to the school," Mollie said.

Cecilia wrinkled her nose—the pig farm had quite a stench, Mollie knew, but then Cecilia said, "It good," and took another bite. Mollie noticed her plate was already half empty, and she was eyeing the applesauce.

"More?" Cecilia said.

"May I please have more?" Mollie corrected and spooned a generous portion onto Cecilia's plate. Then she turned to Catherine. "So, you were out harvesting both tomatoes and apples?"

"A simple thank you will do," Catherine said.

Mollie pictured her mother up on a ladder in the orchard with her arms over her head, picking the low-hanging apples and pears and weaving among the tomato vines in the garden to harvest the last ripe vegetables of the season. So easy to lose her balance and fall, or lose track of her cane, or trip among the heavy vines and not be able to get back on her feet. No one would have found her until they returned home, well after dark. These were tasks Mollie would have done if she'd been at home. She should help more. Then, the worry about the quarantine surfaced again. They were supposed to be so vigilant about the quarantine. She'd promised her brothers she was observing all the precautions, and she was not. However awful they'd been, their request was reasonable. She knew this weighed so heavily on her because she was tired, but still she felt as if she would never get anything quite right.

Tomorrow, Mollie thought again—tomorrow she would take better care.

The three finished their meals in silence. Cecilia's head was dipping even before Mollie could clear the tea and cookies. Catherine had to be done for as well. "Go to bed," Mollie told them. "I'll clear up tonight."

As Cecilia passed, she reached out for a quick hug, then crossed to Catherine. Mollie winced again. Were they going to dispense with all efforts at distance? She put up her hand, but Cecilia didn't notice, and Catherine enfolded her, despite Mollie's cautious expression. Mollie sensed any further effort on her part to modify Catherine's behavior would seem self-righteous and useless, anyway. Plus, as it had turned out, Mollie wasn't even able to keep the cat safe. Why would anyone listen to her?

"Would you like another cup of tea?" Catherine asked, once Cecilia had gone.

Mollie was glad her mother hadn't gone straight to bed. She needed the company. "Yes," she said, and got up to fix the pot and put a few more oatmeal cookies on a small plate.

"How did Tom get involved in that enterprise?" Catherine asked when they were both settled.

Mollie rolled her eyes—here it came. "Don't," she said.

"What?" her mother said. "I just asked how he got involved."

"He came to the school to see if I needed help. Cecilia met him. Then we went to the farm and found the cat."

"Poor thing," Catherine said.

"Poor Cecilia," Mollie said.

"That's what I meant." Catherine smiled. "Poor cat, too, of course, but to lose a pet after everything else."

"I feel badly enough. Please."

Catherine's eyebrows raised. "Why do *you* feel badly?"

"She told me about the cat. She asked to go back several times. I brushed her off."

"Oh, please," Catherine said. "Pace yourself. If you're really going to take care of this child, you must abandon any obsession with being perfect. It's just not possible. That is not how being a parent works. It's not like going to your job, and checking *all* the boxes, which I know you do to a fault."

Mollie sat back against her chair. This wasn't what she'd been expecting. She'd anticipated her mother would have pounced on her again, like she did yesterday when Mollie left for a walk to clear her head. Then, Catherine had acted like it was Mollie's business to be always attached to the child, morning until night, alert to and heading off every disaster. Like there could be no distance at all between her and this new being in her world.

"How were you to know?" Catherine continued. "You've been trying to mother this child for seventy-two hours—three short days! Look at all that's been accomplished since then. You forgot the cat. You didn't see the future. It's sad, but it could have happened to anyone. It could have happened here. We've lost plenty of cats to one thing or another."

"Cecilia said her father poisoned the rats and mice, and then the cat got into it and got poisoned too. We don't leave poison standing out in our barns."

"And here, it could have been a wagon wheel, or you tearing down the road, or a nasty raccoon, or God knows what else. Barn cats have short lives. At least, usually." Catherine reached out and put her hand over Mollie's. "You are trying your best. You are doing your best. No one else is trying to make things right for her as hard as you are. I'm proud of you."

Mollie's eyes filled with tears. "Thank you." She settled against the back of her chair, sipped her tea, and took a tiny bite of a cookie, nibbling around a raisin. She didn't like raisins, but her father and brothers had, so her mother put raisins in the cookies. Mollie realized she'd never told her mother about the raisins, and her mother had apparently never noticed, and was still putting them in although her father and brothers were gone. "Is this what it's like to be a parent? Why is it so different from being a teacher?"

"You mean you wouldn't have raced around after a dead cat all afternoon for one of your students?" Catherine laughed.

Mollie shrugged her shoulders and took another bite of the cookie. "I might have," she said, smiling back at Catherine. "If I realized it was important."

Catherine's face grew serious. "You've had a small taste of what it's like to be a parent. Just a sip, really. But yes, you never stop caring and you *never* stop worrying."

"I've had a lot of students, but not a lot of experience caring for anyone the way Cecilia cared about that cat," Mollie paused. "Or the way her mother cared for her."

"True," Catherine said. Her hand was still over Mollie's.

"Why do you look so sad?" Mollie asked.

"I just want you to be happy," Catherine said.

This too was the last thing Mollie expected to hear. How did Catherine's wish match up with feeling attached to Cecilia, or guilty about the cat? She was exhausted—not miserable. "I'm fine, Mother, really. It was just a hard day. Hard couple of days."

Catherine nodded, and after a few minutes, picked her things up and put them in the sink. "I appreciate having a child here," she said, her back to Mollie, as she pumped water to rinse the dishes. "It brings joy to the house."

"Aren't you upset about what Sam and Dan said? About keeping their children from you? Not seeing your grandchildren?"

"Their children should stay close to home, I suppose. Isn't that what we've asked of families here? When the time is right, I'm confident they'll come around." She pushed the pump handle a few more times, then looked inside the stove, her back to Mollie, her expression hidden.

Mollie knew the stove was cold; putting more wood in and then heating the water for dishes would be an ordeal. "Let's leave those dishes, all right? Do them in the morning?"

"But—"

"I'll take care of them in the morning," Mollie said, her tone firm.

Catherine wiped her hands on her apron. "All right," she said. "Time for bed?"

"Not yet," Mollie said. She remembered the flour sack she dropped near the front door. She swept her dishes from the table, set them in the sink, and wiped the surface of the table with a rag. As tired as she was, she wanted to look at the contents in privacy.

"All right, then," Catherine said. "Good night."

∞

Cecilia pretended to be asleep when she heard the door of her room open. She knew it was late. The sound of the train whistle had come and gone. She'd been crying. She was tired of crying all the time. There was nothing to be done about her family or Daisy. She rounded her shoulders and pulled her knees even further into the ball she preferred to be in before sleeping. She could tell by the way the person moved across the room that it was Miss Crowley, not Grandma Catherine. She made her breath regular and slow and didn't move a muscle.

Miss Crowley's arm reached out over her, and she rested her palm so lightly on Cecilia's forehead that Cecilia could barely feel the cool touch. Miss Crowley stood there for a few moments, barely breathing. She heard the softest of murmuring and realized Miss Crowley was praying. It wasn't a prayer she recognized—Mamusia's prayers were always in Polish. But she was checking on her like Mamusia had done. The hand on her forehead didn't feel familiar, but the cool touch was pleasant. She couldn't make sense of Miss Crowley's words, but it didn't matter. The soft murmuring made her eyes feel heavier. It was good to know someone would check on her when they believed she was asleep.

∞

In her nightgown with a warm wrapper and slippers, the deep chill of the afternoon finally behind her, her face washed and teeth cleaned, and with Cecilia finally settled, Mollie relaxed. Though it felt like the past day had lasted three days, it was only eight o'clock. She'd sit for a couple of hours without being disturbed and go through the papers and the things Cecilia's mother kept in the flour sack.

Diving into the personal things she'd collected and dumped into the sack seemed invasive, but Mollie couldn't see any alternative. How else would she know whether Cecilia was as abandoned as she seemed to be, or understand anything about where the Pokorski family came from? She lit the kerosene lamp and placed the stack of papers on the dining room table.

The top layer was the documents she'd scooped out of the Pokorski parents' bedroom drawer and looked to be mostly business-related. There was the deed to their farm, showing it had been homesteaded not quite ten years earlier. They must have been one of the last families to take possession of government land in Saint Clair County. The boys must have been in her class shortly after they arrived. Mollie wondered how they'd fared at the hands of families like the O'Connells—then, she hadn't even considered the conflicts between Polish and Irish students in her classroom. She'd been far too worried about her own inexperience. Frances Pokorski's beautiful script next to Aloysius Pokorski's "X" made Mollie wonder how they'd ended up together. And, if she recalled correctly, he was a good deal older as well. Sometimes marriages worked when there was an age difference—maybe....

"Stop it," she whispered out loud.

She'd vowed to take a break from all aspects of romance after she broke her engagement to Jim McElpin the week before they were supposed to marry, four years earlier. It had been the talk of the township because she'd refused to disclose a reason. It was bad enough to disappoint Jim without carrying tales to everyone they both knew. The real reason was the drink, that evil stuff. He'd always had a flask with him. Then, the last night they were together, he'd run his buggy into the deep ditch on Fox Road for what seemed to be the tenth time that year. His family had a standing joke about how he liked to check on the crayfish personally. Mollie had not found it funny. Once again, he'd promised to dry out, but it never seemed to happen, and she'd finally admitted to herself it probably never would.

Jim had walked to a nearby farm and the owner—the father of one of Mollie's students—had pulled them out of the ditch. She'd been mortified. When she got home, she'd woken her parents and told them she couldn't go through with the marriage. She'd told them why—too much drink. They had a dusty bottle of wine in the house and took a small glass on occasion and had no patience for drunkenness. They'd agreed about breaking off with Jim. It had surprised her to learn they'd had worries of their own. Taking the high path meant not showing everyone their dirty laundry, so she was not surprised when Jim McElpin—wealthy and handsome—was married less than a year later to one of the Powers' girls, who either didn't suspect his devotion to the drink or didn't care. She only hoped he'd been a straighter arrow for Imogene Powers than he'd been for her. Hard to say, because they now had two little ones and Imogene was stuck, even more stuck than Mollie would have been, given that Imogene had no way to earn a living for herself. Imogene was a fragile bloom; maybe she'd brought out his strength.

Mollie hadn't regretted ending things with Jim but hadn't foreseen that she wouldn't have another option. She hadn't foreseen that so many of the other young men her age would have paired off during her engagement. Then the war took so many others overseas, as if in a pack. She realized she'd been left behind the one time she'd gone to a church dance just before the influenza outbreak. Those dances, which used to be populated with her peers, were now filled with her friends' younger brothers and sisters. Her courting years seemed to have ended so abruptly, making her an old maid in her mid-twenties. What she'd intended to be a romance hiatus had become permanent.

She wouldn't have thought Tom Reid would be the only one left. Tom, like Jim McElpin, was exempt from the draft. Jim was exempted because he managed the large family farm, Tom Reid, because of his management of the hardware store—a necessity to keep the farmers in the area productive—as well as the Reid family farm, and his age. She'd never even glanced at him before the war. She didn't intend to glance at him now, not really. In her heart, she didn't at all mind being a spinster. She had watched the lives of her married friends unfold over the last few years and concluded there was not much to envy or regret.

She was happy on her own. Wasn't she?

There was no point in thinking about Tom Reid. His major attraction was that he was available. He'd never have taken a second look at her either but for the driving lessons she'd been forced to arrange. But, she could hear her mother's voice urging, "No Mollie, he's a good man with a substantial farm and a going business, a better choice than Jim…." She'd cut Catherine off a dozen times as she'd made that pitch, deciding she was best off accepting her life as it was, not making a fool of herself chasing a stale old bachelor who'd perhaps try to trim her sails just as her brothers did. She shuddered; perhaps she was already a laughingstock in his estimation after the drama of the afternoon.

She put the thoughts of Tom Reid out of her head. She had a task to do, and the quiet she needed to accomplish it.

The deed to the Pokorski farm, signed as it was by both husband and wife, made Mollie think about their farm, and her brothers' threat the prior day. It seemed so long ago, but it could also be a big problem. She pulled a paper and pen from her satchel and started a list of things to follow up on. *Ask Mother about the farm* was the first item on the list. She needed to figure out if Catherine owned the farm in her own name, or if it had been conveyed directly to the brothers when her father passed. This was home, and she needed to know whether it would be hers forever or whether she only lived here at the whim of her brothers. Their behavior left little doubt of what they would do when Catherine passed, or sooner if they could take over Catherine's care in the city. With Cecilia wanting to bury her pet here, it was obvious she, too, was beginning to consider this her home.

Below the deed were the immigration papers of Aloysius Pokorski, which showed that he had come to the United States in 1864 at age five. So, he was fifty-nine when he died, even older than she'd estimated. Perhaps more than fifteen years older than Cecilia's mother. He'd come to the United States during the Civil War. She'd heard that men emigrated and fought to pay back their passage. Perhaps it had been something like that. Maybe his father had served as a soldier. Yes, that was it, she thought, seeing that a Josef Pokorski's discharge papers from the Union Army were next in the stack. Aloysius and Frances had named their oldest son—Josef—after his grandfather, Mollie realized, which made her wonder why they'd moved so far from family.

Next, some receipts for farm crops from a few years ago, which Mollie set aside. Then, Frances Pokorski's birth certificate. She was born in 1878 in Warsaw, so she'd been forty when she died. She'd come to the United States in 1885, when she was only seven. Mollie did the math—Josef had been about twenty-four when he died, so Frances would have been sixteen when she had him. Why would she have married and started a family so young, and with a man so much older? Mollie sat back in her chair. Maybe it had been a forced marriage? The nuns used to say an unmarried girl would be better off dead than pregnant out of wedlock. Maybe the arrangement was born of desperation, and maybe that was why they'd moved so far from family and to a place where they had no roots. Maybe that was why Frances had made such an unlikely match.

Mollie shook her head—she'd been twenty-two when she broke off her engagement to Jim McElpin. There was no way she'd have had the strength to do that in her teens, or without the support of her parents, or the security of her education and the farm. Certainly not if she'd been in trouble, as Frances may have been. And then, with the first baby, she'd have been stuck—like Imogene Powers, now Imogene McElpin.

The remainder of the stack of business papers was uninteresting, just receipts for purchases for the farm and for crops they'd sold at the elevator, a passbook showing fifteen hundred dollars in deposits, made over the past several years. It was more than Mollie might have expected, but not a fortune.

She'd have to see a lawyer—she didn't know what Cecilia's status might be as far as the Pokorski farm and any bank account went. Perhaps she was the sole heir, or perhaps the land would revert to the state, depending on whether they'd staked long enough to satisfy the conditions of the Homestead Act. Maybe her mother would know how long a family had to occupy and care for a piece of land before it was theirs free and clear.

She added that to her list: *Does Cecelia inherit property or money?*

She set the stack of business papers aside and dug deeper into the flour sack. There was a layer of dried corn husks. She went to the front door and dropped those into the bushes and returned to her seat. Cecilia had said that the flour sack was where her mother kept belongings, ones she didn't want anyone else to see. Mollie assumed the word, "anyone," meant Mr. Pokorski. That would have to be the case, since both Cecilia and her mother knew about the hiding spot.

There was another passbook, and Mollie was surprised to see that there was more than twelve hundred dollars in that account. The deposits started with a hundred dollars ten years ago and then grew by dribs and drabs over the years. Frances Pokorski's elegant signature appeared next to every deposit. Twelve hundred dollars was what Mollie made for a year of teaching. It seemed remarkable that Cecilia's mother could have saved so much. Maybe someone in her family was sending her money that she was setting aside? Below that was a knot of colorful ribbons, like the ones Mollie remembered Cecilia wearing at school last year, all smoothly pressed. Cecilia's mother must have had them ready for this upcoming year, which would have started a few weeks ago, but for the influenza. Mollie set the ribbons to the side. Without question, Cecilia would want to wear them, and they would make her feel more connected to her mother. She decided not to dwell too much on the ribbons—she couldn't melt into sadness one more time today. She'd beat herself up for her inability to anticipate a child's feelings about a pet, something a mother who tucked away hair ribbons like treasures would surely have appreciated.

Then, a map. Mollie opened it up and looked at a long pencil mark from Kansas to Chicago to Emmett. It took little imagination to decipher that this would have been the route home that Josef traveled. She wondered why he'd been sent home early. She'd read of horrible diseases and lung damage from mustard gas and a debilitating mental condition they were calling shell shock. She remembered how skeletal—both in appearance and temperament—Josef had seemed that one time she'd seen him in church. She'd also read that returning servicemen had been the source of the influenza for many, and suspected Josef may have transmitted the disease to the Pokorski family. Once again, she wondered how and why Cecilia was spared. She must have a strong immune system. Perhaps it was divine intervention. Maybe Cecilia was like Mollie—unlikely to contract any illness. Strong as a horse.

Mollie folded up the map and looked deeper into the bag. There was a bunch of letters tied together, and she undid the string. It looked like Frances Pokorski had received letters from a woman in Chicago named Maria Elisia Pokorski. Mollie felt uncomfortable opening the letters— she'd never in her life read mail not meant for her—but she had no choice. The letter on the top of the pile was from May of last year, 1917, so a year and four months ago.

Frances, Aloysius' mother passed in January. I am so sorry to tell you like this and sorry for the delay. I wanted to write sooner, but Filip wouldn't hear of it. She was asking for Aloysius and you, and your boys, of course, and I was able to tell her how well you are doing, and that gave her some peace. I will try to write again soon.

Mollie thumbed through the letters to see if there was anything more recent, but nothing. From a letter in 1915, she could tell that Maria Elisia was Frances's sister-in-law, married to Aloysius' brother, Filip. It appeared Maria Elisia was the only one in the family who wrote to Frances, and from the way Frances had kept the letters to herself, it seemed their communication was a secret. As she skimmed the first few letters in the stack, Mollie noticed Maria Elisia mentioned Hugh and Josef, but never Cecilia. She'd referred to Frances' boys, not children. That was strange. Was it possible that the family didn't know that Frances had a younger child, a girl, or was it a coincidence? And why all the secrecy and the rift?

Mollie heard footsteps above. Her mother was awake. Why? She quickly scooped the letters up and dumped them into the flour sack on top of some wrapped items she could see in the bottom but would look at later. She sorted the other documents into neat stacks, waiting to hear Catherine's footsteps on the stairs. Nothing. Perhaps she'd gotten up to open or close a window and would go back to bed, but Mollie couldn't be sure. She wasn't ready to discuss the letters and the identity of a relative.

She had a conundrum. It was possible to say nothing. How many months would it be before Maria Elisia wondered why she hadn't heard from Frances? Probably many, given that the last letter was sixteen months earlier. But even as she considered whether she could get away with silence, Mollie knew that was not the right thing—the moral thing—to do. It would not have been what Frances Pokorski would have wanted for her daughter. She was going to have to write to Maria Elisia, tell her what had happened, and tell her that Cecilia had survived. And then, face the fact that Maria Elisia might come for Cecilia and take her back with her own people, as Dr. Murphy had been advocating all those weeks Cecilia was completely on her own in that bereft house. Then again, what if Frances had kept knowledge of Cecilia from her family for a reason? What if she *wouldn't* have wanted Mollie to write?

No longer so clear about how to proceed, Mollie decided to go to bed and sleep on the problem. She would ponder the next best step and find the right path forward. What stunned her was that even though it had only been a few days, and even though her head told her Cecilia had been little more than a stranger, she had no desire to ship Cecilia away. She and Cecilia and Catherine felt like they belonged on an island of safety and health, and Mollie wanted to protect that island, just right for the three of them. And, unless she was badly mistaken, Cecilia wanted to stay put on the farm as well, not go off to strangers in another state, whether or not they were blood relatives. Perhaps she could just wait until Maria Elisia wrote again—or not—and let her know about all that had happened. By then, Cecilia would have settled in, and they could stay together.

Chapter Ten

The next morning, Tuesday, Cecilia was at the kitchen table eating a bowl of oatmeal when she saw Mr. Reid pull up in his truck. He stopped at the end of the walk, opened the door, got out, and slapped his leg to get Lex to come along. Then he took a small rectangular wooden box, about the size of four loaves of bread bundled together, from the back of the truck.

Was Daisy in there?

She was, Cecilia realized.

He set the box down and knocked at the door.

"Miss Crowley," Cecilia yelled, "Mr. Reid here."

"Already?" Miss Crowley said, coming down the stairs. "It's barely light."

"Not hardly, Mollie," Grandma Catherine said. "It's after eight. He needs to open his store at nine. You were up late last night." Grandma Catherine nodded toward the papers divided into neat stacks on the dining room table.

Cecilia left the kitchen and went to the door to meet Mr. Reid. The box was sitting next to the door. She saw he'd made a plaque and affixed it to the top of the box. It said, "Daisy."

Miss Crowley was right behind her. Cecilia noticed her cheeks were pink and her eyes were sparkling. Her blouse wasn't buttoned all the way to the top, and she was in her stocking feet, sorting among the boots by the door to find her shoes. She looked pretty, which was not something Cecilia had ever thought about Miss Crowley before.

Mr. Reid looked at Cecilia. "Where do you want to bury Daisy?"

"Where should she be?" Cecilia asked, looking at Miss Crowley.

"Under the willow tree," Miss Crowley said, "out back," as though there was no other place to consider.

Mr. Reid bent down and touched the lid of the box. "Do you want to look at Daisy one last time?"

The muscles under Miss Crowley's face seemed to tighten. Cecilia could almost hear her thoughts. What-can-you-be-thinking, her face said. But Mr. Reid was not looking at Miss Crowley. He was looking at her.

She remembered discovering Daisy on the floor of the barn, seeing parts of the inside of Daisy's body she was never meant to see. She didn't expect she'd ever forget that moment. It had been horrible. Then she thought of never seeing Daisy again. Her eyes filled with tears.

She remembered making a drawing of Daisy that Mamusia had praised and figured she could do the same again from the image she'd fixed in her memory. "No," she said. "I not need to see Daisy."

"Are you sure?" Mr. Reid asked.

"No—thank you. I never see my family."

∞

"Let's go," Mollie said. "To the willow." She led the way and grabbed a shovel that was leaning up against the side of the house.

Tom first tried a spot that had the remnants of a stone foundation of some sort, then a spot with thick twisted roots.

"You need to dig a *deep* hole," Mollie said. She had visions of something getting at the cat again, creating a scene even more grotesque than yesterday.

"I understand," Tom said.

Under a large branch with trailing vines covered with yellow-green leaves, Tom could dig deep and wide enough to accommodate the coffin.

Mollie saw Catherine watching from the back window. She knew her mother was trying to stay out of the way. Why hadn't Catherine just come outside? Mollie felt irritated yet again. But the sun was out, and the drops of water on the plants around the house sparkled like thousands of tiny diamonds. When a brisk breeze blew through the branches of the willow tree, drops of water showered down on the three of them. Mollie couldn't help but laugh. She saw her mother laugh, too, before she moved away from the window altogether.

Tom pulled a small book out of his pocket and handed it to Cecilia. "You know the priest, the one who was here before this...."

"Don't speak ill," Miss Crowley said.

"Anyway, the one who was here before was named Father Rossner," he said. "Prince of a guy. My mother loved him. When she was sick, he came and visited her after dinner every evening. I remembered he kept a wide selection of prayer books in the library in the rectory, all in different languages. German, Spanish, French. I hoped that other...well, the new one, hadn't gotten rid of them."

Mollie knew what was going on. The people in the village didn't like to speak ill of a priest, but the new one, Father Foley, was not popular. He'd made some changes, without any discussion, that made people feel like the church wasn't the beautiful building that belonged to all of them, but was his own private shrine. Such an insult, after their ancestors had sacrificed to build the tall brick building with its elegant spires, so much more ornate than anything anyone had for themselves. They'd built the church with the same love and care that they'd built their new homes.

"Thankfully," Tom continued, "he hadn't gotten rid of the prayer books. So we got lucky there." He held up a small book. "This one is in Polish. I found the Lord's Prayer there. I've always said a prayer or two over my dogs. Shall we?"

∞

Cecilia took the small book and saw it was opened to a page with a line drawing of a man with his hand on Jesus' head. "I not read English well," she said. "Or Polish." But just the sight of the familiar script made her feel like Mamusia was here, which was strange because the cemetery where Mamusia's body was buried felt like nothing. She put her finger on the page and recited the Polish syllables she could remember Mamusia using, moving her finger to the next line each time she came to a pause in the prayer.

When she finished, she looked up and noticed that Miss Crowley had a strange expression on her face. "Did you speak Polish at home?" Miss Crowley asked.

"Mostly," Cecilia said. "Mamusia and I speak English to one another in the day, but Father not like that. Father speak Polish all the time. Never English."

"He and your mother spoke Polish to one another and to you and your brothers?"

"Yes," Cecilia said, surprised she'd never thought about that before. It was just the way her home worked. "Never English—Father's rule."

Miss Crowley nodded. Now, her mouth was pursed as if she was tasting something she didn't like.

"Father Foley told me to give you the book," Mr. Reid said. He handed Cecilia the small volume. "He said he had no use for it."

Cecilia nodded.

It took just a few minutes to lower the box into the dirt, then cover it with shovelful after shovelful of rich, dark earth. Cecilia could barely remember when they'd buried her family. It felt almost as if she hadn't been there at all—it was like a dream. She remembered being taken back to her house that day by the doctor, who'd made her sit in the back of his truck with her mask on, then left her on the front porch with a full basket of food. "Until we can figure this out," he'd said. That was the night she'd heard the whispers of ghosts. This felt sad, but at least she wasn't alone, as she'd been then.

She turned to Miss Crowley. "I forgive you," she said, and took her hand. She felt uncertainty in Miss Crowley's grasp, but then she squeezed Cecilia's fingers. "And now I call you Mollie. Not in school, but here."

∞

That evening, Mollie waited until Cecilia was sound asleep and snoring softly before settling at the dining room table to go through the rest of the items in the flour sack. She heard the rhythmic back and forth of the runners of Catherine's rocking chair on the kitchen floorboards and knew she would soon finish reading her newspaper and go to bed. She sat with her thoughts for a moment, sipping her tea. How could she not have known that English was Cecilia's second language? How could she have so misinterpreted the father's gruff silence—which she now knew was the lack of a common language—when she'd met with him about Josef, so many years ago? She'd dashed up to his wagon in a temper, with no warning, aggrieved by something the boy had done that afternoon, and insisted on a conference right that minute, never considering that Mr. Pokorski might not be able to communicate with her. One more thing she'd missed. She sighed and tried to forgive herself yet again. Now, with both Aloysius and Josef gone, it wasn't as if she could make amends.

Mollie opened the flour sack, pulled the packet of letters from Maria Elisia from its depths, and set the packet to the side to see what was left. She couldn't fathom any option other than going through the deceased woman's most personal things. Not going through the things—choosing not to look for any family background—was even less defensible than intruding. Cecilia was too young to do it. Somebody needed to look—Mollie had no choice. Still, the fact that she wasn't even family rattled, humbled, and saddened her—made her feel like she was not meant to be here, play-acting the role of a new mother for this orphaned child.

"Stop it," she whispered. Somebody had to take care of Cecilia, just like somebody had to figure out where her family might have come from, no matter the ethics of this strange situation.

As it turned out, there wasn't much more to find—just a formal sepia-toned photograph of an elderly stiffly-posed man, his arms around the shoulders of a small tow-headed girl; a photograph of a young Frances, perhaps twelve, posed with another girl with dark hair and dark eyes; and a wedding photograph of what looked to be Frances and Aloysius Pokorski, with Frances looking like an older version of Cecilia, just on the cusp of womanhood, and Aloysius looking somehow nervous and stern at the same time. The wedding photo reminded Mollie that she still needed to ask the priest and the doctor about the whereabouts of Frances's wedding band. It was sad, really, that a person's life could end with just a small pile of treasured belongings. She remembered feeling that way about her father's possessions when he passed—such a paltry pile of remnants for such a presence as he'd been. Yet, each insignificant item had outlasted his lifetime.

The little tow-headed girl in the picture with the older gentleman looked very much like Cecilia might have looked a few years ago. Mollie wondered who the man was—perhaps a grandfather or an older-than-usual father? In the picture with the dark-haired girl, Frances looked just a bit older than Cecilia was now. She looked almost identical to Cecilia—white-blond braids, slim features, light-as-ice eyes, even the same sweet smile. Mollie wondered why there were no pictures of Frances' parents or siblings. Was she alone as a child too?

In the picture of Frances as a young bride, Mollie could predict the beauty Cecilia would become. It was a refined, quiet beauty, so different from Mollie's often disheveled and stained-by-day's-end appearance. At her best, Mollie looked solid and practical, with nothing poetic or soft to suggest she was anything other than a teacher in a one-room schoolhouse. Twenty years from now, she would probably look nearly the same as she did today. Frances' serene expression in the wedding photograph, with maybe a little sadness around the eyes, also suggested nothing in common with Mollie's nature—fiery, sometimes impulsive, and often abrasive.

Mollie dropped her head into her hands. How could she ever build a connection with Cecilia that was anything like the child had with Frances, her natural mother? Would Mollie just be a poor stand-in? She and Catherine had always easily understood one another, even when they hadn't agreed. Was it because of shared blood, or chemistry? Perhaps Catherine had just worked hard to understand and accept her? What if that bond, natural or built over time, was available to Cecilia, just not here, and not with her? What if that source of bone-deep comfort was in Chicago, with Maria Elisia, or some family member Cecilia didn't yet know, but would recognize at first sight? Worse yet, what if no one living in this world could offer Cecilia the comfort and security Frances had provided?

Mollie lifted her head. A child was not meant to lose her mother so young. There was no fixing it. Perhaps she was doomed to make a terrible job of it. Perhaps anyone was. A wave of sadness passed over her, and she had an urge to get up and check on Cecilia again, asleep in her bed. She waved it off—the girl was sound asleep. What was the sense in looming over her?

Mollie placed the photographs of a younger Frances next to one another in a row across the table. She put the youngest version of Frances with the elderly man at the left, the one of Frances with the dark-haired girl in the middle, and the one of Frances as a bride to the far right. A final image she had of Frances—the one where she looked like the mother of three children, hardened by farm life—existed only in Mollie's memory. In a row like this, the three photographs allowed her to see how Cecilia would mature—she could only hope Cecilia's life wouldn't wear as heavily on her as Frances's life had. For Cecilia, maybe the last photograph in the series could reflect love and ease. Perhaps that was what Mollie, whatever she was to Cecilia now, should aspire to—salvaging a childhood for the girl, despite these awful odds.

Turning from the photographs, Mollie placed her hand on the stack of letters from Maria Elisia, then drew it back. She'd read the most recent ones and had left the rest, the older ones, for later—all she stood to learn was what had caused the rift between Frances and her family. She gathered the photographs and placed them on top of the stack of letters. After she got to the bottom of the flour sack, she planned to look over everything again before she decided what to do. It had been weeks since Cecilia's family passed. No decision needed to be made tonight.

Next in the sack were four pencil drawings. The first was of a robin perched on the side of a nest of eggs. The second was of a midsummer stalk of Queen Anne's Lace, a weed that Mollie had seen thousands of times along the dirt roadways. The artist had perfectly captured its airy, fragile span, and somehow even managed to suggest its color—the palest ivory. The third drawing was of Daisy the cat, curled in Frances' lap, with Frances' hand resting lightly on the animal's back. Mollie set that one aside to frame. Cecilia would treasure it.

Mollie gasped at the final drawing, dropped it on the table, and then pushed it away.

It was a drawing of Mollie, in the classroom. She was wearing one of the several fungible dark dresses she considered her teaching uniform. It had streaks of white chalk across the bosom. A man's white handkerchief, handy for wiping all manner of mishaps, hung from her belt like a flag of surrender. Her hair was drawn tightly back from her round face. A few flyaway tendrils of frizz had escaped, as they always did by the end of the day. Her expression was chilling—she looked unforgivingly stern, her lips set in a long, narrow line. Her glasses— she'd worn them when she started teaching to help her look older, and now it was just a habit—were perched on the end of her nose. The glare from the glasses obscured her eyes altogether—the artist had captured the image of two shiny discs where eyes should be. Her hands were clasped tightly in front of her waist as if she was holding back from pounding a table or throwing a piece of chalk against the board—both things she did when sorely tested. She looked tall, even towering, though she was of medium height. It was the perspective, she realized.

This is what she would look like to a small person—Cecilia—seated at the front of the class.

This uncannily good—yet terribly unflattering—drawing was Cecilia's. The others—all drawn by the same artist—must be Cecilia's as well.

Mollie examined the intricate detail of the variegated pencil shading in each drawing. The authority with which Cecilia executed the images was breathtaking, much more sophisticated than what she would expect of an eight-year-old child. When she looked closer, she saw small signs that indicated a child had made the drawings—a smudge at one corner, a slight error of proportion between the mother and the small bird, a tulip next to the Queen Anne's Lace that wouldn't have been growing in that same season, or along the side of the road.

But the picture of the nest conveyed unshakeable maternal attention. The picture of the weed was rendered as if it was the most perfect of roses and, because of that, it looked precious.

But the drawing of her—well, it was terrifying, no other word for it. She looked huge and mean, electric with ominous energy, ready to pounce. That was how Cecilia perceived her. That observation made Mollie realize how truly desperate Cecilia must have been for help when she'd left the Pokorski farm with Mollie on just a few minutes' notice, abandoning her precious cat. She must have been the last person Cecilia hoped to see—truly, her last resort. She set the drawings next to one another. Each was remarkable.

Mollie had never seen such sensitive work by a child in all her years of teaching. She was reminded of the china Catherine prized, pieces Catherine's grandmother Irene painted by hand. The china was so precious to Catherine that Mollie had never once seen it used for food. The china was a marvel of pastel colors and delicate brush strokes, representing dandelion heads, milk pods, Queen Anne's Lace, and Black-Eyed-Susans. People fell in love with that china before realizing that Irene had the audacity and the vision to paint wildflowers and nuisance weeds onto the precious and refined canvas of translucent bone china. Mollie could barely reconcile her impression of Cecilia with her impression of the artist capable of the drawings spread out in front of her, an artist as gifted as Irene. Once again, she was reminded how she had underestimated—in fact, completely misunderstood—Cecilia.

And Frances had saved these precious drawings—perhaps even more drawings, elsewhere in the Pokorski house—just as a devoted mother would. Mollie never saved anything a student gave her, at least not past the end of the school year, when she cleaned out her desk. Being a competent teacher seemingly had so little to do with being a loving mother. If Cecilia stayed, Mollie would have to try to treat her the way Frances would have, knowing all the while she was doomed to fall short. She wasn't up to the task and wasn't the right person. There was no way to develop the bond forged through all Cecilia's infancy and early childhood, and no way to cobble together the affinity that must be what a mother had with her natural child. For all she knew, Frances shared Cecilia's artistic sensibilities. Mollie felt stiff and unnatural when she touched Cecilia. But she'd have to keep trying. Mollie crossed her arms and dropped her head onto the table. It was impossible to know what to do. There was no map for any of this, and she suddenly realized she was wrung-dry exhausted.

"Are you sleeping?" Catherine said, startling her.

"No. Just resting my eyes."

"I'm on my way up," Catherine said. "It's late. You should go to bed."

"Can you talk for a minute?" Mollie hadn't planned to ask for Catherine's thoughts, yet the words were out.

Catherine sat in the seat at Mollie's left. "What's all this?" she asked.

"This is a sack of things that Frances Pokorski kept hidden at their house. I found it and brought it back here and have been looking through the contents." She handed her mother the drawing of her. "Cecilia drew this."

"Oh, my," Catherine said, studying the drawing. "It's quite severe, isn't it?" She held the drawing at arm's length and tilted her head to the side. "She's gifted, isn't she?"

"She is," Mollie said, handing over the other three drawings, and waiting while Catherine inspected them.

"Lovely," Catherine finally said, and laid the drawings on the table, frowning a bit at the unflattering one of Mollie. Then, she gave a soft sigh and shook her head over the one of Daisy and Frances.

"I am so taken aback by how she must have felt about me," Mollie said. "I look mean—like Sister Mary Alexander used to look to me when I was small."

"Goodness," Catherine said. "I haven't thought about her for years. I wouldn't have remembered her name. She was a stiff old soul, wasn't she?"

"Mean is the word—" Mollie started, "Why, she—"

Catherine put her hand up to stop what was to come next, then quickly crossed herself, making Mollie wonder if that was how Frances had responded to Cecilia's fears. Wouldn't it have been better to let Mollie know how scared the child was so she could make some accommodations? Was she so frightening, so forbidding that even Frances hadn't wanted to approach her?

"I can't imagine how she feels about being here," Mollie finally said, her cheeks hot with mortification. She had no idea she'd grown so stiff and humorless. The drawing made her look old and brittle.

"Perhaps you were having an unusually bad day?" Catherine said.

"Maybe," Mollie considered the explanation overly generous. She suspected Cecilia had reconstructed the image from more than a single memory.

"She seems to be an unusually sensitive child," Catherine added.

"If she felt that way, others must as well." Mollie took the drawing from Catherine and shuddered. "I can't pretend her perspective is an exception."

"There's always room and time for improvement," Catherine added. "That's a good thing about teaching—and mothering. Both professions demand growth. Still, I can understand how painful a picture like that must be when you work so hard. You ask more of yourself than you ask of the students. I'm sorry."

Mollie nodded, unable to speak, and put the drawing with the others, making a neat stack with it on the bottom. She sighed—once again, embarrassed by how little she'd grasped of Cecilia during a whole year of the child sitting in the front row of her classroom, so close she could have reached out and patted her on the head, had she ever been so inclined. How had she not known about this gift? How could she not have known the child was bright enough to not only read English, but understand Polish as well? How much else had she missed as she so efficiently managed her classroom? How had she made no accommodation at all for language differences? How many other students perceived her the way Cecilia did, the way she'd perceived Sister Mary Alexander?

"Mollie," Catherine said, as she stood. "You're still a young woman. You can change—grow. Discomfort isn't always bad. Sometimes it's ordained. Perhaps this pain is your sign that a thing needs attention."

"I suppose," Mollie said, not wanting to listen to another of her mother's missives about what God sent. Her comment about Sister Mary Alexander had been a rare slip.

Catherine's lips tightened.

"I also found some letters," Mollie said. She tapped the tied bundle of letters with her index finger. "From a woman in Chicago. Looks to be the wife of Cecilia's father's brother. Her name is Maria Elisia."

"So they would be Cecilia's uncle and aunt-by-marriage?"

"Yes."

"Interesting that the letters are from the aunt, not the brother."

"I suspect they were close friends as girls, Maria Elisia and Frances." Mollie pulled out the picture of Frances next to the dark-haired girl. "Perhaps that's her?"

"Perhaps."

"She's the only one who stayed in touch with Frances, over her husband's objection. Frances seemed to have some money of her own. Maybe Maria Elisia was the source?" Mollie said.

"I can't imagine Frances had a way to earn any income."

"There's nothing recent from her, but she's written several times over the years. I can only assume Frances was in correspondence with her."

"Not surprising. It would be more surprising if the family turned up here with no roots at all. What about Frances' family?"

"Nothing," Mollie said. She pointed to the picture of Frances with the elderly man. "Perhaps her grandfather? Gone now?"

"What are you going to do?" Catherine asked.

"I don't know. In the letters I've read, Cecilia isn't even mentioned. Cecilia has said again and again she doesn't know anyone in Chicago. On the other hand, her blood relatives deserve to know about her, don't they? And how will they know about what happened to the family unless I write?"

Catherine sat down again. She propped her elbow on the table and dropped her chin into her hand. "Why do you think Frances kept her distance for all these years? Is there any clue?"

"Not so far. I haven't read all of them. But it was serious. Filip—Aloysius Pokorski's brother—wouldn't even let Maria Elisia write about their mother's death. It looks as if Aloysius may have found out because the two women corresponded, long after the fact. Or, maybe if Frances was keeping the correspondence secret as well, Aloysius never found out at all."

Catherine shook her head. She didn't need to speak. Mollie knew how sad family conflict made her, and how she wished that Mollie and her brothers got along better. As far as Mollie knew, Catherine spoke about her wishes only to Mollie, which made her feel like she was expected to be the peacemaker. That always made her plead her case to Catherine—never directly to her brothers—and meant the conflict never got any better. Still, there was nothing between the Crowley siblings so dramatic as the division between Cecilia's parents and their family appeared to be.

"Perhaps it's defensible for us to do for Cecilia exactly what Frances did?" Catherine finally asked. "Keep her from bad influences?"

"Maria Elisia actually sounds quite nice in the letters," Mollie said. "And she has two children herself. They would be Cecilia's cousins."

"Still, I think you should follow the course you think Frances would have chosen, as much as you can. She had her reasons."

"Maybe it wasn't Frances's idea to stay so separate. The father sounds like a bit of a bully. Maybe he's the one who severed ties."

"You can't know—"

"Frances made those decisions when she was alive," Mollie said. "If she had known she would pass when Cecilia was so young, she might have maintained more of a connection. It's like Sam and Dan—" She took a deep breath. "They make me so angry, but if I was in trouble...or if you were sick..."

"Well, then, you should pray about it." Catherine stood.

Mollie swept the contents of the stacks together in frustration. Pray. That was always what Catherine advised—prayer. But whenever Mollie prayed, she felt foolish and completely alone. She didn't think God had ordained anything about her life—it was all luck and grit. At least Catherine hadn't advised doing anything dispositive right away. She seemed to think a decision not to decide—to ponder—was defensible. Mollie would read the entire stack before she reached a conclusion.

"Thank you, Mother," Mollie said, then added something she only rarely said—"I love you."

Catherine patted her shoulder. "I love you, too," she said. "None of this is easy. No obvious answers."

Mollie blew out the kerosene lamp on the table before her but didn't stand. She waited for a few minutes for her eyes to adjust to the dark. She could hear Catherine's steps in the room above, then heard Catherine's door close. She liked the feeling of the dark house quieting around her and liked to be up late alone. She remembered how welcome that felt when she was in the thick of the school year. Sometimes, her ears had still been ringing with the activity and bustle of the classroom. Late at night was when she'd always done her best thinking. She re-lit the lamp; she knew she wouldn't sleep anyway. Too much on her mind.

She took the pile of letters from Maria Elisia and spread them out in order across the table. In the first one, written a few years before Cecilia was born, Maria Elisia begged Frances to consider traveling to her wedding in Chicago. There was a long gap between that letter and the next one, sent a year later, which referred to a series of written apologies from Frances. Frances must have asked forgiveness several times. Maria Elisia said she wished that she'd mended fences sooner. The more recent letters from Maria Elisia related mostly to her own children and family, but never mentioned Cecilia. Perhaps the reason Frances hadn't mentioned Cecilia, born after that wedding, and after the apology and forgiveness, was that a visit would have been both irresistible to Maria Elisia, especially after she had children around the same time, and impossible for Frances. From time to time, Mary Elisia referenced the enclosure of cash as a gift; perhaps that was the source of the funds in Frances's secret passbook.

Mollie collected the letters and spread out the drawings. Frances had appreciated Cecilia's talent and had revered her careful work. Frances also had understood how Cecilia felt about her teacher—terrified and intimidated. Frances could not have wanted Cecilia here in this house, based on what she knew. But she'd also left no clear direction, no thread to follow, about how to move on. Aloysius had left even less—just a few legal papers, without even a legible signature.

Mollie was confounded by the practical issues she faced, but even more daunted by the emotional ones. How could she possibly learn about parenting—something that others seemed to know by instinct or, at the very least, learn over time—especially with an older child? And how, under these strange circumstances, could she possibly show Cecilia's real parents—now gone—the appropriate respect, even deference? Should she keep Cecilia from the relatives she had in Chicago? Had Frances ever spoken to Cecilia about these people? Surely when the next letter arrived from Maria Elisia, the postmistress would pass it on to her. Mollie had never been one to kick the can down the road, but this was all so complicated. There was no clear path.

• • •

The next morning, when Mollie woke, the sun was shining through her bedroom window, making her uncomfortably warm. She'd tossed and turned for hours, worried about the best course for Cecilia. Now she'd slept in late, against her will. The house was quiet.

Where were Catherine and Cecilia? Perhaps they'd gone for a walk?

Mollie struggled to remember what day it was. Being at home all the time made the days run together. It was Wednesday, she calculated. Just over one more week of sloth, and then they'd be back at school. She shook her head. She'd be embarrassed if anyone knew she'd been lying abed so late on a weekday. She needed to be back in school as badly as her students did. She quickly dressed, cleaned her teeth, splashed water on her face, then ran her fingers through her hair.

After breakfast, Mollie faced the task in the dining room. The flour sack and its contents sat next to the piles of business papers she had stacked neatly, right where she had left them. The information about Maria Elisia Pokorski still weighed heavily on her conscience. What would she say, for example, if Cecilia asked to look at the contents of the sack, as was her right? I could put the sack away for a few weeks, she thought. Perhaps the child would forget about it. Perhaps Cecilia wouldn't be able to comprehend any of the letters, and would lose interest. Then she impatiently shook her head.

As Catherine had said, secrets were never a good thing. She couldn't go on like this forever, lying when Cecilia asked questions, as she inevitably would. She couldn't hide letters in the future that were virtually certain to arrive. She couldn't make up a fumbling explanation for why she hadn't told Cecilia everything she knew earlier. And when would the time be right? If she held off until Cecilia was more mature, Cecilia might hate her for withholding information. Or she might hate her for keeping her away from real family. If Mollie waited until some member of the family wrote to Frances, and then responded out of the blue, especially with such terrible news, she would sacrifice any possibility of a collaborative solution. There was no escaping this point of decision.

Mollie stirred up the logs to heat the stove, then put the teakettle on to warm. She looked out the front window but saw no one—where could they have gone? When she heard the whistle of the kettle, she poured a cup of tea and sat down in the same place she'd been last night. She placed a blank page of paper and a pen on the table. She'd draft something—she could always go back later and revise. She could change her mind and throw the letter away altogether if she decided that was best. Just drafting a letter changed nothing. It didn't eliminate any options. It was dropping it in the postbox that could make a difference.

October 2, 1918
Dear Mrs. Pokorski,
My name is Mollie Crowley, and I live in Emmett, Michigan. I am sorry to write with sad news. There has been a tragedy in the Pokorski family. The influenza took the lives of Aloysius and Frances Pokorski, and their two boys, Josef and Hugh.
Their cases are the only ones so far in our township. We believe that Josef may have contracted the virus before returning to Emmett from a military base in Kansas. Frances and Aloysius' daughter Cecilia, age eight, survived. She never fell ill. She continues to be very healthy.
I was Hugh and Josef's teacher, as well as Cecilia's. When I learned Cecilia had been orphaned, I brought her to stay with my mother and me. We live on a farm close to the Pokorski farm. We are happy to have her with us.

Mollie hesitated. Should she say that Cecilia was welcome to stay indefinitely? Wouldn't that seem strange, even brazen, after just a few days? But if she said nothing inviting, would this stranger interpret the letter to mean Cecilia wasn't wanted? Would Maria Elisia then come as soon as possible, or dispatch another family member to scoop Cecilia up? She sighed, and put the pen back to paper.

> *I am not married and have no children. Just my mother and I are left on our farm.*

Mollie paused again, tapping the table with her pen. How should she express to this stranger the profound difference in their home Cecilia had made in just a few days? After a few minutes, she started writing.

> *Our home is so much brighter and warmer with Cecilia here— she feels like family. School will open again in a few days, and I will be sure Cecilia is well cared for and attends school regularly. My mother, Catherine, supports this.*
>
> *You may wonder how I learned of you. Frances Pokorski kept a few personal belongings, which I took the liberty of inspecting. Your letters were among these things. It is the only evidence I had of any family relationship.*
>
> *Please respond to me when you are able at:*
> *2775 Bricker Road*
> *Emmett, Michigan*
>
> *Sincerely,*
> *Mollie Crowley*

Mollie found an envelope and carefully copied the address from Maria Elisia's last letter onto it. She slipped the letter into her satchel and deferred the decision of whether to send it until the next time she had a reason to go near the post office. Posting the letter could wait until she'd made up her mind. Perhaps Saturday when she ran other errands? That would give her a couple of days to consider, and reverse course if she decided to do so. Next week school would begin; maybe it would be best to hold onto the letter until Cecilia had made a solid start in school? Mollie thought she knew the right thing to do, but she often forged ahead half-cocked, only to regret it later. The stakes were now too high. She needed to move more carefully, as Catherine was always urging.

And what if these Chicago people were no good for Cecilia?

Mollie was again tempted to hide the flour sack away where no further inspection was likely, along with the draft letter, but no. These were Cecilia's belongings—not hers. There was nothing threatening here, and no reason these things should go the way of the missing ring. Cecilia had lost enough, and Mollie would not be the one to keep her from anything that might afford some comfort or sense of history. She'd leave the papers out, in plain sight, and see what transpired. Cecilia could look at them in her own time. And Mollie already suspected she knew exactly what to do with the letter, and why, but she intended to make a well-considered decision. For now, the letter was safely tucked away in her satchel, where it would stay until she'd decided.

Chapter Eleven

On Thursday, October 10, 1918, the first day of school, Cecilia woke up with a sour stomach. She remembered how excited she'd been last year before the first day. Her excitement had quickly changed to dread; the playground was torture because of the mean O'Connell girls, and the classroom held the terrifying Miss Crowley, who seemed to jump on every mistake. Each day, Mamusia would try to build her spirits on the long walk to the schoolhouse, then listen to her troubles all the long walk home. Often, they stopped at the stream near their farm and waited until her tears were dry. Still, she'd gone to bed each night wishing she wouldn't wake in the morning. Each day seemed harder. By the time the last day of school finally arrived, and she had the freedom of summer ahead, she wished the schoolhouse would burn down and Miss Crowley would move to some other town, as far away as possible. She recalled how Mamusia had scolded her when she prayed for exactly that. "Education," Mamusia had said, "is something no one can ever take away from you." This year, there would be no one in her corner, as Mamusia had been. And she was living with Miss Crowley.

"Mollie," Cecilia whispered, practicing the new name. She was trying to call her Mollie, even in her thoughts. Mollie, at home, was so much nicer than the Miss Crowley of last year's classroom. But maybe Mollie was just Miss Crowley's summer self? Maybe, the old horrid Miss Crowley was soon to return? Maybe *that* Miss Crowley would try for nothing more than to be fair, as she tried to be to all students—not like Mamusia, who had been her ally?

Then Cecilia would feel like she belonged to no one. Plus, she'd be stuck with Miss Crowley from morning until night. Cecelia wished more than anything she could just go back in time to last year, to the long walks with Mamusia, to having a real mother who belonged only to her, to long hours between the end of school each day and the next morning. Then, she'd try harder to like school and be brave—if only she had the chance again.

Mostly, she wished that today was not the first day of school.

Cecilia slipped out of bed, took off her nightgown and put it on the hook. The dress Grandma Catherine made for her lay across the chair in the corner of her bedroom. She'd made it from a length of yard goods Mollie purchased years ago, but never used. The dress was a simple shift but quite nice—tiny pink roses on a light blue background. Blue was the color Mamusia had said favored her best. She dropped the dress over her head and fastened the small buttons on the bodice. She'd chosen the buttons from the big bowl of leftover buttons Grandma Catherine kept in the sewing closet. Mollie had helped her wash her hair the evening before; she could feel as she ran her fingers through it that it was now nearly dry. Grandma Catherine had promised to braid it for her this morning, and Mollie had shown her the ribbons Mamusia had folded into the flour sack for her. She hadn't been able to bring herself to touch the sack or its contents, though she saw it sitting like a rock on the dining room table each time she passed through the room, next to a stack of her drawings and a pile of letters.

The scents of coffee and bacon wafted into her room, and she could hear chatter. Her stomach turned—she didn't think she'd be able to eat. She could almost hear Grandma Catherine saying, "That won't do. What will hold you?" There was no chance she'd be allowed to leave the house unless she took a few bites. Maybe she should refuse to eat, say her stomach was bothering her—it truly was—and stay home? She sat down on the bed.

No, she thought. Mamusia never allowed her to miss school, even when she knew how upset she was, no matter how desperately she hated going to school. "It's not right," Mamusia would say, "to have education available and let *anyone* keep you from it." If Mamusia were here, she would make her get up and off the bed. She slipped her feet into her leather shoes and felt her toes scrunch at the ends. The shoes had been too big at the beginning of the summer. Her feet had grown. She'd grown.

This surprised her. How was it possible, over this miserable summer, even as people died and everything changed around her? Surely she'd have been nearly to Mamusia's shoulder if they'd have walked together this fall. Maybe Mamusia would have sent her along by herself this year, saying she was big and brave enough to make the journey on her own? Maybe Father would have forced that new independence?

Cecilia tied her shoes and went to the kitchen. Mollie had said the first day of school was her favorite day of the entire year. Maybe this year would be better?

• • •

Cecilia liked the way the sunlight glinted off the hood of the Model T as they sped toward the school. Grandma Catherine's masks were freshly laundered and in a box on the back seat. She had managed to find thirty-five different snippets of fabric in the deep basket of remnants, so each child in the class could have their own mask. She'd reminded both Cecilia and Mollie to bring them home at the end of the day so she could wash and dry them. There was also a basket of clean rags on the back seat. They'd use the rags with the bucket of bleach water they'd mixed yesterday. Mollie had said she wanted to wipe down all the desks and surfaces again this morning, even though they'd spent hours doing so last week. "Daily sanitation—maybe even twice daily— is needed to stay safe," Mollie had said. There were several bars of the lye soap that so burned Cecilia's hands in the back seat, too. They'd put those next to the pump in the yard, Mollie said, with a tall roll of butcher paper from the hardware store that would stand in for towels but be easily disposable.

Mollie was dressed differently than she'd dressed last year. She wore a long, dark blue skirt, but on top, she wore a cotton blouse with soft blue flowers. The fabric reminded Cecilia of the dresses Mamusia used to wear at home but looked nothing like anything she had ever seen Mollie wear in the classroom. She had little pearls, like Cecilia's buttons, in the holes in her ears, and had gathered her hair into a loose roll at the nape of her neck instead of a tight bun on top. That bun had always looked like a doorknob to Cecilia. Cecilia could see that she was smiling and glancing at herself in the mirror every few minutes. Last year, Cecilia had wondered if her smiling muscles even worked. Maybe she liked the way she looked?

"You happy?" Cecilia said.

"Of course," Mollie said. "I love the first day of school. Why do you ask?"

"You look—" Cecilia hesitated. "So soft. You are smiling at yourself in the mirror."

Mollie laughed. "I'm practicing the smile," she said. "I'm trying to look inviting. What do you think?"

Cecilia felt herself blush. "I saw my picture—the one of you—on the dining room table." Her face grew hot. "I sorry."

"I am sorry," Mollie said.

"*I* am sorry," Cecilia said.

"No, I wasn't correcting you," Mollie said. "I was apologizing. You must have been so frightened of me. What are you sorry for?"

The truthful answer was that Cecilia was sorry that Mollie had been so scary last year, but she didn't want to say that. She was also sorry that of all the many pictures she'd drawn, Mamusia had saved that one—she couldn't imagine why. "I not supposed to look?" she said, instead. If she'd trespassed, that was something she could be honestly sorry for.

"Of course, you can look at those things whenever you like—whenever you are ready. Those things belonged to your mother. They are more yours than mine. I would have put them away if I didn't want you to look at them. Moreover, you can look at—even touch or use—anything you find in plain sight in our home."

Cecilia nodded.

"Are you sorry because the drawing of me didn't make me look, well…nice?"

That wasn't quite right, but close enough. "I guess," Cecilia said.

"No need to be sorry for that either," Mollie said. "You had no way of knowing I would ever see that drawing. Plus, it's how you felt. It's how you saw me. You have nothing to apologize for."

They rode in silence for the mile between what Cecilia now knew were Fox and Cove roads. She'd read the signs out loud to Mollie on their last trip to the school, as well as the signs on all the other roads.

"Now I live with you and Grandma Catherine. I not like you to see it," Cecilia finally said. "If I knew—"

"I can understand that," Mollie interrupted, then she laughed.

"I not mean that," Cecilia said. She paused. "I not—I mean, I don't mean that I wish the drawing was a secret. I mean, I not—didn't—want to hurt your feelings."

"Well, if I'd only known you were going to be living with me, perhaps I'd have been warmer to you."

Cecelia was silent.

"Your drawing was food for thought," Mollie added. "When I started teaching, I was so young—only sixteen. I thought I had to…well…be harsh like that, or I assumed I did. The strategy became a habit. It's certainly not necessary anymore. So, I'm going to try to seem softer this year. Nicer."

Cecilia looked over at her and smiled. "I like your blouse. You—are—pretty."

Mollie glanced back at her, eyebrows raised, as if it hadn't occurred to her she could possibly look pretty. "Thank you," she said, darting her eyes back to the road.

"I not read—" Cecilia said, thinking of the pile of letters on the table next to her drawings and the big pile of papers printed in fancy script. She drew loops and circles in the air. "Fancy writing."

"Cursive," Mollie said.

"Cursive," Cecilia said. "Who letters from?"

"This time, I am going to correct you," Mollie said. "Who *are* the letters from?"

"Who *are* the letters from," Cecilia said. "And I like when you correct. I don't want to make mistakes. I don't like teasing."

"A woman named Maria Elisia Pokorski." Mollie was still looking straight ahead, but Cecilia could see her grip on the wheel had tightened. "She is married to your father's brother. Do you know her?"

"My mother's best friend was girl—*a* girl—called Maria Elisia." Cecilia smiled. "Mamusia tells stories about her. About things they do."

"The letters are from her," Mollie said. "Did you ever meet her?"

Cecilia shook her head. "No," she said. "I remember Mamusia write—wrote—to her sometimes. You write to her?"

"Do you want me to?"

She thought for a moment, remembering Mamusia's stories. Maria Elisia lived upstairs from Mamusia. They spent nights in each other's apartments, went to school together, to the nuns in the convent, and played silly games Mamusia loved to describe, and even sometimes to play with Cecilia. The stories about Maria Elisia had always made Cecilia wish she had a friend.

Yes," she said. "I want you write to her. I want draw a picture for her." Then, rushing, "I want send picture of Mamusia. She so sad, to lose her friend. Even if they didn't ever see each other. We mail it today?"

Mollie nodded, but she was staring straight ahead. She started to say something but stopped. Cecilia could almost see her stiffen as the schoolhouse came into sight, and she knew if she were to speak, it would be in the teacher voice she remembered from last year. Cecilia's stomach clenched again—and she reminded herself that Mollie was now Miss Crowley again—as Mollie pulled the car into the schoolyard and skidded to a halt, raising dust, and throwing pebbles to the sides of the car. Thankfully, there was no one in the yard. She could nestle into the space before she'd have to face those girls from last year. She remembered Mamusia's advice: "Just be silent and keep to yourself. It will pass."

∞

It was a boon to be early, Mollie thought. She had time to fuss and putter and make sure everything was in perfect order before the students arrived. Sometimes she felt that her propensity to stay up late, then lag in the morning, was the biggest challenge she faced as a teacher. But it was just so hard to get out of bed, especially when it was dark and cold outside. "Just a few more minutes," she'd whisper to herself. A few times, she'd fallen back to sleep, only to be roused by her mother, like a child. She'd felt so guilty on those days she was late. Students were waiting in the icy school yard when she pulled up, and it took precious minutes to start the fire in the woodstove. No matter how robust the fire, the chill didn't come off the classroom for an hour or more. It was hard for children to learn when they were cold—or hungry. Maybe this year, she'd be able to keep up with the early arrivals. Cecilia could be a good influence.

The first thing she did after she and Cecilia entered the classroom was find white unlined paper and colored pencils for Cecilia and settle her at a desk where she could draw. She hadn't missed Cecilia's reference to teasing in the car; those girls had probably given her endless heartache over her small grammatical errors and language struggles. "You won't be sitting next to the O'Connell girl again this year," she said as Cecilia bent over the paper. "I promise."

"Thank you," Cecilia said.

She put the masks in a basket by the door. She'd have to tell the students to be sure to remember the fabric of the mask they chose so they'd take the same one each day. "Don't let me forget to take these home with us," she said. "I have my routine down, and these are something extra. I'm likely to forget. Will you try?"

Cecilia's smile flashed, warming all her features. "I *will* try," she said.

∞

Cecilia was enjoying the scrape and float of the pencil on the rough paper as she shaded the big tree from their yard, Mamusia's favorite, when she heard children arriving in the schoolyard. She swept the unfinished drawing and extra sheets of paper into a pile, collected the pencils and passed it all to Mollie, almost as if they'd agreed in advance that this new classroom activity was just between them. She slipped back into her seat, happy she wouldn't have to sit by a bully again this year.

"You know I can't give you special treatment?" Mollie said as she put the materials into a desk of her drawer.

"I understand," Cecilia said, though it seemed Mollie already had given her special treatment. Last year, she'd waited outside with the other students. She also wanted to be moved all year long but had never found the words. Mamusia had been too scared or polite to ask for help.

"Do you think you can call me Miss Crowley here every time? No slipping? So there's a bright line?"

Cecilia nodded. "Yes."

Mollie tilted her head to the side and squinted her eyes. "This bright line isn't just for you. I also need to be Mollie at home and Miss Crowley here," she said. "I need to be the leader of the classroom, and I can't hear the 'teacher-teacher-teacher' refrain twenty-four hours a day. I insist students use my name. But I try to leave my teacher personality here. I will try even harder now that you are living with me. I think Mollie will do beautifully at home. Like I'm a big sister or a favorite aunt."

Cecilia wasn't sure about that. She wasn't sure what exactly Mollie—Miss Crowley—felt like, but it wasn't a sister, and she'd never had an aunt that she could remember.

"Just never, ever, *ever* slip and call me Mollie in the classroom or the schoolyard."

"Mollie," Cecilia said out loud, just to test the word, then remembered this was the Miss Crowley space.

Mollie waggled her finger, and tried to look stern, and they both laughed. Then, she buttoned up the top button of her blouse and perched her glasses on her nose.

"I wait outside," Cecilia said, standing. She went to the pegs along the wall by the door and shrugged back into her jacket. "I outside when you ring the bell, like the others."

"Yes, you're correct," Mollie said. "Smart of you to think of that. Now run along."

Her tone was as firm as it had ever been. She was most definitely Miss Crowley now. Her back was to Cecilia, and she was writing on the blackboard. She'd written the day of the week, the date, and the year. Cecilia remembered copying from the top right corner of the blackboard last year and having her heart in her throat as Miss Crowley criticized her penmanship. The strict teacher, the one who always seemed impatient with her, was back. Cecilia shrank back into her scared skin, and slipped out the door, hoping no one would notice she'd arrived from the wrong direction.

Chapter Twelve

When Cecilia was gone, Mollie took a deep breath. As experienced as she was, and as much as she loved the first day of school, she had butterflies in her stomach. It was the same as the last minutes before students poured in every previous year. The first day of school was far more of a milestone for her than Christmas or New Year's—this was where her year truly began. This year's delayed start had only heightened her nerves, as had the addition of Cecilia to her home life. She needed a few minutes to collect herself.

Mollie sat at her desk and adjusted the few items she kept on top to their proper places—then took a deep breath and shut her eyes. The first thought that popped into her head was that it had been exceptionally good thinking on Cecilia's part to want to wait outside. She knew she would have forgotten that detail, despite all her intentions to keep home and school separate. She hoped Cecilia would fit in better than she had last year. She'd seemed then a quiet little mouse, simple and skittish. Mollie felt her heartbeat slow and her self-possession return.

This was her space. She was in charge here. It was her ship to sail.

At precisely eight o'clock, Mollie tied her mask tightly over her nose and mouth. She couldn't imagine teaching with it over her face all day. Her throat and lips would be as dry as straw. But she would have to make do. It was time—past time—to start a new school year, her tenth.

She went to the door, holding in her hand the bell she rang to get the students' attention.

She'd known attendance would be sparse, but sighed when she saw only a dozen of the thirty-five students who should properly be there had arrived. She tamped down her disappointment. At least she could put those in attendance a good distance away from one another. And, if things went well for a few days or weeks, more would trickle in. She rang the bell, and the students came running.

On the steps, she first checked the forehead of each student for fever with her palm, then handed masks to everyone. "Put these on," she said. "Keep them securely fastened while indoors."

A few students gave her a dismissive look, but she glared right back—there would not be any laxity about her precautions in the classroom. One kind girl offered to help with the younger students' masks, and Mollie handed her several.

"Wash your hands when you're finished," Mollie told the girl.

When all the students had tied their masks securely around their heads, Mollie sent them all outside again to wash their hands thoroughly. "At the pump," she said, pointing to the hand-operated pump in the schoolyard, next to which she'd placed a roll of brown butcher paper. "*With* soap," she added. "Every time you come in."

Cecilia led the group of younger students to the pump. She was aware of the precautions they were taking and the reasons for each one.

When they were back on the steps, Mollie made the oldest O'Connell girl wait outside with a thermometer in her mouth, just for show. The girl hadn't felt warm, but it wouldn't hurt for parents or students to appreciate she was taking close care. That girl was so hard-boiled. She'd withstand an undeserved blot on her copy. Perhaps a bit of humility would keep her in check.

Mollie remembered what Cecilia said about those O'Connells tormenting her last year. It was funny how family members shared so many traits. All the O'Connells were just about the same, distinctly the meanest children in the schoolyard, even the generation before, when

Mollie was a girl. Hard to say if they were born that way, or if they'd just bullied each other from birth, or a little of both.

All the precautions she gleaned from the reading she'd done over the summer—everything she could put her hands on about the influenza and how best to contain it—seemed simple common sense, perhaps even things she should have been doing all along. Cold weather often brought runny noses and coughs, even stomach ailments that ran through the class like wildfire. Wouldn't it be ironic if her students stayed healthier this winter than in previous years because of precautions she could have had in place from the get-go?

∞

Later that morning, the youngest O'Connell girl approached Cecilia on the playground the instant they were out of Miss Crowley's earshot. "We thought you died," she said.

Cecilia raised her chin up and stared the girl in the eyes. "Your name Louise?"

"Of course, it is—*Louise*—same name. Same name as last year." She rolled her eyes.

Cecilia's knees trembled, but she planted her feet and crossed her arms over her chest. She stood up straight, hoping her stiff backbone would add a couple of inches in height. She tried to imagine what Miss Crowley would say. She—and Grandma Catherine—would tell her to be fierce. Cecilia could picture their narrowed eyes and firm voices. "I not die," she said, making her expression as stern as she could and raising her voice. "You should be ashamed. You're mean. That's a horrid thing to say."

The bigger girl took a step back. "Didn't the rest of your family die?"

"Yes." Cecilia bit her lip. She would not cry. This year was going to be different. She forced herself to look the other girl in the eye and not look away. "They did. They *passed*." Cecilia crossed herself—Father,

Son, and Holy Ghost—hoping the girl would have the sense to be embarrassed.

"Are we going to catch it from you?" the girl asked. "Like cooties?" She raised her hands and wiggled her fingers like tiny, frenetic bugs.

The group surrounding her laughed, then took a few steps back.

Cecilia stepped toward the group; they took another step back. She put her hands on her hips. "No," she said. "Miss Crowley says I'm…" She struggled to remember the word, "—immune." She could see a small spot of dirt below the girl's ear on her neck. It was the kind of spot Mamusia would have found before they entered the schoolyard and wiped away with a wet finger.

"Miss Crowley? How would she know if you're immune?" the girl asked, glaring.

Cecilia hesitated, then decided. She'd already slipped. The girl already knew she'd had a private conversation with the teacher. Better to get the news out there right now when she was feeling brave. She couldn't hide where she lived for the entire year.

"I live with Miss Crowley now," Cecilia said, and lifted her chin. "And I—*I'm*—not sick. I've been with her for…" Cecilia couldn't be sure exactly how many days it had been. "*Weeks. Weeks and weeks.* She studies about the sickness. To keep us all safe—not just me. So there."

"You live with the *teacher*?" the girl said. "With *her*?"

It was as if Louise could barely imagine such a thing—that their teacher, Miss Crowley, existed at all when she wasn't in the classroom. Cecilia realized that's how she'd felt last year, like Miss Crowley was a scary monster under the stairs who only came out in the dark. While now, she felt like what she saw at school was just a bit of what Miss Crowley was like—the worst bit.

Cecilia heard the bell telling them it was time to come back in—perfect timing. She turned and walked away, and pretended she didn't feel the eyes of the surprised classmates boring into her back.

∞

The first day of school had unfolded like every other thing Mollie had carefully prepared during her life—once it started, almost nothing she'd worried over came to pass. The students seemed happy to be back after the delayed start. She'd never had fewer than thirty-five students, ranging in age from five to fifteen. So this group was deliciously peaceful—so few students and so much space. The luxury of just a dozen students wouldn't last, but she'd enjoy the easier pace for now. If she could catch this group up, they'd pull the others along later. She'd been right to re-open the school. She was proud she'd stuck up for herself and her judgment. The argument that school and Mass should be treated the same had worked. And she'd kept a watchful eye on Cecilia, who seemed perhaps a bit more confident than last year. At the end of the day, as she shut the door behind the last student, she was satisfied.

"I'm going to tidy up for a bit, probably an hour," she said to Cecilia. "I stay after school quite a long while most days. You'll have to entertain yourself. Are you hungry? I packed some apples and peanuts."

"Yes," Cecilia said, "and thirsty. I didn't know you stay after so long. I draw."

"You *will* draw," Mollie said.

As minutes passed, Mollie hoped Cecilia would invite her to have a look, but she kept her arm curved around the top of the paper as she drew.

The letter to Maria Elisia was still in Mollie's bag. She'd considered mailing it last week, just after she'd written it, then the day before when she went to get the roll of brown paper to put by the pump. Then, she'd decided to delay a bit more—until Saturday, when she went into town to do errands. She'd been so torn, but once Cecilia had asked that she mail the letter, she couldn't turn back, only delay. She was just waiting for Cecilia's picture, which would probably be done within the hour. As she rubbed the top of each desk with bleach water, she tried to convince herself she would have mailed it on her own. She wiped the doorknobs of the classroom, then went out to the outhouse and sprayed and wiped it down. By the time she was done, everything reeked of bleach.

She'd been putting the work she intended to do at home in her satchel as the day progressed, so was nearly ready to put her jacket on, collect Cecilia, and leave when she heard the rumble of a vehicle approaching. There was a spray of gravel as the driver took the corner too fast. Then a door slammed.

Cecilia's face registered shock and fear.

"Perhaps someone forgot something," Mollie said, and moved close enough to Cecilia to pat her shoulder.

She'd always locked the door behind the last departing student. Once, when she was a young teacher, an angry parent trapped her behind her desk for over an hour. She hadn't passed his son, who'd been absent more than present, on to the next grade. Now, she made sure she always had the option of meeting on the porch or, at minimum, staying closest to the door during any tense conversation. She knew whoever it was couldn't come in unless she chose to open the door. She peeked around the edge of the front window.

It was Dr. Murphy. He had an angry, flustered expression on his face. He rattled the doorknob impatiently, and Mollie's sense of calm and accomplishment evaporated. She held her finger to her lips, warning Cecilia to stay quiet. She nodded toward the telephone, then realized she'd not yet taught Cecilia how to make a call or talked at all about who she should call in an emergency. Too late now—Mollie opened the door and stepped out onto the porch, shutting the door firmly behind her.

"Is that child inside?" the doctor asked, easing a mask up over his mouth and nose.

"Why?" Mollie moved a step forward, which made him take a step back and down onto the highest step. At least now they were at eye level. Further, she was lodged between Dr. Murphy and Cecilia.

"Father Foley has got the influenza. This is what we were afraid of. She's given it to him."

"Oh, no," Mollie said. She crossed herself—Father, Son, and Holy Ghost. She'd hoped that the Pokorskis would be the only casualties in their township. Now, another one. And God knew how many people the priest had encountered.

"A little late for prayer," the doctor said, "and too late for sensible precautions. If only—"

"How have you concluded that he contracted it when he visited the Pokorski family?" Mollie interrupted. "I really can't imagine Cecilia was the carrier, after so long. It's been weeks since her family took sick."

"He didn't visit the family. I didn't allow it."

"They never had last rites? None of them?" Was it possible that the doctor and priest were so fearful the family had been denied a holy sacrament?

"I didn't allow him in the home," the doctor said.

"I've never heard of such a thing. No last rites? You were so squeamish that parishioners were denied last rites?" Mollie shook her head in disgust. "It's not as if no one has died of anything contagious in the parish before now. Isn't it the priest's obligation to administer sacraments?"

The doctor went on as if he hadn't heard her. "He got it from her," he said, and took a couple more steps back, as if it just occurred to him that whatever Cecilia had, Mollie probably had as well. "When we were at your house. There's no other way."

"But it's been so long, and she was never sick!"

"She's the only one in the community who was near anyone infected."

"What about Josef and the others? They were at church."

"As you well know from all your *reading* and *research*, that was likely far too long ago for the church service to have been the source. Their bodies were buried in August. No, it was her, a latent virus, and that's the only explanation."

"I've not read anything about a latent virus—"

"Don't lecture me on medicine," the doctor snapped.

"But how about you? You treated the family."

His face grew red. "I took *every* precaution. I never got within an arm's length of them, always wore a mask and gloves. It was *not* me. Most days, I didn't even go into the house."

Mollie stayed silent. Her respect for the doctor had just fallen a few more notches, as if that were possible. He had just admitted that he'd done almost nothing to treat the family or even ease their suffering, on top of discouraging the priest from administering last rites. But nothing she could say now would help the situation. She kept her lips tight.

"She is the only person who had unprotected contact with an infected person in the township," the doctor said.

"It was so long ago…weeks," Mollie's voice trailed off. "And how do you know no one in the township has traveled?" She thought of her brothers' visit but decided not to bring that up.

"There is so much we don't know about this sickness," the doctor interrupted. "That's why we need to avoid *every* risk."

"So the priest needs to be quarantined immediately—" she started.

"Don't tell me my business," the doctor yelled, waving his pointer finger in the air. "*Of course*, he needs to be quarantined. And *you* need to be quarantined. And that *child*, and your mother. Probably your brothers, too. *And* everyone the priest has seen since we had that meeting on your front lawn. We were doing so well until you got it into your head to act so rashly."

"But we sat outside, and quite far apart—"

Again, he interrupted. "God knows what damage you've done by holding school today. You just wouldn't listen."

"Wait." Mollie put her hands on her hips. "I question whether Cecilia was the one who transmitted it to the priest. I think you've jumped to a conclusion."

"Who else?" the doctor said. "He hasn't been outside the township for thirty days. No one else is sick. Who else would have given it to him? This is all because of your poor judgment. And mine, for not intervening with you." He shook his head. "Never again, you can be sure. I am following you home. You are going into your house with that child and your mother and staying there. You will come out when I say so."

"So, I'm to be a prisoner, on your authority—"

"I will get the sheriff if need be. It may be near to impossible to contain this now." He held out his hand. "Your keys to the school, please. This building is off limits."

"Do you have the authority to do that?"

His eyebrows raised to his hairline. "You mean *legal* authority?"

Mollie nodded.

"I have authority based on my position in this town, and my reputation, and my education," he said, and crossed his arms over his chest. "Show some respect."

Mollie pondered for just a second. She didn't like him and wasn't sure she trusted him, but he was the only doctor in the township. He was the one she would have to call if any of them got sick, as she had learned when her father's health failed. His maintaining such distance from the Pokorskis inspired little confidence, but he was the best they had. "I'll need to collect my things," she said. "And Cecilia."

"Five minutes. If I have my way, you won't be trusted with this position again."

Mollie pulled the schoolhouse keys out of the deep pocket of her skirt and dropped them into the doctor's outstretched hand. She didn't mention that she had a duplicate set at home.

The enormity of what the doctor said was sinking in. There had been a lapse in judgment, probably hers, and now the priest and everyone he'd encountered was at risk. He'd continued to hold Mass, which had kept him from interfering with Mollie's plans for the school, but he'd seen dozens of people. Regardless of where the priest had contracted the disease, he'd seen her mother within the past few days, solely because Mollie wanted to rescue Cecilia and re-open the school. Mollie's rash behavior had provoked her brothers' ire to the point where they enlisted Father Foley in their cause. But for her, the doctor and the priest would never have been on the front yard in Catherine's presence at all. There was no sense in blaming a child. This was all on her. She'd been a fool—and headstrong—to think she could keep anyone healthy. Worry for Catherine flared up. It overcame every other worry, making Mollie desperate to get home.

From the car, Mollie watched the doctor lock the front door of the school and drop the keys into his pocket. Then, he pasted a big paper sign on the door that Mollie could read even from several feet away—CONTAMINATED, it said, in heavy, dark letters, and below that, DO NOT ENTER.

∞

Cecilia had heard every word that awful doctor said. She waited for Mollie to talk back to him, but nothing. Did Mollie fear him? Did Mollie believe him, and now think she was the cause of the priest's illness? Was Mollie scared of her now? She knew Mollie cared about her, but she also knew how protective she was of Grandma Catherine. Was she reconsidering whether Cecilia should stay at the farmhouse? Cecilia shivered. Could the doctor be right? Could Father Foley have gotten the sickness from her?

Cecilia took the pencils and paper and her unfinished drawing from Mollie's desk drawer and slipped them into Mollie's satchel. It didn't sound as if they'd be coming back to the classroom soon, so she took an extra sheaf of paper from Mollie's desk and slipped that in as well. She said a small prayer, like what she remembered Mamusia saying. That priest hadn't been nice at all, but he shouldn't suffer because of her.

This was all her fault.

•   •   •

When they pulled onto the road, the doctor was close behind them. Cecilia held her breath, worried Mollie would say she wasn't welcome at the farm now that she'd cost Mollie opening the school, what Mollie wanted most. But Mollie said nothing, just rushed over the miles with the doctor's car close to her bumper. When they got back to the farm, the doctor watched squinty-eyed as Mollie parked the car in the barn. His eyes followed them as they crossed the road in front of his parked car. Cecilia could see he was staring straight ahead, his jaw clenched. Mollie hustled Cecilia through the front door, and only then did he drive away.

Cecilia sat down at the dining room table, removed the paper and pencils from Mollie's satchel, and began drawing again. Mamusia always used to say that once she began a drawing, it was as if she was possessed. She had to finish it before doing anything else. When Cecilia was upset or scared, like she was now, the feel of the pencil between the fingertips of her right hand and the texture of the paper under her left, as well as the sound of the pencil brushing across the paper, soothed and comforted her like nothing else.

This part of her drawing was of Mamusia. There was comfort in recreating her features and her small, neat body. It had been growing harder for Cecilia to remember her face just so, the way she liked to remember things. With the photographs from the flour sack arranged in front of her, Mamusia was coming back before her eyes. She was wearing the dress Cecilia had liked best, one with light blue flowers, not unlike the blouse Mollie had on today. She wanted to finish the picture today, so Mollie could send the letter she'd written to Maria Elisia. Now that they couldn't leave the house, she didn't know exactly how that would happen, but they would find a way.

Maria Elisia was the "naughty" one, Mamusia always said, with big and interesting ideas, so Cecilia planned to make Maria Elisia as she was in the photograph, a girl just a little older than Cecilia, with Mamusia a young girl also. After all, that was the way Maria Elisia lived in Maria Elisia's imagination. Cecilia knew this because of the stories. In Cecilia's drawing, Maria Elisia was half hidden behind the big maple tree in their front yard. Mamusia was standing on the steps, angled away from the tree. Like a game of hide-and-seek, she'd thought, shading in Mamusia's skirts, then making the sunlight glint off her bright hair. Maria Elisia had dark, snappy eyes, and curly hair, curly like Mollie's, only longer.

An hour later, Cecilia sat back, rested her pencils on the table, and smiled over the drawing. Mamusia looked as if she was just about to find Maria Elisia, behind the very next tree, and Maria Elisia looked ready to spring out and startle Mamusia. Like she was about to pop right out of Mamusia's imagination, so they could be girls together.

∞

Catherine was not on the porch, as Mollie had expected, when they got home. There was no response when she called out. Given that they were home an hour earlier because of the doctor's interruption, Mollie assumed Catherine had gone for a walk, or perhaps was in her garden. She went straight to her room on the second floor and threw herself across her bed. She planted her face in her pillow and cried tears of regret and humility. She didn't understand this illness—no one did— and instead of being cautious, like her brothers and the priest and doctor had wanted, she'd forged ahead. She kept thinking of person after person who might be at risk—Tom Reid, her brothers, the doctor and the priest, and anyone who'd encountered any of them. All the students she'd taught today, even though she wore a mask all day long. They could all be at risk. Why had she been so foolhardy, so impulsive and stubborn, yet again?

When she had no more tears and had quieted herself, she became aware of noises on the other side of the wall, coming from her mother's room. Catherine was never on the second floor at this time of day. She always made the journey down the stairs in the morning, then up again right before bed. What could she be doing up here? And why, why, hadn't she checked when she came in? Why had she been so quick to jump to the conclusion that her mother was fine, just out for a walk? Why hadn't Catherine come to check on her when she'd been crying so loudly?

Mollie found her mother lying across the bed, fully dressed.

"What is wrong?"

"I am just so tired," she said. "I haven't felt well all day."

Mollie pressed her hand to Catherine's forehead, then her own, then repeated the cycle again. She couldn't tell if it was warm, or it was just her imagination. She struggled to remember the symptoms of this flu—all her reading had concerned preventing it, not diagnosing it. She'd been so sure she herself would never get sick, and Catherine had gone nowhere in weeks. When the brothers came, they'd kept their distance, as had the priest and doctor, and, as far as she knew, Catherine had seen no one else. She hadn't thought she'd need to discern whether anyone had the influenza, a summer cold, or even something entirely unexpected, like the heart trouble that killed her father.

∞

"Cecilia," Mollie said from the bottom of the stairs.

Cecilia felt startled. Where was she? She looked toward the voice. She hadn't thought of Mollie since she began drawing. She was so hot—she shrugged out of her jacket. She hadn't even taken the time to remove it and hang it up when they'd come in.

"Yes?" she said, finally remembering all that had happened that afternoon.

"It's Grandma Catherine," Mollie said. "She's not well. I'm going to call the doctor."

"Doctor?" Cecilia said. It must be bad if Mollie was reaching out to the doctor. He'd been so mean and short with her, and then followed them home like they were bad.

"Is it the....?" Cecilia's voice trailed off.

"I don't know," Mollie whispered. "It could be."

"I so sorry," Cecilia said, remembering the doctor's words and anger "She catch it from me, too. Like the priest. All my fault."

"Don't jump to conclusions," Mollie said. "It could be nothing."

But she didn't look like it was nothing. She looked terrified.

Cecilia could only hear one side of the phone conversation. She heard Mollie greet someone named Theresa, then ask when the doctor was expected. Then she could hear the female voice on the other end of the phone grow louder. The person was yelling so loud that Mollie held the phone away from her head. "You brought this on all of us," the woman screamed. "Why should he help you?"

"I am sorry," Mollie said. "Of course, no one meant for the priest to get sick. I am not ready to blame it on the child, although it's a possibility, I acknowledge. For now, I am just asking that you tell doctor when he returns, I need him to call. Regardless of your feelings, he is the only doctor we have. My mother is ill."

She watched Mollie listen for a moment to the loud retort.

"I understand. Thank you." Then she slammed down the phone.

Mollie turned to Cecilia. "She said she does not know where he is. She doesn't want to help us." She crossed her arms over her chest. "I think we're on our own. I need to call my brothers and find out whether either of them has taken sick."

Cecilia listened to Mollie's end of the conversation with her brother, which sounded much more civilized than the one she'd had with the doctor's wife. Mollie's tone was completely different than it had been the other day. Her concern for Grandma Catherine was obvious, and the brother—Cecilia couldn't tell which one—was calm as well. When Mollie finished with, "Well, thank God," Cecilia knew it must have been good news. Neither of the brothers, or their families, was sick.

"I remember the sickness," Cecilia said when Mollie sat down next to her. "I listened for days. My family had fevers. 'Burning up,' I heard the doctor say. They had blood. Father was silly, speaking silly. My brother Josef yelled in pain, pain from his head. Is Grandma Catherine like that?"

Mollie took a deep breath. "No," she said. "No, she's not. None of those things. But I've never seen her lie down, not even go upstairs, during the day."

"It dark outside," Cecilia said, nodding toward the window.

"Yes," Mollie said, and nodded. "It is. This awful day has somehow passed. I'm going to stay with her tonight, in her room. I'll heat up some soup for us, then I want you to go to bed. This morning feels like a year ago."

Mollie looked so worried, so tired, that Cecilia knew she had to comply, even though the last thing she wanted was to rush through dinner and then be in a room alone while the people she cared about suffered in the house around her—again.

∞

Mollie took her mother hot soup and tea and settled in the chair in the corner of her room, where she stayed for the first part of the night. She fell asleep praying—there was nothing more to do than pray—not to hear the terrible sounds of screaming with pain, retching, and coughing that foretold the influenza. Her prayers were not orderly or formal— just a frantic repetition of the phrase, "Jesus, please keep us safe." She was dozing when Catherine jostled her shoulder.

"I need to go out," Catherine said. "To relieve myself. Will you come with me?"

"You're standing."

"Of course, I'm standing." She shook her cane. "With help."

"I was so worried," Mollie said as they made their way to the top of the stairs. She positioned herself to walk down ahead of her mother just in case she was unsteady on her feet, but Catherine had no difficulty navigating the stairs. When she'd finished in the outhouse, and they came back in, Catherine said, "Let's sit."

"All right."

"Mollie, I just felt weak earlier in the day. I'm nearly seventy. I'm older than my mother was when she passed. Older than your father was." Mollie shook her head, but before she could speak, Catherine continued. "It will happen," she said. "Maybe not today, or this year." She inclined her head toward two letters that were now sitting next to the flour sack, beside Cecilia's drawing of her mother. The two letters bore Catherine's lovely, signature penmanship, and Mollie could see they were addressed to her brothers. There were two stamped and addressed envelopes next to them. "I want you to mail those letters to your brothers tomorrow."

Mollie realized she hadn't told Catherine anything about what had happened that day. She had no reason to know they were all quarantined by the order of the doctor. She filled her in, then asked, "What do the letters say?"

"You can read them. They say I want you to stay on the farm. I want it to belong to you," Catherine said. "I want this place to be a place of refuge and respite for their families, too, if the time ever comes, and I would ask you to honor that."

"Of course," Mollie said.

"I need to know you are provided for and can stand on your own two feet. You need the security of a home, no matter what happens. I am going to have my will adjusted, but this should suffice in the meantime."

Mollie picked up the letters and read them. They were exactly as Catherine said—she told Sam and Dan that she wanted Mollie to have a home of her own and assured them that Mollie would make them and their families welcome. Catherine hoped they would be a solace to each other when she was gone, and that this decisive act would put them all on a healing path.

Mollie's eyes welled up with tears. The security of a place of her own no one could take from her? She hadn't imagined the relief.

"I could make an appointment with the lawyer—" Mollie started.

Catherine's mouth tightened. "One step at a time," she said.

Mollie knew better than to push. This was progress. She nodded, then asked, "Why today?"

"Your brother Dan called me as soon as you'd left for school this morning. He had the audacity to suggest that I might want to talk to you about whether you had a vocation. He and Sarah had it all figured out. They speculated that Cecilia being here meant you'd developed a sudden appetite to raise a child, and reasoned that the convent afforded plenty of opportunities for a spinster who liked children, perhaps working in an orphanage—"

"What?" Mollie put up her hand. "Wait. What did you just say? A vocation? Become a nun? *Me*?"

Catherine nodded. "Yes, you. A vocation." She shook her head. "I suppose they haven't considered, or even noticed, your cool feelings toward the Church, let alone your aversion to authority. They hadn't noticed how you hated being bossed, especially by a man. They had it all figured out—a tidy plan. I was so exasperated. I sat right down and started writing. Once I'd begun, the plan poured out of me. I know it's right."

The thought of joining a convent, like the one over near Memphis where the young novitiates learned to be nurses—another job for which she was totally unsuited—made Mollie close her eyes and shake her head, then laugh. She exhaled. "They know *nothing* about me."

"Apparently not. Whether you choose to draw them closer is up to you. I just couldn't stand the idea you'd have no say when I'm gone. At best, it would have been two against one. With Sarah in the mix, offering her opinions, three against one."

"They never listen to me," Mollie said.

Catherine sighed. "The fighting tires me so."

"I'm sorry," Mollie said, and took a deep breath. "I'll try harder."

"Trying to get along better while also having to appease is not the best answer, at least not over the long plow." Catherine smiled. "Making this decision, and writing it out, gave me peace. Now that the decision is made, I feel relieved. Will you mail the letters in the morning?"

"Yes," Mollie said, not knowing exactly how she would accomplish the task given that she was under house arrest, at least according to the doctor. But she made the promise anyway. She would figure out how to get both missives—hers to Mary Elisia and Catherine's to the two brothers—in the mailbox outside the post office first thing, before anyone could see her.

Chapter Thirteen

When Cecilia woke to the sound of the train's morning whistle, it was dark outside her window and the house was quiet. She'd dropped off to sleep without meaning to, while listening for the footsteps overhead, just as she'd listened for signs of life back in the pantry when her family got sick. She threw back the warm covers. Her heart was racing. The floor was cold against her feet. By the time she climbed the stairs to the second floor, she was shivering. She hesitated outside the door of Grandma Catherine's room and listened—silence—then pushed open the door. At the side of the bed, she gently placed her hand on Grandma Catherine's shoulder—still warm. Her breath escaped. She hadn't been aware she was holding it. After a few more seconds, she discerned the rise and fall of Grandma Catherine's chest. She heard Grandma Catherine's soft inhale and exhale.

"Cecilia," Mollie whispered from the chair in the corner, "what are you doing?"

"I sorry," Cecilia said, then corrected herself. "*I'm* sorry. I was...checking. Should I have stayed in my room?"

Mollie put her finger to her lips. "Heavens, no," she whispered, even quieter than before. "It's all right."

"She is all right?"

"Yes, I think so." Mollie stood and stretched and then pulled the window curtain aside. She leaned forward and opened the window just a crack.

A breath of cool, fresh air crossed the room, raising goosebumps on Cecilia's arms. She pulled the covers closer around Grandma Catherine's shoulders.

"Look, the sun's coming up. Let's go downstairs," Mollie said. "She needs rest."

Cecilia tiptoed out of the bedroom. Mollie, following her, shut the door ever so gently. At the bottom of the stairs, in the dining room, she saw her drawing of Mamusia and Maria Elisia on the table. She stopped to write her name in the lower corner, then hesitated. The drawing was not quite right. She took her pencil and considered altering the shading of the skirt—how could she suggest the patterned calico that Mamusia liked, and perhaps even show the pastel color? Maybe if the background of the skirt was lighter than the grass around her feet? She ran her eraser over the surface, lightening the shade, then ran her thumb over the lighter pencil to make it softer—like cotton, washed many times and dried in the sun. Then, she took a pointed pencil and fashioned the tiny cross design she remembered, more precise where the light was hitting the skirt, and a little blurred in the shadows. There, that was better.

Mollie, who had been in the kitchen, starting a fire in the coal stove, appeared at her elbow. She was holding a cup of steaming tea in both hands. She leaned over to see the drawing. "It's lovely, Cecilia," she said. "I am stunned by your talent. You have a gift."

"One day, I'll draw a picture of you," she blurted out. "A nice one."

"When you are ready," Mollie said and smiled. "And not before."

Cecilia noticed two stamped envelopes and two letters left on the table in front of the seat opposite her. "What those?" she asked.

"They're letters Grandma Catherine wrote to my brothers about the farm."

"You mail them?"

"Yes." Mollie hesitated. "Perhaps we should go put them in the mailbox now, along with my letter and your drawing for Maria Elisia. Before anyone wakes up—we're on strict orders to quarantine, remember?"

"Will you obey?"

Mollie's brows rose. "Of course," she said. "I don't like the doctor much and he lost my confidence long ago, but he's not wrong. Until we determine why the priest got sick, if we can, we're all in the same boat. Everyone should stay at home, at least for a few weeks."

"Are you sad?"

"This morning, I'm mostly grateful my mother isn't seriously ill. About the rest, I'm just so frustrated. I tried so hard to do everything right."

Cecilia nodded—that was how she felt, too. She folded the picture into four parts, like the map from the flour sack, the one she and Mamusia had used to trace Josef's path home, hoping the creases could be pressed out when it arrived. She slipped it into the envelope Mollie offered.

"Where is the letter going?" she asked.

"To Maria Elisia Pokorski," Mollie said, "in Chicago, Illinois." She affixed the stamp to the envelope, and said, "Godspeed. Let's go now, before the chickens are up."

"Chickens?"

"Just an expression. No chickens. Maybe someday."

"I like that," Cecilia said. "I like to collect eggs with Mamusia."

They both threw robes on over their nightgowns, and shoved their feet, without socks, into the shoes they'd left by the door the previous evening. In the village, Mollie pulled the car up to the post box on the curb. Cecilia leaned out the passenger window and dropped the three letters into the postbox—the metal cover made a satisfying clang.

As they drove home, Cecilia realized there was something delicious about the morning. Grandma Catherine was better. She hadn't imagined such a thing could happen. Cecilia had hoped and prayed so hard for her family, with no relief, and hadn't imagined a different outcome might be possible. Then, they were out before anyone, still in nightgowns in the car. That felt naughty. And the act of mailing the letters was like turning the next page in a book. It had been so long since she'd felt happy. "Like a bubble," was how Mamusia had described happy. Cecilia had forgotten the feeling, and now it was back.

Cecilia ran to the top of the stairs when they got home, but Grandma Catherine's door was still shut. Cecilia could hear her snoring, so tiptoed back down again. Mollie was refilling the teakettle from the pump in the kitchen and had added coal to the cookstove. "It's chilly this morning," she said. "I guess we missed out on Indian summer this year. Along with so much else."

"Not going to schoolhouse?" Cecilia asked.

Mollie looked at her as if she was silly, as if she didn't remember what had happened with the doctor.

"I remember," Cecilia said.

"No," Mollie said. "We're not going."

"We have tasks to do there?" Cecilia would have liked to go back and draw by herself as Mollie worked. She quite liked the quiet schoolroom, so different from how she'd felt last year, when it had always seemed full of hazards.

"No tasks there. I was totally ready for the start of school—I can't think of a single thing we *could* do."

"Where are masks?" Cecilia asked.

"In the back seat. We could wash them." Then Mollie sat down in the rocker, the one Grandma Catherine always used. It seemed odd to see anyone else in the seat. "Probably just as well that I'm here when Grandma Catherine wakes, so I can..." Her voice trailed off, and she stood and looked around the kitchen, as if for the thing that would occupy her during the long hours of the day with no school. She pressed her foot against the floor and the rocker made its usual squeak.

"When Grandma Catherine wakes?" Cecilia finished the sentence. "We should be here?"

"Yes," Mollie said. She tilted her head to the side and looked at Cecilia, then stood. "Sweetie," she said, "I really like being here with you. It's so much nicer than when I was here alone—I mean, just with my mother."

Cecilia crossed the kitchen and threw her arms around Mollie's waist. She could feel the warmth and solidity of her and didn't sense any resistance from Mollie. She didn't seem to want her to move away.

It was nothing like the stiff touches she remembered from the classroom, little reminders to move along more quickly, or to the right or left. An occasional brush, by accident. She realized she'd rarely, if ever, seen Mollie touch anyone.

"How about we practice your use of 'Mollie'?" She took a bowl of pennies from the shelf. "Let's put a penny aside for each time you slip and call me 'Miss Crowley' here at home. We'll figure out a different game for school, although I think you're far less likely to slip there."

Cecilia nodded, burrowing her face even closer against the warm flannel of Miss Crowley's—Mollie's—nightgown.

$$\infty$$

By ten a.m., Mollie had finished tidying up the kitchen, made her bed, and helped Cecilia make her bed. She'd collected the last of the beans and potatoes and tomatoes from the garden, swept the front walk, snipped the last of the green branches from the berry bush out back for a table arrangement, and organized the pantry. Catherine was sitting in her rocker, sipping the tea Mollie had made, but looking like she was ready to spit over the presence of Mollie in her kitchen.

"Would you like me to change your bedding?" Mollie asked Grandma Catherine.

"Heavens, no," Grandma Catherine snapped. "I am perfectly capable of taking care of my room and things."

"What's wrong?" Mollie asked.

"This is my time," Catherine said. "My place. You are meant to be at the school—teaching."

"It's not as if I chose to be home mid-morning on a perfectly good workday," Mollie snapped. "This was not my plan."

Cecilia was drawing again, shielding her picture within the curve of her arm. Mollie suspected she was making a gift for Grandma Catherine. She was still dressed in her nightgown. "Why not?"

Grandma Catherine had said, when Mollie asked the child if she intended to wear her bedclothes all day.

The rest of the day stretched out hopelessly. Perhaps, if the doctor had his way, she'd be shelved for the rest of her life, Mollie thought. She ached to be back at school, finishing up the first few days, just beginning to see the broad strokes of the year to come. She was meant to be a teacher, not a housemaid. She'd been itching to get back since August, and now she was thwarted again, with no respite in sight. The right thing is often the hard thing, she reminded herself.

"Cecilia," Mollie said in her classroom voice. "Please hurry and get dressed and washed up. Now."

Grandma Catherine raised her eyebrows, and Mollie looked back at her, daring her to interfere. Could she possibly disagree? The child should be dressed. Why, if she—

"Just because—" Grandma Catherine started.

Mollie put up her hand. She walked over to the table and knocked on the surface as though she was knocking on the front door.

Cecilia looked up, startled.

"We are going to have school today, even if it's just me and you. Teaching is what I do, and learning is what you should be doing. Maybe this is providence, divine intervention." She looked over at Grandma Catherine to see if her reference to a higher power netted any approval. "I can help you catch up to where you should be. Let's see where we are, and then we'll figure out a plan."

Cecilia set aside her drawing to review "skills," as Mollie called them. They'd counted buttons from the big bowl of buttons, salvaged from clothes that had worn out long before. Then she'd written the words for each number next to the group of buttons laid out on a big sheet of brown butcher paper. She'd coaxed Mollie into telling her stories about the buttons she found prettiest—the shiny green one in the shape of a leaf; the bright red oversized set of four, held together with a string; and, finally, ten of the most precious little pearl ones cradled in tissue paper and tucked into a little blue box.

Mollie held out her hand for the box and inspected the little pearls. She smiled, but it was a sad smile. "Those were from my wedding dress. Grandma Catherine made it."

"What wedding dress?" Cecilia asked.

"I was supposed to be married. I called it off."

"Why?"

"He liked to drink spirits. I just couldn't tolerate it."

"Drink spirits?"

"Alcohol. Nothing good comes of it. Poison. I wouldn't even have it in the house."

Cecilia nodded. She remembered whiskey. Once she'd found a bottle hidden in one of her winter boots. Mamusia had taken it and dumped it down the cistern.

Calling off a wedding, though, that was a surprise. She'd thought all women wanted to get married, that those left out were those who'd never been asked. The dress must be beautiful—even the dress Grandma Catherine made her for the first day of school was so pretty and precise, and her favorite color, exactly right for her, though Grandma Catherine hadn't even asked. Much nicer than what she'd had last year. Grandma Catherine's dress was one thing that made her brave enough to stand up to Louise O'Connell.

She stood. She wanted to see and touch the festive dress, maybe even draw a picture of Mollie in it, like she'd promised. "Where is the dress?" she asked.

"I gave it away," Mollie answered.

"*Gave the dress away?*"

"Yes. To Rosie Weir. They married right before Edward went off to war, and she needed a dress. No one had ever seen mine, so there was no harm. Rosie is just my size. She looked lovely." Mollie picked up a pearl between her pointer finger and thumb and held it up to the light.

Except for the color, it looked like the smallest pea from a spring pod—Cecilia wanted to draw it, a perfect iridescent globe nestled in a fresh green envelope.

"Grandma Catherine must have cut off these buttons and replaced them with others," Mollie said.

"Why she save buttons?" Cecilia said. "When you gave away the whole dress?"

"She'd slaved over the dress for months. Maybe she wanted a little something to remember it by."

"*Your* dress!" Cecilia said. "Not something to give away."

"That's what she said, but I wasn't going to wear it."

"What if you marry someone else?"

"Even if I married someone else, which is highly unlikely, I wouldn't wear the dress planned for my first wedding. Not to marry a different groom."

"But why not? You still the same bride. No one saw it."

Mollie hesitated. "I really don't know," she said. "You've stumped me. I just wouldn't."

Cecilia shook her head—what a waste. Poor Grandma Catherine.

"I suppose I could still use the buttons." Mollie sighed and looked out the window. "Let's get back to work," she said after a few seconds. "Let's see about your reading."

By late afternoon, Mollie was stiff from sitting in the chair for so long. Cecilia had some woeful gaps in her skills as compared to her classmates, but was so quick to learn. Perhaps it was fortuitous that she had unlimited time to devote to the child, at least for a few weeks. It certainly took her mind off the aborted start of school.

"Let's make dinner," she said. "Then we'll rouse Grandma Catherine, I'll teach you about fractions." She found the measuring cups with lines on the sides in the back of a cabinet and set a few potatoes to soak.

"What are we having?" Cecilia said. "Potatoes?"

She didn't like to tell the child she didn't know how to cook. There'd been no reason for her to learn. She smiled at the memory of her mother trying to teach her to make a few simple meals when she was engaged. They'd all been failures. When she broke the engagement, the cooking lessons ceased, too.

"We missed breakfast. I think we can attempt eggs and bacon and fried potatoes and toast, a simple meal," Mollie said. "We should be able to manage that. Perhaps there is some nice jam in the root cellar. If I can keep a variety of students at different levels lurching forward, I should be able to make the parts and pieces of a meal turn out simultaneously."

"I not need jam," Cecilia said.

"*I don't need jam,*" Mollie said sternly, then laughed. "Do you dislike the root cellar?" The root cellar was a dark hole with stone walls underneath the house, and she'd been afraid of it herself, long after she'd learned to face down that bull in the Garvey's field.

"I don't like it," Cecilia said. "I don't like the cellar under my house either."

"I can get the jam," Mollie said, "so long as you stand at the top of the ladder and hold the light."

"You afraid too?" Cecilia asked.

"I don't like it down there," Mollie said, and a sudden memory came back to her of her brother Sam closing the door behind her and blocking her from rushing back up as she was wont to do. Her father had finally responded to her yelling and disciplined Sam by taking away his bicycle, which was his only mode of transportation, for a month. He'd had to walk to school and couldn't get to town at all, and he had let Mollie know he thought it was all her fault, that trapping her in the basement had been nothing more than a "silly joke," and that she was a "baby."

They were just getting ready to pour the frothy eggs into a cast iron pan coated with butter when Tom Reid pulled his truck to an abrupt stop at the end of the walk, sending up a cloud of dust. She heard the car door slam even through the window and closed front door.

"Stay," he waved to the dog, who looked mournfully from the passenger seat. Tom's walk was purposeful.

"He looks fit to be tied," Mollie said, "doesn't he?"

∞

Cecilia didn't know what that expression meant, but she knew what angry looked like. Mr. Reid, usually such a nice and gentle man, now looked as angry as Cecilia's father ever had—steaming mad, as Mamusia would have said. Mollie was at the door even before Mr. Reid knocked. She stepped out onto the porch. Cecilia ducked into the little alcove between the dining room window and the bookshelf, a place where she suspected she'd be able to hear every word but remain unseen. Just to be sure, she cracked the window just a bit, and breathed as softly as she could.

∞

"I heard what happened at the school," Tom said. "I'd have come this morning, but I had to mind the store. I'd hoped to call, but people were in and out all day. It seems everything broken needs fixing right now, probably because everyone is staying close to home. And it's my task to get my hands on enough supplies so the town can hunker down and the farmers can stay in production. I didn't have a moment of privacy. But it's just as well."

"Why?" Mollie said.

"About an hour ago, Edward Weir came in, looking for a truckload of supplies. It was all the things I laid in once the pandemic started—

bleach, heavy canvas, large pots to boil cutlery and dishes for sterilization. Lots of gauze. Gloves and all the handkerchiefs I had. He nearly cleaned me out, and those things are dear. God knows when I'll be able to get more. I thought he was hoarding, perhaps considering a new business opportunity, thinking he'd re-sell at a higher price."

"Why?" Mollie said. "Why would he hoard those things? That's not like Edward at all. He and Rosie are the *most* generous people. They'd give you anything you needed—"

"I only got the truth when I resisted letting him clean me out completely. It wasn't hoarding. He was on his way to the convent out past Memphis."

"You mean the convent where they train the novitiates? Whatever for?"

"Thank God he's such a talker, or I wouldn't know. Of course, the doctor told him not to breathe a word, but I go way back with Edward, and his uncles. And you're right—he and Rosie aren't the kind of people to hoard. Or to keep secrets. He had to set the record straight—couldn't help himself. He told me they've had an outbreak of the flu in the convent. Probably due to a teaching nun bringing it from the city—"

"And then the young women contracting the infection," Mollie finished his sentence.

"Yes, that's right. And they may be nuns, but they're in the group that's getting hit the worst. Young people. Young, healthy people." Tom shook his head. "Girls just starting their vocations. Young people just starting their *lives*." He brushed a tear away. "One of the young ladies— only fifteen—passed last night."

Mollie crossed herself—Father, Son, and Holy Ghost—and said a "Please, Jesus" for any other girls who were ailing. She felt embarrassed that she'd been cross over having to stay home. She was just at loose ends—nothing life-threatening. Catherine was safe, though she felt they'd had a near miss. And Cecilia was adjusting, though she'd been with them for less than a week. She could give praise for that as well.

Tom crossed his arms. "The priest had been there to administer communion, every Saturday evening, throughout the summer and into the fall. Novitiates who'd completed their training were going, and new postulants were arriving. That was how Father Foley got it, I'm certain."

"So, it wasn't me." Mollie's voice cracked, and an intense wave of relief passed through her. She sank into a chair and dropped her head into her hands. She didn't have to feel guilty, and she didn't have to worry that everyone in the township was so angry with her they'd never forgive her. She didn't have to feel like people were going to die based on her judgment, or some would say, recklessness. She had kept her students and her mother and Cecilia safe—she'd even kept herself safe. She would not be begging forgiveness for the rest of her life. She didn't have to worry for her job. She raised her head. "I didn't get the priest sick and, with him, the rest of the village."

"Nor did Cecilia," Tom said. "The only contact point between the convent and our village is Father Foley. It was people from the city, not being careful."

"Or," Mollie said, "being careful and still getting sick. We shouldn't cast blame."

"I don't mean to cast blame for getting sick," Tom said, pulling off his hat and twisting it in his fingers. "I'm casting blame for *blaming*, like I heard the doctor did with you. And Cecilia. Persecuting a child like that. They should have just told the truth."

"That doctor might not have had the imagination to consider anything but the most obvious explanation."

"Well, the priest certainly knew better, or should have."

Mollie remembered the priest had sat through the conversation with her brothers, and surely should have considered the convent a risk, as well as Mass, when he was so willing to shut down the school. "You're right," she said. "But you know how the clergy protect one another, as do men in general." She regretted the words once they were out. As far as she knew, she was the only one in the village who had reservations about the Church and clergy, or controversial thoughts about the way things worked between men and women. She always kept her ambivalence to herself. And Tom was a man. Perhaps he'd be taken aback by her observation about men in general.

"It doesn't much matter," Tom said, not seeming offended at all. "Now they're sick in the convent. The one novitiate passed, as I said, and several others are grievously ill. The priest has seen all of them and probably put the hosts right into their open mouths with his bare fingers. Then, he saw everyone in the village. I guess he believed his clerical collar would provide divine protection." He put his hands up, palms open. "I'm sorry," he said. "I don't mean to blaspheme—"

Mollie felt a slow warmth on her cheeks. Tom had just expressed exactly the kind of opinion she usually kept to herself. She rolled her eyes, thinking she'd not known that anyone in the township shared her feelings about the priest and the Church. "Don't apologize," she said. "It's unnecessary."

Tom nodded. "But, regardless of who did what," he continued, "we're all shut down for the duration. The church, the school—"

"Your store?"

"Not the store," Tom said. "People need the things I sell. The grocer will stay open as well. And the post. Anything we don't *absolutely* need daily will shut down until further notice."

"I wonder if he'll ever apologize to me—the doctor," Mollie said, realizing as soon as she said it that not the doctor, nor anyone else, would ever apologize to her—the doctor hadn't even called her back to check on Catherine after her frantic entreaty to his wife last night. "Thank you," she said, after a minute, realizing Tom had come here simply to relieve her worries. "I'm here, and we're in quarantine, I guess until further notice, but I am *so* relieved to know I'm not at fault. That my precautions worked or seem to have."

"Yes, we won't know for a few days if anything spread among the students who were in school yesterday, but you seem to have done well, Mollie." He patted her shoulder, then pulled his mask out of his back pocket as if he'd just remembered it and slid it over his head. "I won't forget this again. Let's keep you all well. Call me if there's anything you need. Oh, and by the way—," he grinned.

"Yes?"

"I didn't promise anyone to keep anything a secret. I only did my duty, making sure I had the facts before I let anyone take more than their fair share of the blame. You'd better believe I'm going to let everyone know *exactly* what happened. Your reputation is intact."

She smiled—just about everyone she knew would be in and out of the hardware store, for some necessity, over the next few weeks. She could just sit tight—it was going to be fine.

∞

Cecilia heard it all from her position by the window—it wasn't her who'd made the priest sick, and Grandma Catherine wasn't sick at all. So, it was just that they would need to stay home, just the three of them, until the sickness passed through the village. Cecilia didn't mind. She'd quite enjoyed working with Mollie all day, just the two of them. Each time she struggled with anything, Mollie explained it again. She helped her to sound out difficult words and seemed to understand that she needed to get up and move around every little while. They'd taken walks both in the morning and the afternoon, and explored the barn across the road, which had a long rope with a knot on the end, on which she'd swung in wide arcs. Then, Mollie swung on the rope too, her skirts drifting around her, and told Cecilia her father hung it when she was a girl. The moment made Cecilia think of friends—she hadn't any—and wonder if Mollie was also friendless. She'd not heard her speak of any girlfriends, other than the lady she'd given her dress to, and that didn't really sound like a friendship anyway—just a good deed. It was a little like last year, when Mamusia had been her only friend. Now it was Mollie, and Cecilia didn't much care when she went back to school.

Chapter Fourteen

The next two weeks passed in a pattern like that first day back at home. Mollie went into town each afternoon just after the train came through. She saw the closed signs on most public buildings, including the church, from her car. She dashed into the post office, always checking for a return letter from Maria Elisia, then picked up the few things they needed at the grocer. She kept a mask on all the time and didn't seek out gossip. No one knew anything more than she did about the flu spreading, or, for that matter, about the healing process. No one seemed to know when or if it would be safe to take up their normal lives. She kept to herself.

At home, she took more responsibility for cooking than in the past, as her mother was resting more. That puzzled Mollie, as Catherine didn't appear to be sick. Her cooking was barely edible, but no one complained. She taught her class of one each day, marveling at the speed and acumen Cecilia showed when given individual attention. Not that she'd vied for attention last year. She'd just sat passively. Her speech was improving quickly—sometimes, it seemed by the hour. At this rate, she'd likely be ready to join the third graders, not the second graders, when they went back to school.

If they went back to school was more like it. The Detroit newspapers said pitifully little about the flu pandemic, though it had changed everything. What was more newsworthy? It would be helpful to know at least when this might be over. Maybe by Thanksgiving? Or could it be until Christmas, God forbid? Perhaps she should be making plans for how to keep all the students at grade level, just as she was working to keep Cecilia on track. Should she make packets for them to use at home, and offer to serve as a visiting teacher? Mollie shuddered—all the miles she'd have to travel between farms. On roads blocked with snow, through winter weather! And she'd need to leave Cecilia and Catherine at home alone. She decided to wait a bit before making a long-term plan.

∞

Cecilia, standing at the kitchen window scraping the lunch plates, was the one who saw Mr. Reid's truck first. It was the Saturday before Halloween—a cold, gray, rainy day, more like winter than summer, and sixteen days after that first day of school when they'd been shut down almost before they began. It had been so long since anyone had been by, she was halfway up the walk with excitement before the passenger door opened.

She stopped. The people in Mr. Reid's truck were strangers. When she saw the man get out of the passenger's side of the truck, she took three steps back. The man looked exactly like her father; slender, with rusty red hair, pockmarked skin, and flinty blue eyes that were too cool for the smile on his face. The woman who got out after him was tiny, not more than a head taller than Cecilia, and slim, like Mamusia had been. She had dark hair pulled into a loose bun, and snappy brown eyes. She carried a large empty bag slung over her shoulder.

Then, Cecilia saw there were two young children, a boy and a girl, in the truck bed behind the cab—she hadn't been able to see them until they stood up. Both looked at her with level gazes, but neither one smiled. The boy looked to be a little younger than Cecilia, and the girl a little older. They both needed help to get out of the truck bed. Mr. Reid was the one who lifted them down to the gravel roadway.

"Cecilia?" the woman asked, as she started up the walk.

Where was Mollie? And why did Mr. Reid have such a cautious look on his face? It was as if he was telling her to go get Mollie, but there was really no way to do that without being rude. Plus, Mollie had gone out on a walk with the big black umbrella an hour or so earlier. Cecilia scanned the area—no sign of the umbrella bobbing in the distance. She wanted to turn and run like a startled squirrel.

"Cecilia?" the woman said, again.

She squared her shoulders but didn't take one step further. "Yes," she said. "My name is Cecilia."

"I'm called Maria Elisia." The woman turned and looked behind her. "And this is my husband, Filip. Your father's brother. And my children, Susanne and Basil."

Cecilia felt someone approach from behind. She glanced back. It was Grandma Catherine.

"Why, hello," Grandma Catherine said. She pulled a mask up over her face.

Cecilia hadn't seen her wear a mask in weeks. Then, again, she'd not seen anyone go into the house at all other than the three of them for weeks. It was too cold to sit outside, as they had earlier in the fall when the brothers came by without warning. These strangers would have to come into the house to talk. Perhaps Grandma Catherine was going to ask everyone to wear a mask?

Maria Elisia pulled a mask out of her skirt pocket and put it on. "I'm sure you'd be more comfortable if we put these on."

"Do we have to?" the boy said. "We had them on the whole train trip here. I hate them."

"Stop," the man, Filip, said, his tight voice reminding Cecilia of how her father used to speak to her. "Put it on."

The boy quickly obeyed, and Cecilia took another step back. The little girl, her mask already in place, ducked under her mother's right arm.

"Well, please come in," Grandma Catherine said. "Mollie is out for a walk. She'll be back any moment." She opened the front door and held it open. Once the group had passed, she shot a questioning look at Mr. Reid.

He shrugged his shoulders, then nodded toward the train track, a half mile south of the house. Cecilia heard the train go through an hour earlier—she got his meaning. These people came on the train, and probably walked to his store and asked for a ride. He obliged and brought them without calling first; Mollie wasn't going to like that. Grandma Catherine probably didn't either. They'd been so irked when the brothers, the priest, and the doctor showed up without being invited. Perhaps Mr. Reid hadn't been able to call without seeming rude, the way she had forced herself to stay still when she wanted to run back up the walk and slam the door behind her.

Cecilia followed the woman, the two children, the man, who she knew was her uncle, and Mr. Reid into the parlor, where they almost never sat. Cecilia perched on the fireplace hearth, where she could see the front walk. She planned to run out and warn Mollie as soon as she saw her approach.

∞

Mollie turned the corner onto Bricker Road and saw Tom Reid's truck. Why was he at the house?

Every day since the news about the convent, Mollie had thought several times about Tom spreading the word that she had nothing to do with transmitting the influenza to the priest. It had felt so good to have someone in her corner, looking out for her reputation. Then, he'd called a couple of times to let her know there hadn't been any other cases, which was more than the doctor did. The doctor, as she'd suspected, had never apologized, or let her know that his dire predictions hadn't come to pass—the outbreak had stayed in the convent. The doctor had never even called to check on her mother. Tom also called earlier in the week to let her know the priest was on the mend, which she was happy to hear. Far be it from her to wish catastrophe on anyone else. He'd said they'd decided to unlock the church doors for private prayer. Even though they were becoming closer friends, however, it wasn't like Tom to come by without calling. As she walked closer, she noticed that he'd left Lex in the cab of the truck.

Also strange.

Just as she turned onto the walk and began to shake off her umbrella, Cecilia ran out of the house.

"They are here," she said. "Maria Elisia and Filip, and two children. They come to take me?"

"*What*?"

"She has a big empty bag for my things. They asked Mr. Reid to take them to our farm. They want a look around."

Mollie put her arm around the girl's shoulders and left the umbrella upended on the front porch without shaking and folding it, as she usually would. She went through the door, and neither of them stopped to take off their shoes, as Grandma Catherine always insisted they do.

"Hello?" she said, in the entrance to the parlor. "I'm Mollie Crowley."

Maria Elisia stood and held out her hands, then pulled them back when Mollie didn't extend hers.

Maria Elisia blushed—"*Mi dispiace*...I'm sorry, it's a habit."

"I understand," Mollie said. "I am just very cautious."

"I'm called Maria Elisia," the woman said, stepping back a pace. "Thank you for your letter. We came as soon as we could. Filip—" she ducked her head in the direction of the man, "is Cecilia's uncle. I was Frances' friend. *La mia più cara amica*—dearest friend," she added.

Silence.

"I'm sorry we came without warning, but we wanted to get here as soon as we could," the woman stammered.

Mollie thought that it was odd that a woman's dearest friend hadn't written for many months, or ever come to visit, or perhaps even known about her youngest child—Cecilia—and then felt such urgency she would arrive without warning. She kept silent about that. It was important to choose her words and demeanor carefully.

"How did you get here?" Mollie finally asked.

"We took the train from Chicago," the man said. "Then, we walked to the store, and hired a ride from this fine man, and he brought us right to you." He glanced over at Tom like he was the lord of the manor and Tom was a handy servant.

Mollie knew very well that no one "hired" a ride from Tom—bringing them here was a common courtesy. Tom would have done it for anyone, as would she.

"We're going to see my brother's farm next," the man added.

"Actually, you asked to go to the farm first, as I recall," Tom said. "It was my idea to stop here. It didn't seem right to be disturbing their things without Cecilia even knowing."

∞

When Mr. Reid said that the man—her uncle—had asked to go to their farm first, Cecilia saw Mollie's expression—which had been looking just a bit uncertain—harden. A skeptical look clouded her features.

There were a few seconds of awkward silence.

"It's stopped raining," Maria Elisia finally said. "May we go for a walk with Cecilia? Get to know each other a bit? Before we visit the farm?"

Cecilia didn't want to go but didn't know how to say 'no' without being rude, and it didn't seem that either Mollie or Tom or Grandma Catherine was going to intervene. It also didn't seem any of them were going to go with her. Why did they want to give her privacy with these strangers? Did they want her to go? Not just on the walk, but also to Chicago?

"It's just a walk, Cecilia," Mollie said. "We'll be right here."

"All right." Cecilia said.

"Do you want to go for a walk?" Grandma Catherine asked.

Cecilia nodded, but wished Grandma Catherine could read her mind.

∞

As the four strangers walked away with Cecilia, Mollie watched from the front porch. She noticed the boy hung behind, and the girl stayed attached to her mother's left side. She wondered at the man's command of English, now that she understood Cecilia's father had spoken mostly Polish, as well as his arrogant air. She could see the strong resemblance between the two men, even though Filip looked younger and as if he'd had a softer life. It didn't look like anyone was talking. A lump of bitterness formed in her throat at the sight of Cecilia walking between the two adults. Her back was straight, and her gait was even, but she looked so small.

So, was it ending just like that? Was she meant to let the child go this afternoon? Or on the westbound noon train tomorrow?

The weight of a hand landed on her shoulder—it was Tom's. Her eyes filled with tears. She had no idea what she could do to keep this new life, one she found she enjoyed so much, from slipping away. The dwindling shape of Cecilia as she walked north, toward the train tracks and the cemetery, felt like an omen. She couldn't bear her leaving altogether—but what was her claim?

"Mollie," her mother said, from the doorway. "What are you going to do?"

"What can I do?"

"You can't just let her go like this."

"But what standing do I have to object?" Mollie shook her head, and made no attempt to hide her tears, or to move from under the weight of Tom's warm hand.

∞

As Cecilia and the family of four walked down the road toward the cemetery, the boy—Basil—poked into gopher holes along the edge of the road with a stick. Maria Elisia encouraged the girl, Susanne, to befriend Cecilia, telling the two girls to run ahead if they wanted to. It seemed, though, that Susanne was even less confident than she. Susanne stayed glued to Maria Elisia, much the way Cecilia remembered staying as close as she could to Mamusia. She hadn't heard Susanne say a single word.

Then Maria Elisia began asking all manner of questions—what her favorite color was, her nicest treat, her best subject at school. The questions came so fast. Cecilia was embarrassed that she couldn't come up with much more than one-word answers, or even a nod. Maria Elisia was nothing like Mamusia—she looked very different with her dark hair and snappy eyes, she spoke quickly and with confidence, and she was trying so hard. Mamusia never tried hard. She just sank back into herself.

The man—her uncle, though he hadn't introduced himself as an uncle—picked along the muddy road in city shoes, prissing and fussing like no man Cecilia had ever met. Somehow, he was just like and completely different than her father had been.

Once they'd crossed the train tracks, Cecilia realized they were just a few minutes short of the cemetery. If they kept walking, they would be there.

"Do you want to see the graves?" she asked.

At the graves, Cecilia noticed her uncle hang back, as if he was spooked by the whole experience. The boy and girl played hide and seek around the gravestones. Cecilia knew they should stop. It was disrespectful, but no one told them so. Only Maria Elisia seemed sad. She ran her fingers along the inscription of Frances' name, as if for proof she was gone. Cecilia didn't know what to say or do. If she'd known how this would feel, she would have made sure their walk took them in the opposite direction. It was as if she was there with strangers.

∞

"I don't like them," Tom said, as they waited in the kitchen for Cecilia to return.

Mollie had never heard him say a cross word about anyone. It was as surprising as the day he'd been so critical of the priest and the doctor, taking her side.

"Why not?" Grandma Catherine said.

"City airs. He asked to be taken to the farm before he wanted to come here to meet Cecilia. Not to live here—he scoffed at that suggestion. But to see if he could sell it."

"But it's probably not salable," Mollie said. "I don't know if they'd met their homestead commitment. Even if they had, who is the current owner? Cecilia? A child?"

"Either way, a knotty problem to untangle." Tom sat down on the sofa. "It will be interesting to see how long he hovers once he realizes there's no future in it."

"Are we being too quick to judge?" Mollie said, mindful of how her impulsivity had gotten her into so many scrapes in the past. "Should we consider what Frances—and Mr. Pokorski—may have wanted for Cecilia? She's only been with us a few weeks. Maybe they aren't bad people."

"They don't have to be *bad* people for us to be the better option," Catherine said.

"The woman's as nervous as a cat," Tom continued, as if he hadn't heard Mollie or Catherine. "Talks *all* the time, without stopping. It's as if she's trying to cover something up."

"Maybe just trying to keep you from getting a clear impression of the man," Grandma Catherine said. "Filling any potential silences."

"It didn't work," Tom said. "He cuffed the boy twice in the store, and the little girl won't get more than six inches from her mother."

Catherine and Tom were silent. Mollie pictured Cecilia on the receiving end of a slap from Filip. She crossed her arms.

"She belongs *here*," Tom said.

The pronouncement hung in the air.

"Why do you say that?" Mollie said.

"Well, why should she go with them? She doesn't know them," Catherine started, but then hesitated, her doubt evident on her face. "But they are her people. That should count for something."

"In what way?" Tom asked.

"The woman's not Polish," Mollie said, feeling more confident of her intuition now that she knew it matched Tom's. "I've wondered all along if that mattered—if Cecilia should be in a Polish home. But if she's not Polish, then my not being Polish shouldn't be a factor."

"I don't care what the man is, Polish or whatever else," Tom said. "He's flat mean."

They sat in silence for a few more seconds.

Catherine finally said, "What we should consider is what Cecilia wants and what our instincts tell us. We did not find ourselves where we are by accident. There is always a plan."

Mollie took a deep breath; Catherine was close to falling back on "God's Plan," a phrase that always rubbed Mollie the wrong way. She wanted to ask if it had been God's Plan to take Cecilia's entire family from her, but that was just argumentative. And the topic at hand was far too serious to start a debate.

"God always puts the right mother with the right baby," Catherine said. "That's what I believe. Frances was the right mother for Cecilia, and now you are the right mother for Cecilia, just as I was the right mother for you." She smiled.

Mollie wasn't sure she followed the logic. God had already given Cecilia a perfectly good mother in Frances, it seemed, but she loved what Catherine had just said. She'd always felt there were any number of girls who would have better suited Catherine. Regardless of what happened, it was a moment that would stay with her. She felt chosen by Catherine, maybe for the first time ever.

Tom stood and shoved his hands into his back pockets. "Mollie," he said. "I haven't really answered your question. *Why?*—you ask. The reason why she should stay here is that you love her. And she loves you. That's *why*. Her leaving is going to break both of your hearts. I won't stand for it."

Mollie wrapped her arms around herself, overcome with the relief of someone supporting her, understanding how she felt and what she wanted and needed.

"Can you figure out how to make it happen? To make it so she can stay?" Grandma Catherine asked.

Tom rubbed his chin. "They don't seem to have come here with any plan for lodging, other than to squat at the Pokorski farm. They have no way to leave until tomorrow when the westbound train comes through."

"It's in no condition—" Mollie said.

"It's late," Tom interrupted. "How about I offer them beds for the night? I've got plenty of room."

"Is it safe?" Mollie asked. "The flu—to have them in your home?"

"I'll take the risk. Keep the mask on in the house. I've been lax—I should have had it on in the car, too. I'll drive them out to the Pokorski farm—you and Cecilia can follow if you like—before nightfall, then put them up for the night. Let them see it in its current sorry state. I'll let slip that the farm may revert to the state because of the homestead law, then see if they stick. Although I'm not altogether sure that's the case... perhaps the farm would stay with the child if there was someone to act as guardian. Though I won't mention that. Let them do their own homework."

"Yes, that plan makes good sense," Catherine said. "Let's give this a bit more of a look-see."

A few minutes later, Mollie saw the group of five come to the top of the hill where the track ran across the road and watched them for the ten minutes it took to reach the farmhouse. The sun was low to the horizon. It had been growing dark earlier. They didn't look any more affectionate or relaxed than when they left, and Cecilia's eyes were on her all the way.

What did the child want? What if she already was imagining herself in that family, the perfect stairstep between the younger girl and the older boy, with Maria Elisia knowing and doing for her just what Frances would have done?

When they reached the porch, Tom spoke first. "Did you want to see the farm," he asked, "before it gets dark?"

"Yes," the man said. "Let's go now."

"Mollie, would you and Cecilia like to follow?"

"Yes," Mollie said. "We'll be just a few minutes behind you."

∞

Cecilia kept silent on the ride from the farmhouse to the farm where she'd lived with her family. She didn't know how to ask Mollie if she could stay, and it seemed Mollie was holding back also. She was praying—like Mamusia had taught her—that she wouldn't be expected to go with the family tonight or stay with them in her old house.

As they crossed over Fox Road, Mollie said, "Mr. Reid is going to invite them to stay with him tonight. The house isn't really in any condition—"

"I stay with you and Grandma Catherine? My own bed? Or must I stay with him, too?"

Mollie reached over and patted her shoulder. But she didn't reassure her. She seemed tentative, which was something Cecilia had not witnessed before.

The farmhouse that once had looked like home now just looked lonely, and she wished she'd stayed back with Grandma Catherine. At least it didn't seem she'd have to stay there in the lonely house, with the awful memories, and the four strangers.

"We have to go inside?" she asked Mollie.

"No—we don't have to go inside."

"Is it rude? Should I go?"

"You owe these people nothing," Mollie said, and turned off the ignition. She leaned back in her seat, and a few raindrops dotted the windshield. "I think we should suit ourselves—I don't want to go in there either. Tom will look out for them."

Cecilia watched Mr. Reid and the family of four cross the porch and go into the front door. She thought they'd probably think that she was afraid to go in, or had too many bad memories, but that wasn't it at all. She didn't want to leave Mollie's side.

"Plus," Mollie added, "if we don't get out of the car, there will be no question of who you'll be leaving with. Or where you'll be spending the night."

Chapter Fifteen

The next morning, Mollie woke early after a deep sleep, still thoroughly confused about how to proceed. When was it she'd thought she knew how to do virtually everything without doubt or indecision? Was it only a few months ago? Yes, before the pandemic. Now, in every area of her life, she felt as if she was walking on cracked ice, holding her breath, hoping not to break through and drown. Perhaps she should just stay in bed, pull the warm covers over her head, and see what the day brought? Perhaps these were the moments for which her mother suggested prayer, or saying the Rosary?

But that wasn't Mollie's way.

All she knew for sure about the last eighteen hours was that Cecilia belonged under their roof, with her and Catherine. The night's rest had strengthened her resolve to keep things exactly as they were. She was determined to see that the day turned out in Cecilia's best interest, and that Cecilia ended it right here—in her very own bed under a colorful quilt much the same as the one covering Mollie right now. Cecilia's room was directly below hers, and she listened to hear sounds of Cecilia waking, but there was nothing. It was barely light outside Mollie's window.

Mollie dressed in what she'd worn the day before and was out and in her car within minutes. Frost dusted the grass, and thin sheets of ice covered the puddles on the road. Her instinct told her Maria Elisia was the key—Filip had rushed to Emmett only to see if any value could be pilfered after the tragic deaths. Mollie shuddered; the audacity of it. She abhorred greedy people. And bold, too, arriving without any warning. Yes, Maria Elisia was the person with a bond to Frances, and Frances was the person Cecilia had loved most. Whatever solution was to be crafted here, it had to begin between her and Maria Elisia. She had to steer around Filip, as if he was no more than a frosty puddle on the gravel road.

She tapped on Tom Reid's front door, and he answered quickly—a mask on his face. Mollie liked that he'd chosen to take precautions with out-of-town visitors in his house. Plus, the mask probably gave him some cover. He didn't have to pretend so much to be a gracious host. He didn't like Filip, Mollie knew, and was only tolerating the rest of them.

"Hold up," Mollie said and returned to the car. The masks Grandma Catherine made for her students were still on the back seat. She grabbed one and arranged it on her face, tying the strings behind her head as she climbed the steps back to the front door. By the time she got back to the porch, Maria Elisia was there, standing next to Tom in the doorway. She too was masked. The scent of coffee wafted into the cold air. Tom offered her a cup.

"No thank you," Mollie said, then turned to Maria Elisia. "Can we talk?" she asked. "Just the two of us?" Mollie nodded toward the church across the road. She thought the door would be open, and it would be empty so early in the morning.

"Yes," Maria Elisia said, and fetched her jacket from the rack near the door.

The red brick church with its high white steeples, like upward-pointing icicles, was the pride of the village. Mollie's father had told her that his father, fresh from Ireland, had worked with the other immigrants to build a finer building than any of them had ever had any right to enter in the old country. It was finished before they'd even had the first crops harvested. It was the nicest church for miles in either direction. As she and Maria Elisia walked toward it, she had a feeling of pride. Not spirituality, but pride. This was a lovely place for a child to grow up—she knew that. She squared her shoulders.

They took a seat in a pew toward the back of the church and sat several feet apart. Fall flowers—dried wheat stalks and chrysanthemums and colored maple leaves—brightened the altar and made Mollie wonder if the flowers were replaced even with regular Masses suspended, or whether there was a funeral service planned for later in the day. Mollie could see just the small dots of candles lit for special intentions, way up in front. She'd lit a few of those candles when her father was sick, which was as close as she'd come to praying for help. Had she arrived a few minutes before Maria Elisia this morning, she would have lit another, maybe even sent a missive to St. Jude, the patron saint of impossible situations. She always perceived St. Jude as a man like her father, capable of detangling a fine gold chain with the point of a straight pin.

The building settled around them in hushed silence. But Mollie did not intend to whisper. The church belonged to her as much as to anyone, and to her ancestors, who'd toiled to build the structure. She had every right to be here.

"Why did you come to Emmett?" she asked, turning to Maria Elisia. "What are your intentions for Cecilia?"

"I came with a plan—to take her home with us." Maria Elisia sighed. "Now, I don't know."

"You and I should talk this through," Mollie said softly. This was one time she did not want to press her case and alienate Maria Elisia. She needed to restrain herself.

"Yes," Maria Elisia said. "Two women—we understand one another."

Mollie immediately noticed that Maria Elisia didn't speak of two parents. She hadn't even mentioned Filip Pokorski. Nor did she speak of two mothers, as Mollie was not a mother. Mollie found the omissions telling. Maria Elisia didn't want to include her husband in their conversation any more than Mollie did. And Maria Elisia was either sensitive enough to be specific in her reference to Mollie, or she was underlining that Mollie was an imposter, not a real mother. Maybe she was questioning Mollie's competence to make pronouncements as to what was best for a child? Mollie waited, sensing Maria Elisia was trying to find the right words for a difficult truth, not sure what would be forthcoming.

"My husband—he's not a warm man," Maria Elisia began. "Once his brother and his family left, I never heard Filip speak of them. When I spoke of my loneliness for Frances, he always turned away."

"Why?" she asked. "Was there a rift?"

"The grandfather was—well, also not a warm man. He was especially hard on Aloysius, the oldest. When Filip, being younger, had more opportunities for schooling and such…." She shook her head. "Well, the jealousy."

"Yes," Mollie said, thinking of her brothers' feeling about her privileges as a youngest child and the affection her parents, especially her father, had lavished on her. "I understand."

"Then they had some silly argument." Maria Elisia wrapped her arms around herself and bit her lip. "I lost my best friend. Frances."

"Such things snowball," Mollie said. "I haven't spoken to my own brothers for—" She calculated. "Well, for weeks. My mother decided I should stay on our farm, and told them so. I'm sure they are angry, and I've done nothing to make it right."

Maria Elisia nodded. "Families—some mend themselves, and…."

"Some don't," Mollie murmured, wondering what could mend her strained relationship with her brothers.

"I am not confident that Filip—" Maria Elisia hesitated. "I am not confident my husband can love the child of Aloysius and Frances."

Mollie thought back to Tom's perception that Filip was not even especially kind to his own children and imagined that Maria Elisia had endured many struggles. She wanted to speak but couldn't think what to say. So, she let the silence surround them. Somehow, a bird had gotten into the building, and Mollie heard it flapping its wings above their heads. It was looking for a way out.

"Did you know about Cecilia before I wrote to you?" Mollie finally asked. "Did you know Frances had a little girl?"

The saddest expression clouded Maria Elisia's features. "No," she said. "I did not."

"Why do you think Frances kept that from you?"

"She knew I wouldn't have stayed away, and she knew the brothers wanted nothing to do with one another. She knew...well, she knew Filip would make my life very difficult if I visited against his wishes. She was protecting me."

Mollie scooted closer to Mary Elisia and took her hand. It was tragic that the two women had missed out on their friendship, on sharing each other's lives, because of a standoff between two bitter men. Ugly dispositions, in her experience, did so much damage. She thought about how they'd both experienced bullying in their lives, both she and Maria Elisia, and said a silent prayer of gratitude that she wasn't married to a bully and watching her children cower, and that, thanks to Catherine, her brothers' influence over her future seemed to be dissipating.

Maria Elisia turned to face Mollie. "You want her to stay here."

"Yes, I do."

"But you've never had a child. Why?"

"I've never been married."

"No, that's not what I meant. I'm not asking why you haven't had a child. I am asking, why do you want *this* child? Why Cecilia?"

Mollie looked up at the domed blue ceiling, high above their heads, taking a moment to gather her thoughts. "I've never experienced this feeling before," she said, a few moments later. "Never felt this...well, affinity, with a child. Even though I've been a teacher for years, surrounded by so many children. Her well-being is more important to me than my own. We belong to one another. She belongs here."

"She is like family to you?" Maria Elisia asked.

"She *is* family," Mollie said quickly, before thinking. As soon as she said it, she felt it was true. Cecilia was as much family as a sister or a favorite aunt. It didn't matter how she'd come to join her and

Catherine. It didn't matter that she hadn't known her since she was a tiny baby. "Cecilia *is* family to us, not less than any other."

Mary Elisia nodded. "And Mr. Reid? He's a kind man."

"He is."

Maria Elisia's eyebrows raised, an unspoken question, but a clear one. Were Mollie and Tom romantic?

Mollie wished she could lie and give Maria Elisia false hope that it was only a matter of time until Cecilia had two parents, but that wouldn't be honest. Her feelings were too new and too unexpected. She didn't know if she could ever give up her career and independence to live with a man. She'd never heard of a married woman who had a career or owned her own property. Living in the farmhouse with Cecilia and Catherine and continuing as a teacher seemed more likely. Picturing them as a cozy family of three was easy. Any other possibility seemed far-fetched. Mollie remembered, as though she could hear her voice, what Catherine had said, "No secrets."

"I don't know," Mollie answered.

Maria Elisia nodded, a look of sadness and resignation on her face. She looked like she wanted to tell Mollie something but couldn't—or wouldn't. Mollie let seconds pass, creating a space for a further confidence, but Maria Elisia didn't volunteer her thoughts on relationships between men and women, much less her relationship with Filip.

Maria Elisia reached over and touched Mollie's arm. She smiled. "I think this is best…*il migliore*," she said. "I think Cecilia should stay with you."

Mollie could not bring herself to speak. Tears welled up in her eyes. Moments passed before she said, "Will you please tell me about Frances?"

•   •   •

Twenty minutes later, it surprised Mollie to see the priest open the side doors and light the big candles on the altar. "I saw you come in," he said, from the aisle, several feet away from where the two women were seated. His voice was muffled by his mask. "I thought perhaps you needed a place to converse in private—but people will be coming to say the Rosary in a few minutes. I couldn't wait any longer. I need to be back in the rectory—doctor's orders. Perhaps we'll have Mass next week when I've passed my quarantine period."

There was a time when Mollie would have jumped on that statement with the announcement that she'd be reopening the school at the same time the priest saw fit to offer Mass, but she held back, instead saying, "I am glad to see you upright." Then she felt herself blush. It was poor taste to be suggesting the alternative to upright in conversation with a priest. She knew Catherine would have thought her comment too familiar.

"Yes, I am glad as well. I hadn't known there was such a thing as survival of this illness, let alone a light case."

"That's exactly what I meant," Mollie said. "Are you feeling well?"

"Drained and fatigued, but much better," the priest said. "Thank you for asking."

Then Mollie introduced Maria Elisia and told the priest she and Cecilia's uncle had come to get Cecilia but had decided—here she looked over at Maria Elisia and received a small nod of affirmation—that Cecilia would be staying in Emmett. Mollie's tone was firm, and she looked the priest right in the eye. She dared him to give any opinion that would contradict the plan.

Silence. No objection raised. No opinions volunteered. That humility surprised Mollie.

The priest looked down and shuffled his feet. "I was reckless," he finally said. "I prayed the whole time I was sick that I would be the only one in the town to be ill."

"As did I," Mollie said. "I prayed for you. And our prayers were answered. How are the novitiates in the convent?"

"Three gone, and several more struggling. I had to bring a nurse in from the city to care for them and arrange for a doctor to come out until the cases resolve. The poor chap is running himself ragged, with all the sickness. Hopefully, he will not be next."

Mollie didn't ask about Dr. Murphy and why he wasn't helping in the convent. "We will remember them in our prayers," she said. "And hope for their recovery."

"Through the grace of God," the priest said. Then, he looked up at the crucifix on the front wall of the church and crossed himself, murmuring, "In the name of the Father, the Son, and the Holy Ghost."

"I've been meaning to ask," Mollie said. "What became of Cecilia's mother's ring? Did you sell it?"

"*Sell* it?"

"Yes, I wondered if you'd sold it to cover their burial expenses." It was the most benign explanation Mollie had been able to imagine. She'd offered it to be diplomatic.

"I still have Cecilia's ring. I mean, her mother's ring. The church covered their funeral expenses. I have it in safekeeping for her."

"Frances' ring?" Maria Elisia asked. "I stood up for her at her wedding. I remember the ring. Gold, with small red stones."

"Yes," Mollie said, remembering how Cecilia had described the ring.

"I will get it," the priest said. "Now, before the Rosary service begins."

While they were waiting, Mollie decided to broach yet another difficult subject. "How will your husband respond? Will he be hard on you?"

Maria Elisia looked away. "As I said, he's a cold man. He came to see about the farm, not the child. It's a sad sort of place, isn't it?"

"It's sad now, but maybe better when there was life in the place."

"They were happy?"

Mollie remembered seeing Cecilia and Frances walking to school, Cecilia's bright bows, and how Cecilia had run to her mother in the afternoons. That was enough to make "yes" seem a truthful answer.

"Does the farm belong to Cecilia?"

"I don't know if they'd been there long enough to hold the homestead. They'd made good progress. It takes work—years of work—to establish a claim. You must stay with it. The law requires that you live on the property. Those are the terms. That's what all our families did. My family is just much further along."

"Exactly. Filip is not interested in moving here, nor is he interested in that kind of hard work."

Mollie wanted to keep the fact of the money—the two passbooks in the flour sack—to herself, but she couldn't in good conscience do that, any more than she could overstate her relationship with Tom Reid. "There's some money," she said. "Not a great deal, but some. I'd perhaps need your help to free it up for Cecilia."

"I can't do that without…well, I can't cross him. Can you talk to him?"

Mollie hesitated—she had no problem taking on a bully, but she knew she and Filip Pokorski were oil and water. She wanted the right outcome. Cecilia was too important. She could not bang heads with the uncle, or risk losing Cecilia over money. Yet, the money was uptown in the savings and loan. If Cecilia stayed, Mollie would be asked to manage the accounts, but would lack authority to do so.

"Perhaps if I just gave Filip the funds?" Mollie said, not liking the solution, but knowing that keeping Cecilia was more important than a fight over money, and suspecting he cared very much about money.

"That's not fair," Maria Elisia said. "That would *not* be why Frances—or Aloysius—saved. They would not want us, or anyone in Chicago, to receive a windfall, especially not when Cecilia will need the security. I'd rather see you have it."

"I don't need it. Cecilia does not need the money now either."

"Still, she may want it later. Perhaps Mr. Reid could speak to him?"

Mollie didn't like to ask for Tom's help—again—but as soon as Maria Elisia suggested Tom, she realized he was their best option for Maria Elisia to keep the peace with her difficult husband, for Mollie to get what she wanted and what both women agreed was best, and for a fair distribution of what funds there were. She would have to swallow her pride and let Tom smooth it over if he could. She already knew what she planned to suggest—just tell Filip they'd left some small deposits in the local bank, and the funds would be left untouched until Cecilia was an adult. She could use the money to pay for her education—maybe art school.

"I will ask Tom to help," she said.

"Thank you," Maria Elisia said. "*Grazie.*"

Mollie smiled and squeezed Maria Elisia's hand. "There's just one more thing to do. I need to talk to Cecilia."

Just then, the priest returned with a folded handkerchief. He held it up to get Mollie's attention and said, "I'll leave the ring up here for you." He took the ring out of the cloth and left it on the altar.

Mollie walked up to retrieve the ring as the priest went out the side door that led to the rectory. A slim gold band with three red stones rested on the polished wood of the altar. She returned to sit with Maria Elisia.

"This is it?" Mollie asked.

"It is," Maria Elisia said, reaching out to touch the band. "Frances' ring. Her wedding ring."

"I am going to ask Cecilia to make sure she approves, but perhaps you would hold it for us? Keep it in Chicago? I want her to know you, so she can know Frances. Would that be satisfactory? There's a train that goes. Well, you know. You came here on it." Mollie laughed. "Perhaps when things are better. We can visit."

Maria Elisia, appearing overcome, her eyes shiny with tears, nodded. "Yes," she said. "I will take it. I will keep it safe for her. And I will come back. When this influenza is finally beaten, you can come to visit me."

"We will," Mollie said, knowing she would keep the promise. Cecilia needed—no, deserved—to know this kind woman who'd known her mother so well.

•   •   •

It was still early in the morning when Mollie returned to the farm. She found Cecilia sitting up in her bed, looking as if she couldn't decide whether to leave the haven or stay huddled underneath the covers. Mollie had certainly felt that way herself, though she couldn't imagine the trauma the child had endured. Losing her family, knitting into the strange new arrangement with her and Catherine, then having strangers arrive with the intention of forever taking her away to a whole new life. She sat down on the edge of the bed and opened her arms to Cecilia.

"Put your head down," she said, and rested the girl's head on her shoulder, stroking her hair.

"Is this goodbye?" Cecilia asked after a few seconds, her voice muffled.

Mollie pulled back and looked into her eyes. "Give me your hands," she said.

Cecilia held out her hands and Mollie took them. They felt light and small, but also strong.

"This is very important," Mollie said. "I am going to ask you a question, and we are both going to live with the answer. Do you want to stay here? With me? Forever?"

"I can? You can make that happen?"

"Yes, I can," Mollie said. "At least I think so. But you haven't answered me."

"Yes," Cecilia said. "I want to stay. I want to stay here. Forever. With you."

"Then we will make it so," Mollie said. She smiled, reached out to nestle Cecilia's head against her shoulder again, and reveled in the feeling of Cecilia's soft hair against her cheek. As Cecilia leaned against her, she said, "We will stay close with Maria Elisia. She is going to take your mother's ring for safekeeping, and to hold a part of you. It will be yours when you are grown. If that is alright with you, of course."

She felt Cecilia nod against her shoulder.

Through the bedroom window, Mollie saw mist rising from the pond behind the farmhouse. The few leaves left fluttering on the trees were the last bit of autumn. Soon, maybe within the next days, they'd get their first snow. The season of fires in the fireplace, long, dark nights, and late sunrises had arrived. Mollie had read that a cold snap could curtail the spread of the flu, but she'd also read that people being driven inside would incubate the illness, so rates could rise. It was hard to know what to expect. She vowed to keep her people as safe as she could.

∞

After Mollie left her room, Cecilia waited to see if she could fall back to sleep. She counted frontwards and backwards, considered all the sketches she'd made, and then thought about the long, strange day before, starting with being alone in the farmhouse with Grandma Catherine and knowing that Mollie had gone to try to make arrangements with her uncle and Maria Elisia. She'd been so relieved when Mollie promised she could stay, but it was a bittersweet relief, like the tart taste of the oranges she'd found in her Christmas stocking last year. In her heart, what she still wanted was to go back and see her family and be with Mamusia. But she knew that was impossible. Cecilia didn't necessarily feel happy, but she did feel safe. She prayed if sleep came, she would dream of Mamusia and Maria Elisia as girls, girls just like her. As she lay thinking, she heard the whistle of the approaching train and recalled how the sound had frightened her just a few short weeks ago. Now, she liked the way the sound was almost too faint to hear at first, then loud and clacking, so she could almost see the wheels turning. Then it was soft again, all within a few minutes.

∞

Mollie, Catherine, and Cecilia said their rosaries in the dining room, then went to town to meet Tom and put the Chicago family on the noon train. After the sound of the whistle of the westbound train faded, and they waited for the last view of the train moving down the tracks, Mollie turned to Tom.

She meant to properly thank Tom for his help. She remembered how she'd run to him for help the day Daisy died. It had been wonderful when he stuck up for her after the priest got sick, and when he'd given her hope that perhaps it was not out of the question for Cecilia to remain on the farm. Or when he helped by talking to Filip. She didn't remember ever feeling that she'd had a true friend of her own, not like this. But as she tried to find words to express herself, Tom's gaze on her was too intent, too confusing.

She turned away and muttered, "Thank you, Tom." Then, she hustled Grandma Catherine and Cecilia into the car and rushed off toward home, leaving Tom standing on the platform.

•   •   •

Later that afternoon, after a quiet lunch, Grandma Catherine said, "I have an early Christmas gift for you both. Be a dear and go up to my room, Cecilia?"

Mollie heard the last part of the question with concern. When had her mother begun to avoid necessary trips up and down the stairs? Should she be suggesting that Catherine and Cecilia switch rooms? Then Catherine could have the first-floor bedroom. Mollie recalled the sad day she had to make that suggestion about her father and then move his things. The thought of moving Catherine from the room she'd occupied since she was a young wife made Mollie shudder.

"A gift?" Cecilia said, eyes sparkling. "A *maly prezent*?"

"What is a *maly prezent*?" Mollie asked, stumbling over the unfamiliar words.

"A small gift," Cecilia translated. "A kindness."

"Yes," Catherine said. "An early Christmas gift. Unwrapped." She smiled. "Go to the chest at the foot of my bed and fetch a flat cardboard box—*carefully*."

Cecilia jumped up.

"Place your hands *under* the box, to support the bottom," Catherine said, "or there will be no gift."

Mollie refreshed the hot water in their cups from the tea pot on the cast iron woodstove. A few seconds later, Cecilia entered the dining room carrying a box the size of a bed pillow.

"It is a gift for Mollie," Catherine said, "although I think you'll both enjoy it."

"You can open it," Mollie said to Cecilia.

Cecilia removed the lid of the box, and inside was a nest of shredded newspaper. She carefully separated the shreds and found nestled beneath them four bone-white perfectly plain cups and saucers. Her forehead knotted up in confusion.

"Keep looking," Catherine said.

Below, Cecilia found a palette, some pastel paints, and a set of brushes, some made from the finest possible strands, finer than eyelashes, and one as thick as her thumb.

"We can paint the teacups?" Cecilia asked.

"I thought you might enjoy that," Catherine said. Outside, the rain fell steadily, as it had for several hours.

Mollie wanted to ask what-were-you-thinking, but instead asked, "Wherever did you get them?" Catherine hadn't been away from the farm without her all summer.

"Sarah," Catherine answered.

Of course. Sarah was her brother's prissy wife, the one with a wealth of suggestions on how Mollie could correct her spinster status. Fussy teacups and saucers were exactly the kind of gift she'd expect from Sarah.

"I've had them for a few years," Catherine added.

Then Mollie understood. This gift was no doubt something Catherine had obtained at Sarah's suggestion when Mollie was engaged to Jim McElpin, in anticipation of her bridal shower, which never happened. It would have been Sarah's place to plan the event, and then to cancel it when the engagement fell through. Painting them now felt like an acknowledgment that Catherine thought she was bound to be sadly single forever. Catherine was giving up on her.

"I must have been such a disappointment to you," Mollie said.

Catherine looked stunned. "Whatever do you mean?"

"You thought I'd be a different kind of daughter. More like Sarah."

"Oh, please," Catherine said. "Sarah doesn't have a teaspoon of your spirit. I don't want you to be anyone other than exactly who you are. Don't you remember when I said that you were exactly the right child for me?" She nodded in Cecilia's direction. "And this, this new gift is all due to you. This child in our home. You had the initiative to make this work. Mollie, they are just cups and saucers, not a signal. I thought you and Cecilia would enjoy painting them on some rainy afternoon. This morning, I wondered what I was saving them for. It will be good for you to have a remembrance of today."

A remembrance that has nothing to do with me, Mollie thought, but then she looked at Cecilia, who looked rapturous. The cups and saucers were a perfect distraction from the tempest of the last twenty-four hours. Cecilia had already set two cups on a clean dish towel and was turning them around and around so she could inspect all vantage points. Mollie leaned back against the chair and crossed her arms.

"Mollie, I am so proud of you," Catherine said. "I don't care whether you want to paint a teacup. I truly don't."

Mollie looked at the other two cups that Cecilia had positioned on a clean towel in front of her. She found the prospect of painting them daunting. She didn't know where to begin. The substance of the activity felt appropriate to a skin she'd sloughed off, and, to top it off, she had no talent for painting. Sarah was good at that kind of thing, as was Catherine—she made lines of smooth stitches, perfect buttonholes, and even sewed dresses without patterns. Catherine's mother Irene had painted the stunning wildflower designs on her china two generations ago. Mollie could see Irene's teacups through the glass doors of the dining room cabinet behind Catherine.

Mollie turned a teacup upside down, which seemed to be a more stable option, but then realized she'd have to paint any designs upside-down. Usually women painted flowers on teacups; she imagined some of her favorite blossoms—roses, peonies, and sunflowers—but then discarded each on the basis they were far too complicated. She pictured her fingerprints all over the pristine surfaces. She decided that she'd watch Cecilia take on the project.

Cecilia hadn't yet touched a cup or saucer. Instead, she was sketching. She'd made four simple sketches, just a few lines each, but Mollie recognized the images: the Pokorskis' front porch, with a vine trailing up a pillar and wind chimes hanging from the beam; Daisy with her fat belly lying in a puddle of sun; all five Pokorskis together with the train in the background; and Mollie and Catherine on the front porch of the farmhouse looking as if they were preparing to greet a visitor beyond the frame.

"Those sketches will make for some unusual teacups," Mollie said, "especially the one of the cat in the family way."

Catherine raised her eyebrows and gave a slight shake of her head.

"What?" Mollie said, daring Catherine to object to the mention of pregnancy in front of a young girl.

"Cecilia should make the pictures she likes," Catherine said. "Stop editing."

"I want more cups and saucers," Cecilia said, as though she hadn't heard Mollie.

"Would you like mine?" Mollie asked.

"We can paint together," Cecilia said, but she was eyeing the two cups and saucers positioned in front of Mollie.

"Mollie could do the first wash of color and fill in the spaces," Catherine said. "Cecilia, you could manage the details."

"That could work," Mollie said.

Cecilia slid Mollie's cups over to her towel. She clearly wanted to make all the artistic choices.

"There's a lot of work ahead for this town," Catherine said, meeting Mollie's eyes over Cecilia's bowed head. "We're far from through this. The students are blessed to have you. They will learn to appreciate you."

Mollie nodded, and tears filled her eyes. She was grateful for the activity that would pass the afternoon with Cecilia, still fresh from saying good-bye to Maria Elisia, who even now was speeding by train back to Chicago. She was grateful for Catherine's grace. The cups had been purchased with a vision of Mollie enjoying an activity with other young brides-to-be and wives, preparing for a conventional marriage. Mollie had realized none of that fit her character. After a few awkward and sad weeks, she'd been relieved her engagement had fallen through, then embraced her independence. She knew Catherine had been surprised when she'd chosen such a unique path.

But now, Catherine was making the cups and saucers a shared possession for her and Cecilia, an unconventional family but a family all the same. Catherine had protected a home for the three of them as well. Mollie already knew that the four cups and saucers, no matter how they turned out, would be among her most prized possessions, and the memory of this afternoon, only a few short weeks from when she met, as in really met, really saw, Cecilia would be among her most precious memories. She reached over and took Catherine's hand and smiled. They both rested their eyes on Cecilia's bent head as she carefully executed her imaginative designs, the soft whisper of pencil on paper and the sound of the rain comforting their hearts.

Acknowledgement

My first thank you goes to the teachers, most especially my mother and grandmother, as well as the librarians and booksellers, who have placed books in my hands from my earliest memories until the present. Reading has been my abiding pastime, comfort, and pleasure; it never disappoints. I have dreamt since I was a little girl of holding a book that I wrote. Thank you to Black Rose Publishing for making this dream come true.

I have been privileged to have many wonderful writing teachers and mentors. Many of these experiences have been at the Breadloaf Writers' Conferences, associated with Middlebury College, and the annual Bear River Writing Conference, sponsored by the University of Michigan. At these conferences, I had the privilege of working with Ann Hood, Helen Schulman, and Antonya Nelson. I also appreciate the many wonderful teachers I had in the MFA program at Bennington College, especially Lynne Sharon Schwartz, who assisted in the development of *Like Family* in its earliest stages, and Susan Cheever, who became a mentor and friend. I also appreciate Kathie Giorgio, the first teacher I had when I embarked on this creative writing journey over twenty years ago, who has been a steadfast and encouraging influence, and Melanie Bishop, a wonderful writing coach and the person who encouraged me to gift myself an MFA for my sixtieth birthday. I also thank Robin Black for encouraging me to enroll in an MFA program.

I have the privilege of having a writing partner, Mary Holden, and writing friends—Hika Anani, Eleanor Marsh, Lys Paulhus, and Nikki DeLeon Martin—who support me every day and week in the endeavor to build my skills.

I also thank Riley Helen Wendling, the most recent young woman to reside on the farm described in *Like Family*. Riley read Cecilia's parts out loud with me on the porch of the farmhouse Grandma Catherine and Mollie lived in so many years ago. She infused Cecilia's voice with passion and imagination. Riley joins the generations of women who preserved the legacy of the farm for our family, through personal, national, and international struggles.

Most of all, I appreciate having been married to Matt Feeney, a creative force, for over forty years. His love of music and my love of writing have been wonderfully compatible. It truly makes a difference to live each day with a kindred spirit.

About the Author

Michele Feeney, a lawyer in Phoenix, Arizona, is a native of Michigan. She pursued her passion for creative writing for 20 years before she earned an MFA from Bennington College in 2022. She and her husband Matt have raised five children, biological and adopted, and welcomed two grandchildren. They made navigating the COVID-19 pandemic a family affair. While doing so, she remembered a story told to her by her grandmother and was inspired to imagine how families and community members navigated their way through the influenza epidemic of 1918. *Like Family* is her first novel.

Note from Michele M. Feeney

Word-of-mouth is crucial for any author to succeed. If you enjoyed *Like Family*, please leave a review online—anywhere you are able. Even if it's just a sentence or two. It would make all the difference and would be very much appreciated.

Thanks!
Michele M. Feeney

We hope you enjoyed reading this title from:

BLACK ROSE
writing™

www.blackrosewriting.com

Subscribe to our mailing list – *The Rosevine* – and receive **FREE** books, daily
deals, and stay current with news about upcoming
releases and our hottest authors.
Scan the QR code below to sign up.

Already a subscriber? Please accept a sincere thank you for being a fan of
Black Rose Writing authors.

View other Black Rose Writing titles at
www.blackrosewriting.com/books and use promo code
PRINT to receive a **20% discount** when purchasing.

Made in the USA
Monee, IL
21 November 2024

70763970R00132